With very ...

THE KILLING OF
ELLIE SWALES

Olga Merrick

ALSO BY OLGA MERRICK

Untouched Departures
A Rake of Leaves

THE KILLING OF ELLIE SWALES

OLGA MERRICK

chadgreen books

First published in 2017

Cover Image: from a photograph by
Tia Driver-Williams and reproduced with permission

ISBN-13: 978-0992957766

chadgreen books
are published by Chadgreen Publishing
Telford, Shropshire, United Kingdom

Printed and bound in Great Britain by
BookPrintingUK, Peterborough, Cambridgeshire

DEDICATION

To my three sons, James, Adam and Chris,
and in memory of Tim

1

Why Josh killed Ellie Swales, he had no idea. Chrissakes, she was his Gran. Course he didn't mean to. *Shouldn't have done it to me, Gran. You... you... stupid old lady. Not my arm. Mustn't touch it. I... just don't like it. And no, I don't know why.* He prowled the room as he muttered the barely coherent words. *Look what happened to Andy's? Both of 'em, and his legs... and that boot with his foot still inside it. And his head...* He almost gagged, held his face in both hands, wanted so much to cry and be hugged better by her, by his Gran.

Backwards and forwards he paced, unable to look at her inert body, Josh rocked as he walked. He had to swerve to avoid knocking over the small table next to one of her high-riser chairs, with its vase of artificial and out-of-season roses and daffodils. There were souvenirs and bric-a-brac on shelves, on more small tables, collected over the fifty odd years she had been married to Josh's grandfather, dead these past two years.

She described each one of them, every time he came home on leave, as if it was the first time he'd seen them. He didn't mind, not really, though wouldn't have minded if she'd shut up sometimes. Her common-sense voice and nodding head, and her teeth clattering, badly fitted as they were, in her pleated face. All the time telling him he was lucky to be alive, just like Granddad had survived his war. What about Andy, his best mate ever? Couldn't say he'd been lucky, lucky not to live maybe... no arms, no legs, and a face blown to bits.

Josh was sure Gran had grown older since his last leave. Her eyes reminded him of little dried blackcurrants, and she'd just had a perm that morning. You could tell: those white curls were so tightly woven on her head that bits of pink scalp were sneaking through, making her look like the fairground candyfloss she used to buy him, when he was a kid, down at Dreamland Fairground.

Now her body lay on the floor, crumpled, almost in an ancient, foetal position, one of her walking sticks beside her, and the other a few feet away where she had tried to reach it. He remembered she had grasped his arm for support, not knowing. And he had pulled away, violently. He remembered that much before the blackness overcame him and the ear-splitting sound of explosions returned. Then the numbness and painful deafness after the bombs, and the screams and cries. Were they his or Andy's? *You can't know what it does to me when someone pulls my arm. Like I pulled his, Andy's, and look what happened...*

When he came to, the sounds had gone; the bombs and screams and the ringing in his ears. Now he was pacing the small room, his frame spare with the honed muscles of a professional soldier. And he was restless, touching things, looking out of the window but still hoping no-one could see in. Unlikely: Gran's bungalow had those little square latticed windows, double glazed. It was set back from the pavement by her neatly kept lawn and a tree on the edge where the gardener hung the birdseed container. 'My outdoor television,' she called it. She had quite a nice turn of phrase for things, he reckoned.

Now he daren't look at her or touch her, and kept saying to himself 'what the fuck have you done?' His body was shaking. From fear or what? Again, he peered through the window: nothing, nobody. He wished she had those lacy net curtains though, like most old people had, so she could be a twitcher of her neighbours and other passers-by. He muttered to himself, dared a quick glance at her body. There it was, she was... curled up, inert, dead. He almost bent to touch her, only almost: decided against it, couldn't. He tucked one hand under his other arm and shuddered. She was probably going cold. How long had it been? He had no idea: when the blackness overcame him, time went away.

Eighty-five years and eight days old. (Her birthday cards still on the mantelpiece and bookshelves). Take away the eighty-five and you'd have the baby she had once been. Curious thought. *Wonder what you looked like as a baby, Gran? Wonder why I'm wondering that? Losing it again are you, Josh? Like they said you would, every now and then? Told you not to concern yourself over it; perfectly normal reaction after trauma. Yeah right. They never said what I might do during these blackouts though, did they? Like kill your own grandmother?*

'Now what do I do?' he hissed to himself. Money first, he supposed. *Gotta try to be level headed, logical. Best make it look like a burglary.* He opened the drawer, with a teacloth from the kitchen. *Don't leave fingerprints on the handle.* It was the drawer in her small side table, next to her riser chair: with the oversized reading lamp on it that hurt her eyes, she said. She always kept her spare cash in the drawer beneath. 'My slush fund' she called it, and grinned every time she said it. And he would dutifully grin back. He was a kind man really. Twenty-nine, going on thirty, never married, never had a serious relationship. Plenty of talking pillows available in the bars across the world. Even in the war zones if you knew where to look.

There was £400 in twenty-pound notes. He took it all, not that he needed any money. His wallet, in his jeans back pocket, bulged with £300 of his own, straight from his army account. But if this was to look like a burglary, instead of a loving grandson accidentally killing his grandmother, then the money must disappear. He left the drawer open. What's he to do next? He took out his mobile from his jacket pocket and rang her number. Her phone, jangling on its loudspeaker, made him jump even though he knew it would ring. He spoke the message to her answerphone. 'Gran, it's me. I'm on leave for a few days. I'll be around in about...' Automatically, he looked at his watch. 'Say an hour or so. It's three o'clock, no, nearly three-thirty now. Just gotta do a bit of shopping first. I'll ring again when I'm on my way, so's you can put the kettle on,' he said and laughed. He added, 'Love you lots,' before folding down and sheathing his mobile. Had to make it sound real. Felt a bit self-conscious though, saying those words. *Like speaking to yourself,* he supposed he was.

What next? Should I empty out more stuff? Best had. That decided, he went through, down the narrow hall to the bedroom, and pulled open a few drawers, flung the contents about and did the same with the wardrobe. *How long has that bedside table door been hanging off? Couldn't Dad have come round and mended it? Maybe not, Mum always finds jobs for Dad to do when Gran asks him to do anything. Mum and Gran don't get on, never have really.*

Josh felt bad doing what he was doing. She'd been a good grandmother to him over the years, better in many ways than his own parents. He had often suspected he wasn't the be-all and end-all of *their* lives: Gran was the one he remembered mostly from his childhood. Mum and Dad were always working, saving up for those exotic holidays in exotic places, always holidays for two adults only. 'You wouldn't like it, Josh. You'd be bored. We'll pay for you to go on a school trip instead.' Gran used to look after him while they were away. And Gramps, of course.

From the bedroom, he went out into the tiny hall again and through to the dining room. He stubbed his toe on one of the table legs, swore, kicked it and dislodged some of her papers that were balanced on top of a plastic folder. They slid to the floor. A voice inside his head told him to pick them up. He told it back, *Later*.

There was no sun left. He could see beyond the dining room to the conservatory that he remembered as always being warm and sunny. Instead, a wintry gloom had set in, with drooping trees dripping with dying leaves, and blackened summer borders that had been caught by the first frosts replacing the warm-season colours. *Everything dies in winter, except over there. Any day, every day was a killing day. Look at Andy...*

But Ellie Swales wasn't dead as she lay there, curled up in that foetal position. She lay still, numbed in shock, the numbness temporarily cushioning her body from the pain that would come later. Her mind, though, was not fuzzy like her curled up body. It was sharp, clear... in shock yes, that such a thing could happen to her. That it was Josh who had done it, her grandson. The one who she loved so dearly and thought he loved her back. No, not thought, she knew he loved her. At least, the Josh who went away to war had loved her. Was this a different man? One with the same name? He certainly was a changed man. There was a darkness about him that showed in his eyes. They mirrored his soul, his troubled soul.

Despite her confusion, her discomfort and fear, Ellie still wanted to reach out and help him. For the moment though, she thought it might be wiser to lay still, let him decide what was to happen next, let him make the pace. Something told her, some ancient instinct, to lie very still. She could do that, had learned the trick way back from one of her visiting nurses. 'It lessens the pain, love. Preserves your crumbling bones for a bit longer.' Following the advice enabled her to live with the present as she remembered the past. She loved doing that when she was alone.

Now she could hear Josh crashing about from room to

room: winced when she heard something break. *Not too much, son, don't destroy all my precious things.* She'd guessed why he was doing this, to make it look like a burglary. She knew, had seen it on TV, about burglars ransacking every room to find valuables. Well they wouldn't find much here. Of course they wouldn't. Besides it wasn't a real burglary, only Josh covering his tracks. *'Not me, officer, wasn't me. I'm the poor sod who found her.'*

She knew he'd be back later. Hadn't he said so on his mobile and on her answerphone? He had to make his alibi tight first. It had sounded weird though, like an echo, his voice in two places.

By slightly opening one eye, the right one that was uninjured, she could tell that it was one of those grumbly days, no sun only thick dark clouds. Good. At least her grandson could sneak away in the growing darkness, hopefully unseen. In any case, there would be few about in the road at this time of night. They'd all be safely behind their pulled-together curtains, central heating up to twenty-odd degrees and telly full on: drinking tea and waiting for their ready meals to warm up in the microwave. 'Bungalow City-on-Sea' settling down. That's what Josh calls it, not Birchington. She almost smiled. He wasn't a bad boy really, well, man now.

The place fell silent, apart from the central heating pumping in and her grandson's furtive steps. She sensed him near her again, standing over her, could smell his sweat and hear his shallow, nervous breathing, felt the tension in him. How still could she make her body? Still enough to fool him? Please God yes.

He touched her shoulder, gently. *Don't flinch, Ellie, you'll give the game away. He must not know you're still alive. Else all his efforts at a fake burglary will have been for nothing. Then what will he do? What would he do?* She dreaded to think. He was – after all – a trained soldier, trained to kill. Yes, she must keep very still...

She heard him say, 'Sorry, Gran. Love you,' and then he went. Away from her, out of the room and into the small hallway. She heard the click as the front door shut behind him.

Ellie felt as if she was floating, hovering. Hovering over her own body. Her head seemed to have lost its initial pain and now was sort of numb yet light like a balloon, her body weightless. She could almost imagine being able to float from room to room, to survey the damage Josh had obviously caused. The dining room might not be too bad: maybe some papers she'd been sorting earlier swept onto the floor from the table. It would take her a little while to pick them up, but she'd manage. They'd be numbered anyway, top of the page in her spidery handwriting. The story of her life. A chair or two might be upturned but damage should be slight.

In the bedroom, she guessed her ornate chest of drawers, given her by Ben on their fiftieth anniversary – the year he died – was probably emptied: sweaters and underwear strewn about the floor with Ben's photograph among them, the smashed glass distorting his smiling image. She'd heard the smashing of glass. The bedside cabinet door was surely hanging lopsided and open. Bibs and bobs on the floor. It wasn't Josh's fault: she'd been meaning to get it fixed for some time and she just kept forgetting, even though Julie, her cleaner, reminded her about it every Thursday morning. The wardrobe door was probably hanging open too, with clothes half-dangled off their hangers and the bed stripped of its linen. *Have you made a good job of it, Josh? Done it before, have you?*

Miffed, and horrified, too, of the bedroom's rape, she came back into herself, to where she lay, on the floor of her small lounge. The curtains had not been drawn but darkness mantled the room anyway. She doubted anyone would trouble to look in. Wouldn't want to tread on the damp grass, would they? It felt more comfortable in here, away from Josh's attempt at trashing the place. Except it was getting colder... Bringing her mind back to the present meant she felt the pain and discomfort, the drying blood on her forehead where she had stumbled and hit the hearth, and the swelling over one eye. Her left arm and leg tingled with pins and needles. Perhaps it would be a good idea to move them slightly, in case they got too cold... She was dying for a cuppa.

Thinking of tea, she remembered Uncle Stanley and Aunt Willow (such a lovely name) who once had a café up on a hill, called Boulders End. Near the Peak District it was, but she could not remember exactly where. She used to stay with them sometimes during the school holidays. Mum would put her on the train and Aunt Willow would collect her at Cromford Station.

Uncle Stanley and Aunt Willow served teas with home-made bread to any tourists that passed that way and sometimes to serpentine lines of cyclists. Leastwise, Uncle Stanley did after his accident and Aunt Willow got a job in the town. *He's not able to go out to work anymore, love,* she explained to Ellie. *But you and he can serve the customers, can't you? There's not enough money comes in here so I have to go out to work instead.*

Ellie enjoyed looking after Uncle Stanley, and the occasional tourists who stopped by. She'd make them local-cured-ham toasted sandwiches, with or without cheese, a shilling and sixpence with and a shilling without. They also served home-made scones with butter and blackcurrant jam, made from their own fruit bushes at the bottom of the garden, and pots of tea served in pretty floral pots with matching china cups and saucers. Uncle Stanley would beam at her when she took the money and put it into the little wooden drawer that served as a till. She remembered it pinged when you shut it and he would clap his hands and give a little jig on the spot. He was such a dear soul.

She had tried the local school but did not want to stay. The other children laughed at her. 'You talk different,' they said, and they made fun of her disabled uncle when he occasionally met her from school, with his twisted, ungainly walk. But he wasn't slow-witted like they said he was, the accident had taken away his ability to walk a straight line. That was all. He was gentle and kind. He would never slap her like Da often did, especially on Friday nights when the pub turned out. Ma always said, 'go to bed.' But she liked to sit on the stairs until the others had gone to sleep and stopped their fidgeting and stupid giggling. She even stayed downstairs with Mam sometimes. If Da came home drunk, he'd get the belt off to her. Uncle Stanley would never have done that.

She had really wanted to live with her aunt and uncle forever and enjoy being their only child instead of one of five at home with Mam and Da. At their place, she had her own sunshine-yellow room that overlooked the breath-taking Derbyshire hills and valleys. It had pretty furniture and a hand-made curly rug on the floor by the bed. At home, she shared the bed and one blanket with two sisters, and the room with two brothers as well. Lennie, the little one, often wet the bed and the smell of urine constantly pervaded their room. Ellie learned to hold her breath until she could burrow her nose into her thin nightie. It was a way to get to sleep.

They piled their coats on top of the one blanket in severe winter weather but it was never enough. Their room, at the back of the two-up, two-down house, looked onto the backyards of similar terraced houses, grey and grimy with foundry smoke. At Uncle Stanley's and Aunt Willow's, if she ever stayed down there in winter, she had a rosebud-patterned eiderdown on top of two woollen blankets and flannelette sheets. Nice and cosy and warm, and cool cotton sheets in the summer with a pretty yellow, daisy-patterned bedspread over one creamy blanket. The room that looked out to those wonderful Peak District hills and valleys...

Ellie was cold now, even though the central heating was on. Usually, at this time of night, she would light the gas fire for extra heat. She had a cut-down walking stick that she used to prod the fire switch to ignite the coals. Not now though, especially as she was laying half in and half out of the fireplace. If only she could move and get a cup of tea.

Ellie really did need one, and to be shifted. She had soiled herself too: she could feel a warm, damp patch on the dress beneath her. If only Trisha (*Don't call me Pat, Mother, it's so old hat. Everybody calls me Trisha*) would come back with Josh. Between them they'd get her up and into her riser chair. *But Josh thinks I'm dead.*

A tear of self-pity rolled down her cheek as she lay there helpless. She mentally shook herself, tears and pity would not solve the problem, they never did. Besides, if she stayed on the floor much longer, in this cramped situation, she really might die. She tried shifting her body to a more comfortable position but pains shot through her, making her feel nauseous. Wouldn't do to be sick, she might choke on her own vomit. People did that, she'd read.

2

Ellie had a decision to make. When Josh returned should she let him know she was still alive? What would his reaction be? Anger? Relief? Fear that she knew him to be the 'burglar'? *He might kill me then anyway, stop me telling the police, or even his mother.* If she continued to feign death he would no doubt ring for the police and ambulance, pretend he'd discovered his grandmother killed by a burglar, judging from the look of the place. He could prove his innocence, his alibi, by the phone call he'd made earlier, leaving her a message. She presumed he had not been seen by any of the neighbours, prayed it was so.

If she was not feeling so uncomfortable she could almost see the funny side of the situation. But wet knickers and multiple bruising did little to make her smile. Plus, her craving thirst, like she had swallowed the dust from a vacuum cleaner bag. This awful clogging in her throat. The feeling of helplessness was overwhelming, making her want to cry again. She felt very, very frightened. Until she remembered her alarm. Around her neck on a cord. One press would connect her with "someone of your choice, or our incident centre, with fully trained staff round the clock."

Silly me, why did I not think of it before?

It would be a bit of a struggle to reach it but 'no pain no gain' as Mother used to say. She gently rocked her body from side to side to try and free her 'dead' arm. Five minutes on, not much progress and lots more pain in her hips and shoulder. She pressed her lips together in effort and determination. *Come on, Ellie, you can do it. I can't. Yes, you can. Can't. Can. Oh this is bloody stupid, get on with it, you silly old woman.*

Ellie did not often swear, and never on Sundays when her good neighbours drove her to Church. But recently she had stopped going, too much effort with these crumbling bones. One journey too far, as the visiting specialist had told her last month. Saying 'bloody' had given her that little ounce of extra push needed to release her arm. The relief was wonderful despite the added pain elsewhere. Weakly, she rubbed away the pins and needles, from her arm and left hand: gradually a hint of warmth crept back into them.

As if in prayer, she brought both hands together up to her chest to feel for the alarm cord. The effort produced agonising pain in her shoulders like someone wrenching her arms from their sockets. Beads of perspiration enveloped her forehead, salty against the bloodied wound and stinging. Keep going, Ellie, you're doing well. *I'm trying to find the alarm, not having a wretched baby!* She'd only had the one, Paul, who married Patricia, Pat. Now known as Trish because, *Pat is old hat, Mother. So is Ellie, Pat, but I'm not changing it now. I've lived for eighty-five years with it. Same as you've lived for nigh on fifty years with Pat or Patsy or Patricia. Depending what your mother wanted to call you. Trendy Trisha, that's what you are now.* Ellie sneered to herself and humphed. *Glad I called my son Paul, you can't muck about with that, can you?*

At last she could feel the small plastic hardness beneath her dress. Another rocking movement to give her courage and strength to extract it, then press...Something rang, but not the little alarm bell. No of course not, it was the phone over there next to her chair. She could not answer it and prayed whoever was on the other end of the line would stay on long enough to leave a message. She'd hear it well enough, it was permanently on loud.

'Hiya Gran, it's me again. I've finished shopping. I'm on my way. Get the kettle on, will you? Love ya... see you in a bit.'

A feeling of terror swept over her. He hadn't even commented on the fact that she had not picked up the phone. But of course, he knew. Or thought he knew; thought she was dead, as dead as she had been when he left earlier. But she was not dead, she was still alive if not kicking. Alive, in pain, soiled and crying for help and dying for a cup of tea. And now her so-called killer was returning. So was the dread of confronting him.

For a moment, she felt animosity towards her grandson, along with the foreboding of his return. If only he'd examined her more closely after her fall, he might have felt a pulse in her neck or wrist. He must have had *some* first aid training in the army, specially going abroad to those far-flung battle grounds, like Afghanistan. All this mess and discomfort could have been avoided had he been more patient. *I know you've got battle fatigue, Josh. They don't call it that anymore though, do they? Call it by letters nowadays, PTS something. Don't know what they stand for, I'll ask you when you get here...*

A car drove by, Ellie watched the light reflected on the wall, as it sidled across the floor where she lay, then disappeared. Could be the man from the end bungalow, the one with big, white chalk stones lining his narrow driveway. They remind her of lights along an aircraft runway: not really necessary to guide him into his garage, she would have thought. But his wife said he was a bit of a fusspot, liked order in everything. Ben had been a bit like that, but not over the top as much as Mr Whatever-his-name was. (She'd forgotten).

The headlights had picked out her bookshelf on the opposite wall to the fireplace, near to her chair, and the wide window ledge in front of her that divided the fireplace and the other wall. She had seen her little china ornaments and seashells illuminated, the dancing lady in a red ball gown that she and Ben had bought in Blackpool one summer: the little girl with a school satchel, wearing a red beret. Made her think of her schooldays, when they couldn't afford shoes, let alone satchels for all five of them. She and her siblings went to school, summer and winter, in wellies or the cheapest plimsolls. One day, the headmaster had stood them out in front of all the other teachers and pupils, and presented each of them with a pair of shoes from the Town Council's Charity. The Mayor was there, beaming, fat, and wearing his heavy gold chain of office over a bloated belly. They had to bow their heads to him and thank him, out loud, in front of the whole school. Ellie had never known such humiliation nor ever blushed quite so red.

Her specs were up there too on the window sill, where she'd left them after reading a letter from her brother, who still lived up North. Briefly she saw her birthday cards decorating the bookshelf, hiding all her paperbacks. She didn't buy hardbacks nowadays, too heavy. Didn't buy many books at all now: no need with the home-library visiting every week. Nadia, the travelling librarian, such a lovely lady, so obliging and as exotic as her name. Smartly dressed and always smelling of expensive perfume. She didn't do it for the money, no need, she said. just enjoyed meeting people on her rounds. *Wonder why you didn't trash the bookcase, Josh? Just taking my money from the drawer will make it look like the burglar knew where there'd be money. It'll make the police suspicious straight away. Maybe there's not a real burglar in you after all.*

The road returned to darkness. Luckily, her neighbour opposite had switched her porch light on, above the door and Ellie's eyes became accustomed to its scant glow. But she was still cold, and damp, still thirsty, and suffering pain everywhere. She felt rather than heard someone at her window. Were they looking in? Could they see her? Dare she take a peek to see who it was? Curiosity overcame caution.

She jumped in her skin, it was Josh. Too dark for her to read any expression on his face, but she knew it was him... the shape of his head. At the same time a car drew up, its headlights halo-ing Josh and the holm oak tree behind him at the path's edge. A few leaves were missing on it now, after the autumn gales, and autumn almost into winter. She heard the car door shut, not slam. Must be an older person, or a newish car. She could hear their muffled voices, as they spoke to each other, but not what they were saying. Not that it mattered: she was going to be saved. He couldn't hurt her now, not with someone else with him.

'I've rung her twice,' Josh said. 'Told her I'm home, on a few days leave, and to get the kettle on. Didn't take much notice of her not answering though, thought she might be having a ten-minute shuteye.'

They had the front door open by this time and Ellie could hear them both quite clearly. She identified Nadia, the librarian, and her powerful, carrying voice. Would make a good stage actress. What a relief to know it was her with Josh, she'd know what to do.

'Let's hope she's all right, Josh. It's unusual for her to have the lights out and her curtains not drawn by now.'

They turned on the hall light, then the front room lights. The sudden brightness blinded Ellie and she squeezed her eyes shut. Nadia gasped when she saw her lying there, crumpled and quite still. 'Oh my God! What's happened here?'

'Bloody hell,' said Josh, 'what's been going on? Looks like Gran's been burgled.' He pointed to the open drawer.

'Never mind about that, let's see if she's conscious,' and Nadia knelt down close to the old lady. 'She's freezing cold and damp, probably peed her pants.'

'She's dead, isn't she?' said Josh.

'Don't think so. Hope not. No, dead people don't shiver, and look, her eyelids are moving. Call 999 and ask for an ambulance, Josh,' and to Ellie, 'Ellie, can you hear me, darling, it's Nadia, your library lady?' She took off her coat and covered the old lady with it. 'Tell them her age and that she has fallen and is unconscious.'

Josh took out his mobile and dialled. 'Erm, ambulance please. Yeah, it's for my Gran: she's eighty-five and has fallen down. I think she's unconscious. How long what? I don't know, I've only just got here. I'm with a friend of hers, the library lady. The address? Yeah, it's 25, Acacia Crescent, Birchington. No, I don't know the postcode... CT7... wait a minute, what do you say, Nadia? Right it's CT7 8NV.'

Ellie could hear his every word, even when he left the room and was speaking in the hallway. The ambulance would soon come and she felt warmer already with Nadia's coat about her. She could smell the lady's rich perfume on the collar. Josh re-entered the room.

'Well the place has been trashed. Told you it was a burglary. Better call the police as well hadn't I?'

'Yes, you best had. Do you know if your grandmother has a hot water bottle? We could do with warming her up. I don't like to move her. Pity, because we could light the gas fire.'

'Dunno. Yeah, probably in one of the kitchen cupboards.'

Ellie felt so much better, even though she was still in pain and uncomfortable. Just to know that help was here and more to come. She kept her eyes closed, it meant she did not have to talk yet. Save that for when the ambulance arrived, she thought. Not that she was going into it. Oh no, she just needed help to get up and change into decent, dry clothing: a cup of tea and the gas fire lit. *Take more than a fall to defeat me.*

What to do about Josh? To admit she knew it was him would open up a hornets' nest.

3

The police arrived before the ambulance, by a full minute. Ellie heard them entering her small bungalow, firm footed without being too heavy; taking in every detail, she imagined, and being in charge. Josh blustered with his answers, Ellie thought. He should let Nadia do the talking, she was good with words.

A policewoman was kneeling down beside her, feeling for a pulse, handling the alarm around her neck. 'Pity she hadn't been able to use this,' she said. But to whom, the old lady was not quite sure: she still kept her eyes shut, waiting for the ambulance crew.

Josh was explaining about his phone calls, how they should be on her answerphone. Telling the policeman about being home on leave and how he always called on Gran as soon as.

'More like a Mum she's been to me. Spent most of my time with her, when I was a kid. Hope no bastard's hurt her, I'll kill 'em if they have. You know what I mean, mate.'

And the policeman's polite reply, 'Yes sir, purely hypothetical.'

She heard the eerie whine of the ambulance siren and its abrupt finish as the vehicle pulled up outside her bungalow. The next hour passed in a scrambled-egg mix of conversations, questions and answers, and her 'miraculous recovery' from unconscious to consciousness. At first, she refused to look at Josh or Nadia, concentrating fully on the trained medics, ignoring even the two police officers. After much argument and failed persuasion, Brian and Kerry, the paramedics, gently raised her to sitting position and into her chair. But not until they had shushed everyone out of the room while they undressed her. Then they had drawn the curtains and changed her into clean and dry clothes that Nadia had found in her ransacked bedroom. Ellie was now seated, warm and comfortable, and looking into Kerry's anxious face who knelt in front of her.

'I know we can't force you to come with us, Mrs Swales, but you did take a nasty fall and I think you should have an x-ray, maybe even stay in overnight.' *And if I do, they'll never let me out. I want to die in my own bed, not in hospital, or a hospice or a care home.* Even the name made her shudder, 'Care Home'. *They'd have me sitting in adult nappies, teeth by my side in a glass and me waiting for God, watching endless television. No thanks.*

'You two have done a wonderful job, patching me up and giving me back my dignity. Thank you. I wish you were on my daily care team,' she added and laughed. 'You're so gentle and know just how to handle these crumbling bones.'

The colour was returning to her face. She'd at last had a cup of tea lovingly made for her by Josh, 'I know how my Gran likes her tea, white with half a spoonful,' and she felt better able to deal with the policeman's questions and to face both Nadia and Josh. Time now for survival tactics.

'No officer, I have no idea who it was, or even when they came in. I really don't remember anything.'

'Retrograde amnesia,' whispered Brian, the paramedic, and nodded knowingly at the policeman who asked to be called just Dave and 'my fellow officer's name is Katie.' Ellie was brought up to call all policemen 'officer' and cannot imagine in a million years referring to the upholders of the law as 'just Dave and Katie'. Bad enough calling the paramedics Brian and Kerry. *Wouldn't have happened in my day.*

They all helped to straighten the place after 'just Dave'

made notes as to what was missing and what was not. She stated quite firmly that 'No, there's no need to bring in the CID or whatever. What's done is done and if they've only taken money, well...'

If he had any ideas about the perpetrator the policeman kept them to himself. He sent his colleague, Katie, around the estate, to ask if any of the neighbours had seen anyone suspicious or heard anything, apparently without success. *Well she wouldn't get answers, would she?* He daren't look at the grandson, but promised himself that he would come back often and at odd times to visit the old girl.

The paramedics reluctantly packed their cases and returned to the QEQM (Queen Elizabeth the Queen Mother) hospital in Margate making Ellie promise to ring if she felt the slightest bit unwell. Nadia fussed about like the proverbial mother hen and Josh continued threatening the unknown invader of his beloved Gran's bungalow.

The two police officers took their leave after promising to alert any local patrol cars to pay particular attention to Acacia Crescent. Ellie was certain she saw 'just Dave' glance suspiciously at Josh. She smiled a secret smile, it gave her a kind of comfort to know she was being looked out for.

'Here you are, darling, eat this.' Nadia had rustled up scrambled eggs on toast fingers, with more tea. Ellie realised how hungry she was, having eaten nothing since the breakfast porridge made by her morning carer. She tucked in gratefully, spooning the egg onto bite sized pieces of toast, her gnarled fingers grasping each piece.

Pat aka Trish arrived. 'For God's sake mother, what's been going on? Josh?'

'Gran's been burgled, Mum.'

'My God! Are you OK?'

'Of course I am, and before you ask, I don't remember anything about it. The paramedics called it, mmm...'

'Retrograde amnesia,' added Nadia. 'Often happens after a blow to the head. Your mother-in-law fell over and hit her head on the fireplace. But she's OK, nothing broken apparently.'

'They took all my money, about £400 I think I had, don't quite remember the exact sum.'

'That's how much I drew out for you yesterday. All of it gone?'

Ellie stared at her daughter-in-law. 'Well they're hardly likely to leave any behind, are they?'

Trisha tutted, 'As I keep saying, Paul and I don't like you having your door open all day long. Anyone can walk in. They could have killed you.'

They nearly did, leastwise Josh nearly did.

'Perhaps your mother-in-law could have some kind of remote control fitted on the door? What do you think, Ellie?'

Trisha looked at Nadia as if she hadn't seen her before. She seemed to bristle, almost squaring up to her, Ellie sensed. She could read her daughter-in-law's mind. *What's it to do with you? You're only the library lady, not my mother-in-law's minder.* Ellie thought she'd better intervene before there's a spat.

'It's a thought,' she said. 'I could talk to my electrician. There's the key box outside for the carers, they know the code.' Perhaps I'll leave the door shut for a while and only those who know the code can come in.' *Does Josh know the code? He can always ask his mother. I am so tired. Why don't they all go home and leave me be?*

As if on cue Trisha said, 'I think we'll leave you now, Mother. Are you coming home with me, Josh?'

'I think I ought to stay with Gran, at least for tonight.'

'I'm fine dear.' She managed to smile at him. 'Leave your Gran to get some sleep. Come around tomorrow eh?' *I don't need you here tonight, or any night from now on...*

'I'll draw you out some more cash tomorrow, Mother.'

Ellie nodded a dismissal and smiled once more. *These false smiles are cracking my face. Just go, all of you, especially him.*

They trooped out together, all three of them. Nadia waited until Trisha and her son were in the car then said to them through the car window, 'I've just remembered, haven't given Ellie her new books.' And before they could say or do anything, 'I'll pop them into her.' She ran back to the house, punched in the code, and retrieved the key from its box.

'It's all right Ellie, only me. I forgot to give you your library books with all this shenanigan going on.'

The old lady was in her chair, where they left her. Her colour's a bit high, Nadia thought. She patted Ellie's hand. 'You all right, my love?'

'Yes dear, I'm fine, well as fine as one can be after a burglary and a blow on the head.' Then, 'What brings you back here?'

'Your books,' Nadia laughed. 'Silly me, I forgot to leave them with you.'

'Has Trish gone? And Josh?'

'Yes'

'Good, fancy a cuppa with me or a glass of sherry?'

'Tea would be good, I'll put the kettle on.'

Ellie felt sorely tempted to tell her friend the truth, but loyalty to her grandson stopped her. She thought it might be a good idea to get Nadia to change the code. *I'll ask her later, before she leaves.* They settled down to enjoy tea.

'You've made it right, dear, plenty of milk so's I don't burn myself. Think I might take my co-codamol now. They'll make sure I have a good night's sleep.'

'Are you sure you don't want company tonight? I can always ring Jack and tell him where I am.'

'No, I'll be fine. There is one thing though, do you think you can change the key box code for me? And ring the carers with the new number?'

'Of course I can. What about your daughter-in-law, though? She won't know it. Want me to ring her?'

'No, it's all right, I'll ring her tomorrow, I'll tell her then. She's coming here before she and Paul go on holiday.'

'Again? They're never home.'

'Some do of hers, works affair or yet another musician-of-the-year concert. I'm not quite sure.'

'Don't those two ever go where your son wants to holiday? Seems to me it's always her choices.'

Ellie grinned, 'His choice, to pander to her.'

Nadia said 'humph' and went out to change the code. Then she rang the care centre and gave it to them.

'Right, it's 1085. Can you remember that?'

'I should do, it's the month I was born and my age.'

'Good, now let's get you to bed. You've taken your tablets. I'll get you a hot water bottle and a library book. By then you should be all tickety-boo.'

Ellie looked up at her good friend, 'You're very good to me, Nadia.' Her face crumpled a little around her rivulets of wrinkles, and her rheumy eyes fill with uncried tears. The librarian patted her hand again.

'And you're worth it. By the way I cancelled tonight's carer, no sense in paying for her now I'm here.'

'Bless you, darling, you're like a daughter to me.'

Better than my daughter-in-law, that's for sure.

Half an hour later and she was tucked up in bed with the minimum amount of pain, despite the bruise on her forehead and a body of crumbling bones. Her friend left, promising to put one key on the inside hook where Ellie usually kept it, and the other one safely locked away in the coded box outside. Nadia washed up the cups and things and left the front room tidy. She kissed her old friend goodnight and sleep tight and they laughed like children when Ellie replied, 'Don't let the buggers bite.'

But Ellie cannot sleep, despite the tablets and the hot water bottle. Her mind refuses to rid itself of the day's events. *Will he come back tonight and try to finish me off in case my memory returns? Does he even believe I've lost my memory? He's different somehow: not the Josh of old.* She senses a danger in him, a menace that was not there before his last tour. And something else, but she's not sure what. He paces the room like a caged animal. There is a hardness about him, a restlessness. No longer is he the soft little boy who used to beg her to tell her tales. *Tell me like it was, Gran, in your days.* And she would tell him stories of her childhood, like the time she and Gracie had dived into the North Sea and nearly got washed away by a giant wave, until a fisherman rescued them. She told him about the seals and the puffins, the guillemots, and the wild geese that flew over their little house every winter and spring. She described her horror when Gracie ran across the big road and straight into the path of a huge lorry, leaving her on the opposite kerbside with their younger sister, Rosie, and baby brother, Lennie.

'She only wanted to play in some grass.' She had to explain to little Josh that they didn't have gardens or playgrounds, up there in the north, only backyards where the lavvy was, and Mum's boiler in which she did the weekly washing. There was just the street to play in. Gracie had run across to play in the graveyard of the church, it was the only place with grass and she wanted to squeeze and squelch her feet in it. She told him how Gracie lost the lower part of her leg through the accident, and any chance of marriage or a decent job. Nobody wanted a peg-leg for a wife. Sadly, only weeks later, the shock of it all killed her. Gracie, her favourite sister...

The wind has got up. She can hear it moaning outside, and the rustling of the few leaves left. She hears her wrought-iron garden gate screech and slam: there is no lock on it. The sudden sound makes her jump. Was that the wind? There are other noises, all magnified by her lonely state and fear. *Have you come back, Josh? What's that noise in the attic? Don't panic, Ellie, no-one can get in, can they? Did I lock the conservatory doors? The dining-room doors?*

She feels sick and curls up in bed, clutching the hot-water bottle. She looks toward the drawn curtains. *Are they drawn tightly enough? Can anyone see through them? Turn off your bedside light. Not that easy, my shoulder hurts, my arm aches. Just a bit more, there you are.* She sighs with the effort but has managed to switch off the light. Now she worries that an intruder can get in and she won't see him. *Should I put the light on again? Is that a figure I can see through the curtains?* For eighty-five years she has trusted and been deemed to be trustworthy. Now, through one stupid fall she is in danger from her grandson. *Is that him out there? Has he come back?* But everywhere is locked, doors and windows. He will have to smash double-glazed glass to get in. *Can he afford to disturb the next-door neighbours? They don't sleep too well. Him with his arthritis and her with her weak chest. And what about me?* She is trapped in a tomb of double-glazing, door and window locks and a crippled body that refuses to move more than one mile per month. Even then in terrible pain. The gulls outside scream her pain. She'd forgotten the gulls, heard only other, sinister sounds; noises that threatened. Perhaps she should just listen to the sea birds. They weren't a threat, held no terror. She is so tired...so very tired. *Why am I still alive? Why do I want to live? Why not? Because I do: because it's my right, my choice.* Now she feels fatalistic, knowing Josh may or may not get in, may kill her or not...

She sleeps then, a dreamless sleep: the tablets have kicked in. The night envelopes her, protects her, despite the wind outside and foreign noises and maybe-intruders. She is cosseted by warmth and co-codamol. Fear has left her and cannot encroach upon her peaceful sleeping. She dribbles slightly, blows soft bubbles and quietly snores. *Sleep on Ellie, none shall harm you tonight.*

An owl hoots in one of the nearby trees: a fox is out there, rummaging, trying to upturn a wheelie-bin. He goes away hungry from the bungalows. Perhaps he will have better luck at the Chinese Takeaway. Gulls wheel and dive silently overhead, like flying ghosts in the night sky: tide will soon be in and then they will feed.

Two miles away in nearby Westgate, Josh lays in his bed and worries. When will Gran regain her memory? That old bag from the library reckons it could be months, years, if ever. Why did he make that bloody-stupid decision to fake a burglary? There again, how was he to know Gran was not dead? It looked for real to him. He turns over, hears the bed creak, like it used to when he was a boy. *Don't wake the parents up, they're off tomorrow and I'll have the house to myself. Wonder how I can get Gran's money back to her? Don't get your memory back too soon, Gran. I don't wanna do anything bad to you.* His face, in the dark, is enigmatic. Just as well Ellie can't see his expression, or read his mind; she might really have something to be frightened about.

4

The carer calling out, 'Morning, Mrs Swales,' and clicking the front door shut behind her, wakens Ellie. She smiles to herself. She has survived the night. Now comes the price to pay for being alive. Gently pulled and pushed into an upright position, legs swung round to the edge of the bed: her body washed and changed into clean day-clothes with matching bling accessories, and last of all, make-up applied.

'You got some nasty bruising there, Mrs S. You had a fall or something?'

Ellie doesn't want to go into details. 'Something like that, dear. But I'm all right.'

The carer said, 'Mmm,' and finished off the make-up, patting Ellie's cheeks with face powder and blotting her freshly painted lips with tissue.

Ellie finally reaches her chair by the lounge front-window, thirty-four agonising, shuffling paces from bed to front room. She awaits her breakfast dish of porridge with honey drizzled over it.

'I nearly forgot the new code,' prattles the carer. Ellie remembers her name is Tracy.

'New code? Me too,' says Ellie.

Tracy laughs, 'You silly old silly, it's 1085: this month and your age.' She sits down, companionably near the old lady, and drinks coffee. Ellie can smell it, lovely aroma... coffee. Doesn't drink too much of it herself, gives her heartburn. She listens as Tracy clatters on about her family, the two boys at school, her troublesome teenage daughter, her old man who is out of work: she blames the recession, the government, and automation. Ellie nods her head, clucks when it is needed, sighs for the state of the country and remembers her Da being out of full-time work for eight years during their recession. They had meat on a Sunday if they were lucky, mostly stewed bones that Ma used to beg off the butcher 'for the dog". They never had a dog.

Mostly, it would be a stockpot of stewed veg, with stale bread to dip and Ma hoping it would last the rest of the week. No sweets, except at Christmas and fruit very seldom, then only apples and the occasional pear. Tracy talks about her Tom's unemployment like it was a badge of honour. Da used to be ashamed of his: he would roam the streets and nearby villages and farms looking for casual work, anything to bring in a bit of money to feed his babbies and the missus. Da was a riveter by trade, at the steelworks, until they closed down, putting hundreds out of work. Ellie remembers his blackened, scarred hands that only faintly became whiter once he had been away from the steelworks for six months. That was how long it took for his work hands to become out-of-work hands.

'We're going to Spain again this year,' says Tracy. 'Tom, me and the boys. Got a cheap deal on Boxing Day off the telly last year. Lucky we paid for it before he got laid off.'

Ellie and her brothers and sisters never had a holiday, not unless you counted a day by the sea with sand getting in the butties that Mam made. And the breeze nearly batting them silly. They couldn't afford the boat trip out to the islands, or the donkey rides on the beach. But it was fun to look at them and imagine being on one of their backs with the 'Jesus cross' on their fur and their gaily-patterned blankets under small, leather saddles. Once, her brother was allowed to lead the donkeys when the little kids rode them: told her, the best day of his life.

The doorbell rings. Pat *(Trisha)*. 'Mother? I can't get in.'

Tracy hurries to the door, 'Sorry, Mrs Swales, I locked the

door again after me. Anyway, your ma-in-law had the code changed last night.'

'Oh? Not while I was here.' She enters the room and gives Ellie a brief nod. It's as near as she gets to affection for her mother-in-law 'Are you ok this morning? No bad effects?'

'No dear, I'm all right. Bit sore from the bruising, that's all.' She hasn't told the carer about the burglary, and neither – apparently – has the lady who runs the centre.

Tracy takes her cue. 'Right, Mrs Swales, I'll be off. I've pulled out a ready-meal from the freezer, it'll be ready by dinnertime, about twelve thirty or one o'clock. Wendy's coming round tonight and tomorrow morning. Have a good week.' And she was gone.

'Strange how they send a different one every day,' says Trisha.

'Mmm, well that's the way they work. Means I get to see a variety of people during the week and you and Paul on Sundays.'

'Not this Sunday though. Don't forget we're going away later on today.' She completely ignored Ellie's veiled criticism of how little they both came to see her.

'I haven't forgotten. By the way did you pick me up some money?'

'Yes I did, £400: let's hope you don't have any more burglars. Do you want your bank card back as I'm going away?'

'Yes please. Nadia will always draw me some cash out, if I need some.'

'Hmm.'

'What's that meant to mean?'

'Nothing. I thought maybe you might ask Josh to do it.'

Over my dead body.

'I don't want to put the boy to any trouble, he needs a bit of R&R after his last tour.'

Her daughter-in-law looked at her blankly. Ellie chose not

to explain.

'Right then, I'm off. I'll see you when we get back and I'll get Paul to ring you when we arrive there.'

She briefly kisses her mother-in-law this time, trying to ignore the bruising, and makes to leave.

'What shall I do about the door?'

'Just lock it behind you with the spare key, then put it back through the letter box for me.'

'What about the new code, can't you give it me?'

'Sorry Pat, Trish, I've forgotten it. The carer can tell me tonight when she comes to do my eye drops and put me to bed.'

'What about Josh?'

'I'll tell him tomorrow. Off you go now, have a good holiday. Love to Paul.' *As if he couldn't come to see me.*

She heard the front door click shut, then it being locked from the outside, and finally her daughter shoving the key back through the letterbox. It landed with a dull thud and Ellie relaxed. There is a drink of cranberry juice by her side, two co-codamol to take in a minute. Peace of mind and a bruised body to put up with. But she is alive. SHE IS ALIVE.

She decided against putting the money in its usual place. Why not sit on it? She grinned, her nest egg, *her nest egg.* She snuggled under the chenille throw-over that friends had bought her last Christmas and enjoyed looking out at a wintry sun where the gulls were ballet-dancing across an azure sky. The carer has left her a daily paper: she'll look at it later after she's had a bit of a nap. Her arthritic hands shook and fiddled with the bottle of tablets. Two only, then two tonight before bedtime. The doctor said she could take eight a day. *I'd be like a zombie if I did that. Four's enough...*

Picking up the TV control, she clicked it to Radio Four. Should be a morning story any time now, better than watching some stupid program on daytime TV. She lay back in the chair, waiting for the tablets to kick in. The pain seemed pretty bad this morning and she'd been aching everywhere, as if she'd been kicked around like a football. *Concentrate on the radio story, Ellie, forget the pain.* Easier said than done, she thought, but she'd be determined, if nothing else.

Gradually the pain subsided, leaving her with a feeling of euphoria. She was floating again, hovering like yesterday. But she had no need, everything was fine today. Plus, later on this afternoon, Carole, the chiropodist would be coming. *Don't go hovering, stay where you are in comfort and no pain for a few hours. Is this what Heaven will be like? No pain and this lovely warmth? Will you be there to greet me, Ben? I'm so tempted, my loved one, so tempted. But not yet. Let me stay here a little while longer.*

She slept for an hour, all the way through the story and the Archers. She awoke to a tapping sound, like a woodpecker. It was Josh banging on the window, impatient and glaring. Ellie was frightened. He put his face close to the window, distorted, ugly in ill-temper. *I'll not let you in if you threaten me.*

'Gran, I can't get in.'

She nodded through the safe, double-thickness glass. 'The code's been changed and I can't remember the new one. Come back tomorrow morning when the carer's here, she'll know it.' She didn't want him to know a carer would be there this evening. No way did she want him round tonight, or any night. She mouthed the words carefully for him to interpret. He bunched up a fist, as if he was going to punch the window. She thought, *You're suffering, boy, not my fault. Best you stay away till you calm down.*

'Can't you give me the carer's number?'

Ellie shook her head, pretending not to understand. He strode away, in temper and disgust, and she watched him until he reached the bend in the road. He didn't look like a loving grandson. From now on, she promised herself, she would only see him when other people were around...

Time for lunch. She struggled into her two walking sticks and shuddered as she remembered yesterday. It took her ten minutes to reach the kitchen and the high stool that she sat on while preparing her lunch. Today it was lamb hotpot and creamed-rice pudding to follow. Two minutes in the microwave for the hotpot and one minute for the pudding. She had a plastic bowl, with a string carrying-handle that Trish, in one of her kinder moments, had fashioned for her, in which to pour the hotpot. Now she was able to carry it into the front room, still using her sticks, with a small spoon and fork tucked into her cardigan pocket. It would be a slow walk but she'd manage. The hotpot smelled good and her struggle would be worth it.

Damn! Who's that ringing the doorbell? Whoever it was would not see her in the kitchen. Luckily the carer had neglected to raise the window blind. She'd eat at the work surface, on the stool. The ringing persisted, she struggled to the kitchen door and peeped round to see who was behind the glass door. Josh again. He was persistent if nothing else. Well he could wait till it was time for the chiropodist. *I'm not coming out to you, and you're not coming in here. Not yet.*

5

Ellie had slipped into an uneasy peace of half-awake and half-asleep. Half-asleep because eating made her whoozy and her tablets were still having some effect. They gave her a brain of cotton wool and made her tongue raspy, like a pot scourer. The half-awake condition was coupled with the shock of Josh's appearance at her window this morning. He reminded her of one of those huge herring gulls that often strutted the pavement. His slightly hooked nose a bit like the bird's arrogant and sinister beak. It could break anything with it. What about him? Could he break anything, everything? Could he break her?

She lay back, reclining in her chair, and mused about the animal kingdom outside her front window. Urban foxes, who raided overfull wheelie bins, tearing black bags to pieces with their sharp teeth and rummaging among the contents for remains of all the readymade meals. Bungalow City and meals in wheelies. She smiled at her own almost-pun. *Wish I could still write. Even now there are untold stories in my head. The words could roll smoothly enough: barely a whisper on the page with my trusty ball point. It's persuading them to flow down this aged arm and squashing them out through these contorted, arthritic fingers that's difficult: almost impossible.*

She thinks about the hierarchy of the animal kingdom. After the urban foxes come the gulls, zooming down like jet planes, clawing their way through the foxes' leftovers. Bits of bread, meat, and apple pie, all strewn about by these furred and feathered litter louts. Then come the crows, strutting about, black and iridescent: afterwards the pigeons, and next, the tiny dunnocks (sparrows they call them here down South). Last of all, the sea breeze takes its share, blowing and buffeting the remains of paper and cardboard high into the air, like kites.

Remember the kites we used to make, Gracie? You and me and our Joe, for the little ones, Rosie and baby Lennie? He'll always be baby Lennie to us because he didn't make it through the war, did he? I was away in the Land Army with Rosie when the German pilot dropped his load on our street, so's he could make it back to Germany. Lennie never recovered from his injuries. You were already gone, Gracie, run over by the huge lorry that dreadful day and not surviving the shock.

Remember how we used to make those kites... out of sheets of newspaper, folded and folded again, then into diamond shapes and stuck on a cross of thin wood? And we'd make pigtails with the left-over bits to trail behind when they were up in the air. Remember? We used to run along the sands with the kite trailing behind, sometimes struggling to get it airborne, sometimes it would bump along the ground and refuse to rise into that cold, north-east wind. And Joe shouting, 'Run Ellie, run!'

Rose is in America now: Texas, in a town called Austin, like the car, and Joe's still up North, old like me and twice as crotchety. He still writes a decent letter though, in his spidery hand. No spelling mistakes, thanks to Miss Goodman. She was a stickler for spelling; if you got a word wrong she'd make you write it out ten times. You never forgot it after...

Ellie shifts slowly, uncomfortably in her chair, her crumbling hips cannot be replaced anymore, so it's the pain or co-codamol. She remembers back to their schooldays. Poor Rosie, she was no good at writing her essays. Ellie would help her little sister, night after night by the light of a flickering candle, and Mam used to tell them to get to bed and finish it in the morning by God's sunlight. Mum liked her God: suppose He helped her cope with Da and five children. She didn't have it easy...

Ellie drifts off again until her doorbell rings. A voice through the letterbox says, 'Ellie, it's me, Carole, the chiropodist.' *Heavens, is that the time already?* 'I can't open the key box, have you changed the code?'

She puts her chair into riser position and shouts out, '1085.'

'Thanks, dear.'

Ellie hears the key turn in the lock: she has acute hearing for her years. She smells the waft of Carole's perfume over the remains of her hotpot and rice lunch, and hears her bump through the door with her box of tricks that doubles for a stool. It carries all her tools of trade, plus the little silver-grey bowl she uses to wash her clients' feet.

Carole pokes her head around the door, all smiles and bobbing her expertly cut blonde hair. She smells nice too, Ellie doesn't know the perfume.

'Hello Ellie, what do you want me to do with this?' and dangles the key.

'Put it back in the box when you go out, that'll do.'

She pops it onto a little side table near the door, with the photo of Paul and Trisha on it.

'Ok if I just get some water in my bowl?'

'Of course, dear.'

Carole returns and unstraps her small sitting stool from her vanity case, squats on it: drips some sweet-smelling liquid into the bowl, and takes off Ellie's slippers, placing her feet gently into the warm and perfumed water. Ellie feels the benefit already. The next hour is spent enjoying foot massage, nail clipping and general pampering. Meanwhile she tells Carole about the burglary and all the drama that followed.

'My goodness! Poor you. But you're ok now?'

'Sort of.' She wants to tell her about her grandson's part in all this, but she daren't. Perhaps it's best to stick to the amnesia story.

'I don't remember what happened. Only that I ended up half in the fireplace and half out of it.'

Carole examines her bruise. 'Bless you, it's turning purple *and* you've got a black eye coming.' She continues with her gentle foot massage.

'That feels good.'

'Would you like me to paint your toe nails today?'

Ellie smiles. 'But nobody will see them.'

'Tell you what, how about I give you a manicure and paint your finger nails. I could do them a pretty pink to match your beads.'

The old woman laughs, shows her mouthful of dentures and huffs and puffs, constantly short of breath nowadays. 'That would be lovely, dear.'

While her nails are being painted Carole wraps Ellie's feet in warm towels. They chat. Carole tells her about her latest trip to the Pyrenees and their chalet up in the mountains.

'No snow yet, but it won't be long.'

Ellie tries to imagine the scene. Carole often sends her postcards.

'When the eagles fly in the Valley of the Eagles, that's a sure sign of snow.'

She has told Ellie about the Valley of the Eagles in Andorra, the tiny country that nestles between Spain and France and the people who speak both languages. Bonjour in French and hola que t'al in Spanish. What they say for 'hello'.

The hour passes. She puts the old lady's slippers back on her feet while Ellie waves her newly polished finger nails in the air. Carole says, 'money in the drawer?'

'No dear, not today. I'm sitting on it – like a nest egg,' she

35

laughs. They both do. Carole extracts a twenty-pound note and gives Ellie five pounds' change. 'Right, I'll make the tea now, or do you prefer coffee?'

'Tea please, Carole. There's coffee there if you prefer, and a little box of iced fancies.'

'Ooh lovely. Are you having one?'

'Yes please.'

Ten minutes later they sit by the window sipping and munching. They hear the front door opening and closing, look at each other, Carole querying and Ellie, her eyes shuttered, hiding her dread.

'Hello Gran,' says Josh.

6

He carried a huge bouquet of flowers and was smiling. More like his old self, Ellie thought. He looked at Carole and Ellie introduced them. 'Josh, this is Carole, my chiropodist, Carole, my grandson, Josh.'

They said 'Hi' to each other and Carole added, 'What a gorgeous bouquet. Would you like me to put them in water for you?'

'Yes please, dear,' said Ellie, and to her grandson, 'Thank you Josh, they're lovely. Just what an old lady needs to cheer up.'

'How're you feeling today, Gran?'

She moved her head from side to side, and shrugged her shoulders, 'Not too bad, ticking over.'

He knelt down in front of her, examined her face. 'That's a nasty bruise you've got, *and* a black eye. Looks like you've been in the ring with Amir Khan.'

Ellie managed a weak grin. 'Yes, I feel like I have. Never mind,' she added. 'I'll get over it.'

Carole came back in with the flowers. 'They look magnificent. You're a lucky lady to be this spoiled.'

Yes, with my money, no doubt.

Carole asked Josh if he wanted tea or coffee as the kettle was still warm.

'No, you're all right love, I've not long had one. Went to the cafe down the road as Gran couldn't remember the new code for her key box. Wouldn't say no to one of those cakes though.'

Carole looked sharply at Ellie then down at her lap. Not

for her to comment.

'By the way,' Josh had crumbs around his mouth, 'how did you get in?'

'I rang the carers and they gave me the new code,' interrupted Ellie. 'Shouted it out to Carole through the letter box.' She laughed. Josh stared at both women, shrugged. It made sense, he supposed.

'Any news from the police?' he asked.

'Erm, no, not yet. They said something about calling around later.' She left the sentence unfinished. Would he take the hint?

'That's good. Hope they catch the bastard.'

You don't really mean that, do you Josh?

'Time I went,' said Carole. 'I have to call on Mrs Greenway next, number 29, just up the road from you, Ellie. D'you know her?'

'Yes I do, nice lady. She often calls in to see if I want anything at the shops. Husband's a bit of a fusspot, specially about his car.' Ellie smiled and Carole laughed. Josh looked bored.

'I'll see you out, Carole, and put the key away for you.'

'That's all right, Josh. You stay with your Gran; I'll leave it on the hall table. Will you stay till the police get here?'

'Probably.'

She waved goodbye to Ellie and blew her a perfumed kiss.

'Bye you two,' and she was gone.

'Seems a nice lady.'

'She is, she's lovely. Makes a grand job of my feet and did my hands as well.' She showed Josh her newly-painted nails. 'And she's so gentle. Doesn't hurt, hardly at all.'

'That's good, Gran.'

Ellie began to feel uneasy at her grandson's restlessness. There's an unburned energy about him, she thought.

'Josh, why don't you sit down, lad? You're like a caged tiger pacing up and down like that.'

'I know Gran, I'm sorry. It's just...'

'Do you want to talk about it? Is it something to do with your last tour? Afghanistan, wasn't it?'

'Yeah. And yes, I wouldn't mind telling you about it. You're a wise old bird, Gran, better than talking to one of those shrinks back at base.'

Eventually he sat down, folded and clenched his hands time and time again: licked his lips and almost rocked his body back and forward like a baby in a cot. *Whatever you do Josh, don't confess about yesterday, else you'll have to kill me again. I don't want to go through it again, love... might be for real next time.*

'My mate, Andy. Remember I told you about him before? We'd been together right through our army careers, passed out together, and been on every tour together. Best mate I ever had.' He got up and walked around, even went out of the room and walked down the hall to the dining room and to the conservatory beyond. Ellie stayed quiet. He'd be back in a minute when he'd got control again. He came back into the room and sat down on the edge of his chair.

'Andy was brought up in an orphanage, some church charity home or whatever. Said he hated it there, hated the bullying and the bed-wetters, and the crying: the awful food. He used to go to see an old man, Foxy, he called him: don't know what his real name was. S'pose he was a bit like a Granddad to him: used to make him toys and things. Used to tell him stories too, like you did to me.' He grinned, his face fogged and he went into his head. Ellie stayed silent. *He'll begin again when he's ready.*

The room was growing dim in the winter twilight. She wanted to draw the curtains, shut it out, put the lights on, and send the screaming gulls back to sea. She was not afraid of Josh anymore. Whatever he did yesterday had been an accident, unintentional. She was still alive and she knew, deep down, that he would find a way of returning her money. He wasn't a thief, or a murderer. But he was sorely troubled, she could tell.

'Andy's dead, Gran. Stepped on one of those IEDs (improvised explosive devices) buried in the road. Bastard Jihadists! There wasn't much left of him... I was following him... in his footsteps. He saved my life and got blown to fucking pieces doing it.'

She winced at his swearing but understood. Still she stayed silent, knowing there was more to come before he was fully unburdened. For a few moments, he wasn't there with her, lost somewhere in his mind. She could tell he had left the present and was back there in the war zone...

'No! No!' He was screaming, punching an unseen foe, pushing away the severed limbs, the shattered foot in its debris-covered boot. The noise of the bomb rang in his ears, threatening to damage his eardrums forever. There was bile in his throat, mixing with the dirt and spew of the surrounding desert. Josh rubbed his eyes, felt the grit that scratched his eyeballs. He pushed the horror away: his dream, his nightmare, the noise of that bomb... so close...

Why? Why Andy? Andy, his best mate forever. They had joined up together, trained together, and been through all hell, side by side. Now Andy was gone, blown to pieces by the IED. Blown away, right there in front of him. Hadn't he, Josh, tried to put those pieces together again? Humpty Dumpty... sat on a wall.

Andy had been walking ahead of him, sweeping the bomb detector from side to side; helmet and face-mask on – punishing in the blistering heat. The padded protection suit that held in the sweat, rubbing your armpits raw... and the boots that helped grow blisters on your heels and soles that you salt-washed at night and hoped they would be better come daybreak.

He would not walk in front of Josh anymore, his best

40

friend from forever days. Andy was the arm he picked up, the tattered tunic-sleeve still smouldering. Over there lay Andy's head in its ravaged helmet, and what was that? A bit of rifle, a mangled piece of metal that would fire no more. Another arm sat stupidly on a sand-covered rock, like it was waving, 'I'm here Josh, over here.'

Fragments of uniform with remnants of Andy's body inside. But it was the boot, cradling his best mate's foot, which made Josh vomit on the desert floor. Afterwards he cried like a baby: like when he was a little boy and Gran used to cradle him better, rocking him in her strong, warm arms. But here in the desert there was only a keening wind. Only the vultures up there keeping their sinister watch.

'Get away,' Josh shouted, waving his arms and his rifle. 'You won't have him. Not Andy. Not my mate.' He fired the gun, causing them to wheel and dive away, finally resting within sight of him, a grim reminder of their permanent hunger for all things flesh. He wanted to cradle his friend, whisper soothing words to him. 'It's ok, Andy. The ambulance will be here soon. Hush mate.'

But there was no Andy to hold. Not unless you counted a scorched arm, a severed foot, a mangled rifle. Or that head still in its helmet. He couldn't look at that. No, no. And that stupid arm up there on the rock. Waving.

A crafty vulture winged down towards it, grabbed it between powerful talons and made to rise once more. Josh fired. Again and again. The noise raging in his ears, the anger raging in his heart. He was a good shot: both predator and arm thumped onto the ground, both shot to pieces mingling in a bloodied mess of flesh and feathers.

Josh sat on his haunches, looked at what he had done and wondered how he was gonna get that arm into a body bag? How could he separate the feathers from Andy's flesh and bone? He cried then, sobbed, tears running in rivulets down his blackened face, mixing with snot and dribble from his nose and mouth. He was so alone, so wanted himself and Andy to be together again. In the barracks with their mates, drinking a brew and telling bawdy jokes. He wanted to be a child again, feel Gran's arms around him, and listen to her telling him to 'Hush now pet, it'll soon be over. It's only a bad dream, bonnie lad.'

A hand touched his shoulder, a hand at the end of a clean uniform.

'Come on son, time to go.'

Josh's nightmare was over.

Josh blinked and looked at his grandmother again. 'I moved forward as soon as I could. The air was full of smoke and dust and flying bits of God knows what. I couldn't see Andy, only one of his boots at the side of the track. When I went up to it, his foot, or what was left of it was stuck inside it. Bits of flesh and bone sticking up in razor-sharp fragments, and lots of blood and I dunno what. I heaved my guts up. Then I had to look for the rest of him. Fuck sake, I thought. Sorry, Gran. There must be more than one boot. All I could find were bits of clothing, his belt buckle, and his mangled-up gun. I found small chunks of his head and hair inside and outside his helmet, and an arm that was almost intact, can you believe? It was stuck on a rock and looked as if it was waving at me.'

She watched as he shuddered at the awful memories, wishing she could cuddle them away like she did when he was but a tottie lad.

He got up again, went to the bathroom and she heard him throw up. He was gone for some time, but eventually she heard the tap running and knew, by the sounds, that he was washing his face. He flushed the toilet as well.

'Ugh, that's better,' he said when he came back into the room. He ran his fingers across his mouth, backwards and forwards. 'Want the lights on, Gran?'

'Yes please, Josh. Can you draw the curtains as well?'

'Course I can. Shall I make a fresh brew?'

'Good idea. There's beer in the fridge if you fancy anything stronger. There's fresh ham in there too. Do you want a sandwich?'

'No, you're all right. Or do you want me to make you one?'

'I'll have one later, the tea will be fine for now.' She wanted him to continue with his story: he needed to decontaminate his tortured mind of all that hurt and pain.

'That tastes good,' he said after scalding his mouth on the hot brew, almost like a punishment, a flagellation. 'Where was I? Oh yeah, finding bits of my best mate. Not that there was much else to find. I was determined though; he was going to have a proper burial. The others rocked up then to help. Somebody found a few more bits, gave me a body bag to put everything in. Another soldier lit a fag for me and I don't smoke as you know, but I dragged that one down. Dunno how long I sat there, cuddling Andy's remains. They took me back to camp and the doc gave me something. It made me sleep, anyway. Next thing I know I'm on the plane, coming back here with Andy's coffin and his personal effects in my rucksack. Terrible feeling, you know.' He turned to her. 'Waking up and being somewhere you don't recognise. I don't remember being put on the plane, don't remember much at all really... after Andy was blown up.'

You must know how I feel then, Josh. Except I do remember: my amnesia is not real.

'Foxy's address was in there with his other things, somewhere in Highbury, London,' he continued. 'Don't know yet if he's dead or alive. I don't know how long ago that Andy last saw him. There was no-one else. Andy's parents died when he was a kid. Foxy was the only one he ever talked about.'

Highbury? Wasn't that where Delia Shackleton's daughter lived? Her who was put away as a serial killer... the mother, not the daughter? Ellie blinked and returned to

Josh and his story.

He jumped up, almost spilling his mug of tea. 'Do you know what he said to me once? "He got it all wrong, Josh. This is what it's really like out there, not the stories he used to tell me." We both knew 'out there' wasn't story book stuff, not those putrid smells and the noise: the screaming and the shelling, with the planes overhead and bombs under your feet. I mean, during the day we eat dust and desert heat, and at night we freeze to bloody death. You never know if the local coming towards you is friend or foe. Will he shoot you, stab you, or offer you sweet mint tea? I don't know why we're over there. Hearts and minds be buggered. The only way they want our heart is on the end of a dagger. 'D'you know?' he added, 'they've awarded Andy a posthumous medal. What for? What good is that gonna do? Who will take it? Treasure it?' He shook his head, held it in his hands. Ellie bent to touch his arm. He flinched and tore his arm away. Then she understood, knew why he had done what he did yesterday: pulled away from her, not wanting to be touched by another human being. She had fallen because he jerked away from her: all that agony inside his tormented mind. PTSD.

'What does PTSD stand for, Josh?'

'Post-Traumatic Stress Disorder. They reckon I've got it.'

She shrugged and nodded, understanding. 'What'll you do? Will you try to find Andy's Foxy?'

He sighed. 'S'pose I'll have to. It's the least I can do, I reckon, for Andy. I do miss him, Gran.'

'Of course you do, lad. But you'll just have to remember the good bits.' She winced at her unfortunate choice of word. 'All the great times you had together. I think it'll do you some good to find Foxy. He's a part of Andy after all: a part you didn't know, his boyhood.'

'Reckon you're right, Gran. As always.' He grinned. 'Anyways, I'd better go now and let Mother's cat out, or in, depending where it is. Would you like me to make you that sandwich now?'

'No, you're all right, Josh. I'll make it myself in a wee while. I'm going to watch television for a bit, catch up with the news. Can you see yourself out, pet? Lock the door and then put my key back through the letter box, there's a good lad.'

'Don't you want it in the locker? For the carer?'

'Oh yes. Sorry, I forgot. There should be two keys on the hall table, one for them, one for me. Leave mine on there, will you?'

He nodded, gave his grandmother a genuine kiss of affection. She still seems to have a memory loss about yesterday, he thought, and was relieved. *I'll get the money back to you Gran, somehow. I am so sorry for what I did. Believe me I didn't do it on purpose: then I panicked and made it look like a burglary. What a twat...*

7

The police did not come to see Ellie that night. She knew they wouldn't. It was a white lie on her part: didn't want Josh to be aware how vulnerable she felt, how alone. Not that she thought there was much to fear from him now. He'd purged himself of Andy's awful death by talking to her here, quietly, just the two of them like it used to be. More here than at his parents: they were always away, leaving grandmother and grandson together. Theirs had been a good, strong relationship, until yesterday. Maybe it would be again. She hoped and prayed so...

Time to have a bit of supper now. There's that tasty bit of ham in the fridge her neighbour bought for her from the supermarket. Off the bone too, they cut it as you order it so it always tastes nice and fresh. She struggles out of her chair, painfully: stands up and takes hold of her sticks that hang on the radiator. *Take the pain Ellie, it won't last long, thirty-one shuffling paces into the kitchen. Get the ham out of the fridge, sit yourself on the stool, butter the bread, spread it with a smear of mustard, ham on top, slices together, cut it into quarters, and into a freezer bag: you can carry it easily that way. Then back into the front room again on your sticks. Thirty-one paces, sit down again: bliss! Food and drink: I've got a cup of cranberry juice on the side, to help swallow my co-codamol. Twenty minutes after eating the sandwich and taking the tablets, the pain will be no more, at least for a few hours. The carer will come after that to get me ready for bed. Afterwards I'll watch the box.*

THE KILLING OF ELLIE SWALES

What's on tonight? Holby City followed by a new six-part drama. Wish they wouldn't do that. A week's a long time to remember what went on in the last episode. Still, they usually repeat some of last week's to give you a reminder. What's that noise? I'm not expecting anyone, well the evening carer a bit later on. I'll take a peek... Fifteen paces back to the door, look round doorway see who's there. No-one. Strange, thought I heard a noise. Wonder if the conservatory doors are locked, and the dining room doors leading into it. Josh was out there earlier; he wouldn't have unlocked them, would he?

All the suspicions return. *Does he still want to silence me, forever? I won't snitch on you, Josh, promise. Please don't hurt me again.*

The wind howls, rain patters on the front room glass panes, branches graze the bungalow walls and windows. Only the gulls are silent, or gone out to sea, or hiding in the cliffs beyond her road. She remembers when she and Ben used to walk the lower road beneath the cliffs, right along towards Westgate. Past the war-time coastguard's lookout, now occupied by all those sinister pigeons. Odd they were: it was rumoured that once a wild pigeon had mated with a white dove, and the chicks then mated with each other. Now the old lookout resembles a dovecote of very mixed crossbreeds and its occupants clearly do not like humans. Ellie knows most people scuttle by it on their coastal walks. She and Ben did, always.

Sometimes they walked in the other direction, as far as Minnis Bay where all the beach huts were. Gaily coloured ones, some with stripes, and the new ones that they erected in the Millennium year, of unpainted, natural wood. In the darkness, she smiles a sad smile. They got blown away before the end of summer that year. The October gales came early, in September, just days before the children went back to school. She remembered the devastation, buckets and spades, picnic crockery, kettles, towels, deckchairs and windscreens all blown everywhere, mixed and mashed so that no-one would know what belonged to who. The huts themselves collapsed like a pack of cards, wooden slats and broken doors scattered everywhere, as if a marauding gang of giant vandals had attacked the Bay.

They never repaired the new huts, merely transported the devastation away on open trucks, with the broken pieces of wood carelessly tossed in the back. Such a waste. It was the year that Ben died. He never saw the carnage, was too ill to accompany her on that last walk to the Bay. She never went herself after his death. Age, loneliness and arthritis overtook the will to keep fit. Her walks were shorter, limited to down the slope to the first bit of promenade: until it was best not to walk at all. Sometimes Paul or Trisha would push her in the wheelchair, down to the beach and a little way along the promenade. In the summer, they would stop at the seafront cafe and have tea and one of their freshly-made jam doughnuts. They'd look at the cargo ships far out to sea. On a clear day, they fancied they could see the east Essex coast on a misty horizon, beyond the wind turbines. The cafe's gone now, not enough business to keep it going.

Ellie was glad she and Ben had decided to move down to Kent from Northumbria. They still hugged the coast but it was much warmer down here, the North Sea not so savage, more benevolent, and kinder. Tonight though, she had a feeling of nostalgia for her northern home, a longing to be back among her own folk. Here, the neighbours were agreeable enough, of course they were, but to hear that sing-song 'Geordie' accent again would make her feel warm inside. She thought a lot about the old village nowadays, and the folk that had lived around the village green, where she spent her early teenage years working for old Mrs Hegglestone and her daughter, Amy.

THE KILLING OF ELLIE SWALES

They were good years, by and large, except for the war years and what had happened to poor John Morris. He'd come home on leave, just a seventy-two-hour pass, before going back to Northern France. No-one had ever seen enemy planes so near to the village before, but this one was in sore trouble, with its coughing and spluttering. Maybe the German pilot thought he could land it in the farmer's field: the plane thought otherwise, lost height as it whined and spiralled totally out of control. The people stared, mesmerised. They wanted to run, but where? None knew where the plane would land or crash, which house might be hit, which ones saved. Ellie was rooted to the spot until she remembered poor old Mrs Hegglestone still waiting for her cream from the farm. Ellie used to walk over there every morning, let the farmer's boy give her a bit of a fondle. Didn't matter to her really: sometimes he liked to squeeze her breasts, other times her bottom. Then he would clear his throat, hide his blushing face in his red kerchief and hand her the filled jug of cream. 'Here, give that to the old lady from me. Hope it makes her feel better.' Small price to pay for it, his clumsy fondling.

It was on her way back over the village green that fateful morning when the plane crashed and burst into flames. Johnny Morris had seen her in its flight path and ran like an Olympic sprinter towards her, pushing her way away from the hurtling giant. She rolled over to the grass and ended up behind one of the horse chestnuts that ringed the green. Johnny caught the full force, had no time to run anywhere, before it blew up in his face and left bits of him scattered everywhere. Miraculously she was unhurt, apart from being hit by a few small branches that shivered and shuddered themselves off the tree. Hardly scratched she was, and plenty of willing hands to pick her up. More than wanted to try to find Johnny, or what was left of him or the pilot. They would both be charred to cinder. There was a gaping hole between two houses where the pilot had tried to get to the fields beyond the village green and its houses. Both dwellings lost every pane of glass but kept their occupants and a few blackened marks on their outer walls.

The funeral was the saddest you could wish to attend: full military honours of course. Johnny's widowed mother trying so hard to be brave. It was when the officer presented her with the folded Union Jack that she broke down completely. Neighbours pressed to her, hugged her in her grief, lent handkerchiefs, and half-carried her over the road to the pub where the reception was to be held. The landlady had a stiff drink waiting for her, already poured. They sat her down by the fire in the best chair, coaxing her to 'Finish every drop' and telling her, 'It'll do you good, pet.'

The army took the pilot's charred remains away and when someone said, at the funeral, 'Good riddance,' Johnny's Mum said, 'He was someone's son as well.' Ellie thought how charitable that was of Mrs Morris, a real Christian. It was one of the ladies from the Post Office who had made the remark. Everyone knew their mother had been killed by the Germans in Occupied France only months before, so they forgave her. Their mother was French and had married their father after the First World War. Only she could not settle here in the cold of Northern England and returned to her beloved France. Six months later she was dead, at the hands of those who occupied her beloved land...

Ellie was tired now, still in pain but with two tablets left of her daily dose. The carer had been and gone after helping her into her night clothes. Ellie said she'd already eaten in response to the girl's concerned, 'Will I make you a wee sandwich, Mrs S? It's nae bother.' She said that she'd be fine and wanted to stay up to watch TV. 'Off you go, pet. See you tomorrow.' She was glad to be alone after all her visitors. Tiredness, however, set in; bed seemed a good idea after all.

THE KILLING OF ELLIE SWALES

I'll make a cup of tea and take those last two tablets. Think I'll have an early night, won't bother with Holby or the new drama. Feeling old, may not even make the tea. Where's the tablets? Sure they were here earlier. Then she remembered she took them after her ham sandwich. *Best make sure the door is locked. Did I ask Josh to pop the keys back through the letter box? Ellie, you're losing it, you silly old woman, it's the carer who's just left. Go to bed. Like go to gaol, go directly to gaol, do not pass go, do not collect £200. What was that game? Used to always play it at Christmas with Josh and Paul and Trish. Monopoly, that's it.* She smiled. Josh always hated losing, used to throw the dice all over the place if he was last, and scatter all the little hotels and houses. She rose, slowly, shuffled painfully towards the door on her two sticks. The searing agony each step earned her was almost unbearable. Pity, in some ways, her grandson hadn't killed her, at least she would be free from all this pain...

8

Josh took the scrap of paper out of his pocket, wincing when he saw the burnt edge. He knew, if he put it up to his face, he would smell the cordite, the dust of the desert, the inside of Andy's pocket. Foxy's address was almost faded but he had memorised it, indelibilised it on his mind, Lower Ground, 10, Harbourne Road, Highbury, N1. He was walking away from the station, hoping that the AtoZ of London he had was up to date enough and correct. Also, was the old boy still there?

The area was pretty trendy, he thought, and like much of London, multi-ethnic, along St Pauls Road anyway. Plenty of odd or strange fashions, but it was the capital city after all. Although he saw one smart guy go by, long navy overcoat, striped scarf tied in that ridiculous way, folded in half and looped through itself so you ended up having a scarf that barely covered the V opening of a coat or jacket. The guy also had highly polished leather shoes, defo an ex-officer type. You could spot 'em a mile off. He carried a takeaway cup of coffee, latte probably, the *in* coffee, and a copy of a broadsheet, the Times or the Telegraph: more than likely, the Times.

Josh watched as a no-hoper went up to the guy, holding his hand out, presumably asking for some odd change. He grinned to himself when the guy told the no-hoper to 'fuck off mate'. Then he turned pale as he watched the tracksuited beggar pull out a knife. After that, the scene speeded up: the guy deflected a stab that came in his direction with the speed of light and a well-trained forearm. The next minute, 'tracksuit' was on the ground with a highly-polished leather shoe on his neck, just under his jaw, and the knife was in the guy's hands. He put pressure on his well-polished shoe and Josh watched the tracksuit's complexion change to a bluish red around a pair of popping eyes. 'Serves you fucking right,' he thought.

The foot was removed and 'tracksuit' made a hasty, if limping, retreat. The guy carried on drinking his latte and licked away milky foam from his upper lip. He caught Josh's eye, briefly noted the short hairstyle and upright stance, and nodded and grinned in an unspoken fellowship. They walked off in opposite directions.

Josh smelled many different foods as he continued along the main road: Turkish, Greek, Chinese, Indian, and Jamaican. *Blimey, you could eat a different nation every night here.* He even found Vietnamese and Indonesian. Two shops he could identify with, a butcher's and a second-hand junk shop. Oh, and a charity shop. As for the rest, he could have been anywhere but England.

His copy of the London AtoZ *was* up to date and he found the street fairly easily. He was pleased he had decided to come by train and not by car. The side-streets off the main road were badly signed, with markers stuck on the end of brick walls, if there were any at all.

He passed two or three side-turnings until he came to Harbourne Road, noted quite a few newish cars parked outside the two and three storey buildings. He put the age of the buildings about Edwardian or late Victorian, mostly painted cream or pale grey, over rendering with stone framed windows. The front doors were variously painted black or British racing green, dark blue, and the occasional red one. The street looked a fairly prosperous one: maybe the officer guy lived here. Josh wondered if he had a Jag, or some other classy car parked outside his house.

Harbourne Road proved to be a three-sided square with a small green park at the bottom end behind high, wrought-iron gates. The numbering of the houses was confusing, with no apparent pattern or sequence. Foxy's house, he reasoned, would be down there, somewhere near the park and the railway. The thought of that oddly pleased him. He could not think why.

A thin, watery sun followed him along the street of parked cars, reflecting off their paintwork and glass headlamps, making his eyes water. There was no-one else in the street, or any cars moving. Maybe they're all at work or indoors tapping away at laptops, talking on mobile phones, being clever, or playing computer games. A tall, black guy emerged from number seven as Josh passed it. He scarcely glanced at Josh, flashed his key at a parked Porsche and climbed in while taking out his mobile, pressing keys and gluing it to his ear. Josh heard the deep-throated car engine come to life and watched it pass him as he approached number nine. The black guy still had his mobile glued to his ear and drove one-handed towards the park. He turned right just before the entrance and roared, unseen, around the far side of the square and out onto St Pauls Road, presumably.

Foxy's house was at the very end, situated right next to the park entrance. Out of all the houses he had passed, his seemed the most neglected, with peeling paint on his lower-street door and badly-fitted curtains at the grubby window. His door was under the stone steps that lead to the upper house, and looked dilapidated. It had once been red but was now a faded pink, with scraps of whitened wood showing through. All the other houses had smart pots around their fronts or street doors, with interesting shrubs or a few winter-flowering plants. Foxy's had three broken steps leading down to his basement door and no plants, unless you counted the weeds growing out of the cracks.

There was an iron grill covering his door, reminding Josh

of prison bars. He recalled a visit he had once made to friends in South Africa. The whites lived behind barred gates with guards and dog patrols, while the black population roamed free but lived in corrugated shanty towns with little domestic comfort. Is that what they called equality and freedom? Was this here any different? He could see a bell push, the old-fashioned kind, white porcelain and brass: only the brass had not been polished for years and had taken on a rusty tint with freckles. He walked down the three crumbly steps and pushed the bell. Inside he heard a low drilling sound rather than ringing. Guttural, as if the bell, too, was on its last legs.

Clouds gathered above him, blotting out the sun that had guided him here, and threatened rain. He automatically turned up his jacket collar, hunched his shoulders and waited patiently for someone to open the door. No one did, so he rang again, heard the drilling sound again. Still no answer. He fidgeted from step to step, ready any minute to give up, begrudging a wasted journey even if it had been made for Andy.

He heard a bolt being scraped across and the door opened no wider than six inches, anchored as it was by a thick safety chain. A wrinkled face appeared, one side of it anyway, showing suspicion and weirdness through the gridded gate.

'Yes? What you want?'

'Are you Foxy? Sorry mate, I don't know your surname.'

'Who's asking?'

He hopped from one foot to the other, a bit chilled now and wanting to empty his bladder. 'My name's Josh, Josh Swales: I'm a friend of Andy's.'.

'Where is he then? Has something happened to him?' Then, 'He's dead, isn't he?'

Josh did not know what to say. He stood there, head bowed, shuffling his feet. 'Yeah, I'm afraid so. He asked me to come to see you if anything happened to him.'

They stood looking at each other through the cage. Foxy slowly removed the chain from the door and Josh saw his face; the other half, covered with dreadful scarring, as if someone had peeled off the first layer and gouged the life out of the second. It was raw, angry, and red. Josh felt sick. It looked like gangrene from a wound, an ulcer, maybe shrapnel. Andy had told him he got it in the war. Said he didn't know the details, the how and why and when. Foxy would never tell him. All Andy had told Josh was he had half a face. The other, damaged half, reminded Josh of an old man he'd once seen in an Afghan village. He lived on his own after his wife and children had been killed; shot by the Taliban for giving a soldier sweet tea on a hot and arid day. The old man had escaped his family's fate because he was out in the fields at the time they were slaughtered. He returned before dusk to a house full of flies and blood and staring eyes that still held the terror in them.

Josh and Andy got to know him over the weeks of their patrol. They would share sweet tea and a soldier's sympathy with him. It was Andy who noticed the man's face first. Thought it was a particularly nasty bite from a particularly spiteful insect. Daily it grew and festered. They gave him clean field dressings to put on the wound, but the poison seeped through, yellow then brown and later, black. When, one day, Josh removed the dressing to apply a fresh one, the wound had trebled in size and was black with foul smelling pus oozing from it. Back at camp, they told the army medic who said he really did not have the time to treat anyone other than their own. Eventually, reluctantly, he went with them to the old man's crumbling house. When he attempted to take off their makeshift dressing it stuck to the wound. The old Afghan barely flinched, yet they guessed how much it must have hurt.

The army medic mouthed the word 'gangrene', and swallowed back his vomit.

'Nothing I can do for him.' He cleansed and redressed the wound. All three of them held their breath at the putrefaction, patted the old man's shoulder and left. They never went back.

Josh dared himself to look at Foxy's face. Maybe a shrapnel wound, cut to pieces those years ago. But no gangrene, no smell, except for a certain staleness that crept from the hallway behind the old man.

'Suppose you'd better come in. Here.' He handed him a large key. 'Unlock the outer door with this, it's easier done from your side.' Josh made the inner door just as the rain fell in large icy patters and followed the old man along a worn, carpeted hallway. The rail along one wall was loose with some brackets missing. He noticed the old boy leaned on the other wall, walking painfully with heavy breathing. He could almost hear the creak of his bones. He thought of Gran.

As they got to the first room he smelled stale fish. Yesterday's meals on wheels? It was nearly always boiled cabbage or fish that pervaded old people's houses. Gran's smelled like that sometimes, but not as strong as this. *Her* place was regularly cleaned and windows opened. Foxy's place was like a reeking tomb that hadn't been invaded by fresh air for months or even years. He thought of a Dickens book, read to him and the rest of the class years ago, about a strange old woman. That was it, Miss Haversham in Great Expectations. Maybe Foxy was the male equivalent?

He led him along the small hallway into a combined sitting room-cum-kitchen. There were two armchairs either side of a coal-effect gas fire and a small table with one chair in the window. The table had the remains of today's meal on it. Definitely fish and a few scrapes of mashed potato and a couple of peas, abandoned by the eater. There was a silver-foil throw-away container with a spoonful of rice pudding left in it and a jar of plum jam with a teaspoon stuck in the top.

'My name's John, by the way, John Hollander. It was only Andy what called me Foxy: and my old friends. Nearly all dead and gone now.' He motioned Josh towards the fire grate. 'Do you want a cuppa?'

It was said ungraciously, but Josh didn't think the old man meant it so. Gran would have called him brusque. Foxy beckoned to one of the armchairs. 'You better sit yourself down there.' And he shuffled into the kitchen end, filled an ancient electric kettle and unhooked a couple of mugs from a shelf next to the stove. 'How d'you like it?'

'Milk and two, please sir.'

'Call me Foxy, Andy used to.'

He winced when he heard him use past tense, as if he had resigned himself to his young friend's fate even before he knew how he'd died. Foxy seemed to read his thoughts.

'How did he die?'

Josh hesitated, trying to choose the right words. There weren't any. 'He got blown up. A roadside bomb, an IED.'

'Not much left of him then.'

Josh saw the television in the corner nearest the window. Apparently, the old man kept up with the latest news then.

'I came back with his coffin,' he said. 'We flew back in the same plane.' He didn't tell Foxy about cuddling Andy's body bag, or picking up the pitiful remains and try to fill it.

'He told me how you used to tell him stories about other wars, historic battles and things. He told me to tell you, if he never made it back to tell you, that it wasn't like that. Not real war, not like we've been through.'

Foxy stared at him, brought the two teas over and placed the mugs either side of the small fireplace. 'I know son, but he was just a lad then. What was the point of telling him the truth? This is the truth,' and he pointed to his scarred face. 'This is what war does, if it doesn't kill you. It scars you forever.'

Josh didn't mean to stare but the scar was mesmerising.

'I 'spect you want me to tell you how it happened?'

He nodded. Did he want to know? Yes. What had this old man's war been like?

'Seventh of September 1940. Hitler bombed London. My Mum and my little sister, Queenie, died: killed outright when our house got blown up. I was in the kitchen and got thrown into the fire by the blast, right where the kettle was hanging. My clothes caught alight and the kettle fell onto my face. The water was near boiling.' (So it wasn't shrapnel). 'Over four hundred killed that day, in London, and over 1600 of us injured. Orphaned and injured in one day I was.'

'How old were you, Foxy?'

'Five, and little Queenie was two. Blessed release for her, really. She was one of those Mongol babies: would never have grown up properly.'

Down's syndrome, Josh wanted to correct him, but what would he know about 'political correctness'? What did he care anyway?

'Ironically, my Dad was killed that day, somewhere in France.'

He stared at the old man. 'So who brought you up?'

'Orphanage, just like Andy. S'pose that's why I took to him. I never married you know,' he added, and laughed without humour. 'Who'd want to marry an ugly mug like me?'

Josh sipped his tea and noticed the slightly sour milk: little white bits floated on the surface. Didn't matter, he'd tasted worse.

'How long have you lived here then?'

'Since 1946. I got fostered by a couple after the war ended. Mr and Mrs Carter. Never called them Mum and Dad though, always Auntie and Uncle.' He lost himself in his memories. 'They were good to me, fed me and clothed me, loved me like their own son, even with these scars.' He touched his face, making Josh feel his pain.

'As I say though, I never married, didn't even have many girlfriends come to that. Anyway, when the old couple died they left me this flat and the furniture. Everything bought and paid for, I didn't need to buy a thing.' He said it with pleasure and Josh wondered if he had a stash like Gran, in a side drawer or somewhere. He quickly put the thought away. *What the hell am I turning into? Some kind of monster?*

'I worked in a factory down the road from here, not bad wages for a young boy. Mr and Mrs Carter left me a little nest egg as well as everything else. I was tempted to get something done about this.' He touched his face again. 'Could've had more done on the National Health once it got under way, but it was painful and would have took a lot of time. Plus, I was worried about losing my job.' He fell silent again and Josh did not know what to say to fill the stillness.

'Tea all right?'

'Yeah, ta. It's fine.'

'Mine tastes a bit rancid, reckon the milk's off.'

'Do you want me to go and get some more for you?'

'Erm,' he hesitated. 'I wouldn't mind. My legs are playing up: started first thing when I got out of bed. I knew it would rain.'

Josh had forgotten about the downpour. He turned around and looked out through the grimy curtained window. It was blowing a gale out there, even moving Foxy's curtains, although the window was not open. There was no double glazing and the putty looked like it hadn't been replaced in donkey's years. There was a lot of jobbing to be done here, he thought. It occurred to him he could offer to do some for him, but dismissed his own kindness. He needed all his energy to survive from now on. *I'll go and get him some milk though.*

'Anything else you need while I'm there?'

Foxy looked towards the kitchen. 'Yeah. Bread, I could do with a small loaf.'

'White or brown?'

'Can you get me one of those fifty-fifty loaves? Please? Thank you, son.' Foxy shuffled over to the window table and found his wallet on a shelf above it. Like Foxy, it had seen better days, as Josh's gran would say. He opened the decorated leather wallet. 'Andy brought this back for me from one of his trips.'

Josh recognised the design but couldn't remember which bazaar they'd bought them in. He'd got one each for Dad and Granddad, and a fancy purse each for Mum and Gran. Mum's went straight into a drawer after a brief 'thank you dear', Gran had kissed him and beamed a grateful smile, and transferred her money to it from her old purse. The memory made him feel guilty again after the 'accident'. Once more he hoped Gran's memory would not return, at least not enough to remember it was him who had caused her to fall.

'It's all right, I'll get them.'

The old man gave him a lopsided smile, which did nothing to improve his looks. If anything it made his face look more horrific. Josh shuddered, but not so it showed. Poor old sod, he had little enough going for him. He doubted Foxy had many friends or even acquaintances. Didn't he just tell him most of his friends were dead and gone?

'You'd better take the keys with you, save me coming through again to let you back in.'

Josh nodded, put on his jacket that he'd hung on the back of the only dining chair. It was dry now but, looking out again, he could see it was still raining. He shrugged. *Been in worse situations, and colder than today, a bloody sight colder...*

The convenience store was crowded. Different, too, from those down in Kent, lots more ethnic variety foods. He remembered a song the girls at his junior school used to sing when they were skipping in the playground. 'Picking up paw paws, put 'em in a basket, picking up paw paws, put 'em in a basket, picking up paw paws put 'em in a basket, you-oo are my darling. *What is a paw paw anyway?* A sign over one of the exotic fruits enlightened him 'Paw paws, papayas, £2.20 each'. They looked a bit like a smooth-skinned pear and a bit like a pear-shaped melon. There was a picture of one cut in half and he saw hundreds of black pips inside. He'd give it a miss. He found the aisle for the bread, and the milk was on a side wall in the fridge. The two check-outs were both busy but nobody had more than a basket load. He stood behind a large West Indian lady who smelled of exotic spices herself. She had a loaded basket of items that Josh could merely guess at. When she saw he only had two items, she said, 'You wanna go in front?'

'No, you're all right, love. I'm not in a hurry.' *Not in a hurry to get back to a scarred old man and his stale basement flat that smelled of fish or boiled cabbage, whatever.*

The black woman, when she smiled, had a gap in her front teeth. Gran used to say that meant you were lucky. She had lipstick on her teeth, bright red like her lips which made him unconsciously lick his own teeth. *As if he would ever wear lipstick!* Josh thought she was a happy person who lived life like it was one big joke. She was beautiful in her unique, West Indian way. Good shining skin, huge brown eyes that lit up when she smiled and hair, well cut, that framed her face in a pleasing manner.

'Looks interesting,' he said pointing to her basket's contents.

'Yeah, we're having a family meal tonight.' She had a deep but singsong voice. 'My grandparents are over from St Lucia for a visit. Thought I'd give them and the rest of us a taste of home.'

'I know St Lucia. I been there. It's where the mountains called the Pitons are, right?'

She laughed, 'Spot on, young man.'

Further conversation was cut short when she reached the checkout. As she left she said, 'Happy memories of the Pitons.' Josh nodded and half smiled at her retreating back. *Just goes to show, not all Londoners are reluctant to talk to strangers, like Gran always says.*

The rain had stopped by the time he paid, and he walked out once more into a wintry sunshine that reflected off the wet pavements. There was a traffic build-up he noticed, then realised it was turning-out time for the schools: also, possibly, early leavers from shop, factory and office. Several women walked by with checked or striped tunics showing under their coats, care workers he surmised. Pity they didn't call on old Foxy, he could do with a bit of TLC.

Despite the thin sunshine, Josh shivered. Time to get back to Kent: let Mum's cat out. He would drop the milk and bread off and say his goodbye, duty done. He had no desire to see Foxy again, he wasn't his responsibility. Besides, he had to go back, not to Afghanistan straight away. Probably a stint in Germany, six months maybe, then an English posting for three months and possibly back to Helmand, or somewhere like it, by autumn of next year.

The tracksuit who had bothered the guy earlier today knocked against him and muttered, 'Sorry man.' They eyeballed each other, Josh angrily, and 'tracksuit' with a half-apologetic but begging smile.

'Spare your odd change, mate?' He held out his hand and hopped from one foot to the other. Mindful of the knife Josh knew he was carrying, he switched the large plastic milk bottle to his right hand – it would make a weapon – and the bread to his left hand.

'Sorry mate, no change.'

Tracksuit looked at him with disbelief mixed with desperation. *Must have had a rough day's begging.*

'You sure?' He was whining now, nasal. *Wanting another snort, are you?*

'Course I'm sure. How about you piss off and leave me alone?'

Tracksuit's right arm sidled around to his back at waist height. Was he going for his knife? Two seconds to act and Josh did: he swung the two-litre bottle of milk at the man's head, causing him to stagger backwards as the knife clattered to the ground. Josh picked it up and tossed it into a nearby skip. It gave a satisfying clank against the metal sides of the near-empty skip. *Now go and find it, you tosser.*

Several people had witnessed the incident. None offered to give a hand up to 'tracksuit' and no-one looked Josh in the eye. Not their business, not their war. They hurried by, anxious to be gone. Incidents like this happened there all the time.

Now Josh was angry. Tossers like that were a drain on the economy. Took up hospital beds and free prescriptions to try and get them off their habit. It was taxpayers like him who forked out for their NHS treatments and their no-hope habits. He thought briefly of those poppy fields in Afghanistan. Mad. *Why are we there, defending them... while they are growing opium?*

He looked around for 'tracksuit' and realised he'd legged it, without his knife. Sorted. He was nearly at Harbourne Road when the guy he'd seen earlier walked past him. Turning back, he said to Josh, 'Saw you earlier, didn't I? When that tosser tried to knife me?'

Josh grinned and they fell into step. 'Yeah, just seen him again. He tried it on me. I whacked him round the head with this.' He lifted up the two-litre milk container. 'I threw his knife into an empty skip.'

'Nice one. Waste of space, types like him. Vermin.' He

paused. 'You a serving man?'

'Yeah, yes. Was with the Tigers[1], now I'm with the Loggies[2].'

'Oh really? So was I, till they took me out of Iraq and stuck me in that building on the Thames. I'm out now: not a desk man. You in bomb disposal?'

'Sort of. Not the real stuff, close-up and all that. My mate and I were deployed to look for roadside IEDs. Only he found one. Blew him to pieces.'

The guy looked at him, concerned. He guessed what Josh was going through. 'You on R&R?'

'Yeah, I flew home with Andy's body, what was left of it.'

'Happened to two of my men.' (Josh had guessed right; he *was* an officer). 'Only they didn't die. Both had their legs blown off. One had brain injuries, the other lost his arm as well.'

They fell silent as they walked, shared each other's pain.

Josh said, 'This is my turning.' He hadn't noticed the pub on the opposite corner before.

'Fancy a drink?'

'Yeah, that'd be good.' He held up the milk and bread.

'Better deliver this first. He's an old man, kind of took care of my mate Andy when he was a kid. I'll be back as soon as, that OK? My name's Josh, by the way, Josh Swales.'

'I'm Mike, Mike Beresford.'

Josh tucked the loaf under his arm as they shook hands, briefly. 'I think I've heard of you,' said Josh. 'Didn't you get a gong for gallantry some time ago?'

Mike grinned. 'Yeah, I was more frightened meeting Her Majesty and shaking hands with her than diffusing a bomb, I can tell you. Eight years ago it was.'

'Right,' Josh laughed. He suddenly felt good, the best he

---

[1] Princess of Wales Royal Regiment, the PWRR
[2] Royal Logistics Corps, the RLC

had felt since coming home on the plane. 'I'll be back in five. Just drop this off to the old man.'

'Not the scar-faced chap, is he?'

'Yeah, that's the one. Foxy. Funny old guy, but he's Ok.'

'I see him from time to time when I shop round here.'

Josh said a swift goodbye, promising again to join his new friend as soon as. He quick-marched towards Foxy's, noticed that the Porsche man had returned home and was climbing out of his car, his mobile still glued to one ear. They nodded to each other as Josh passed him.

It was getting dark now and street lights were beginning to flicker on as he turned into Foy's side entrance. He had trouble with the iron-gate lock in the gloom. There was an overhead light above the front door, unlit. The metal security gate at last squealed open so he could unlock the inner door and let himself in. He called along the darkened hallway, 'I'm back, Mr Hollander... Foxy.' There was no reply. *He's probably fallen asleep.* As he reached the living room, he could see him through the open door, head flopped to one side hiding his scars, mouth open and quietly snoring, and spittle drying on the side of his mouth.

Perhaps he should leave before the old man woke up? He put the milk into the grubby fridge and the bread on the work surface by the stove, switched on a light in the kitchen area of the room so he would not be in total darkness when he did wake up. What to do with the keys?

'Who's there?'

Josh jumped. 'S'all right, Foxy, it's me, Josh, Andy's friend. I've brought your milk and bread.'

'Oh, yes. Thanks, son. Would you like another cuppa?'

'No thanks, you're all right. I gotta be off now.'

The old man struggled out of his chair, switched on a table-lamp and shuffled over to the window to close the curtains.

'Nights are drawing in now, aren't they?'

Josh nodded, anxious to be gone: looking forward to a pint with the guy, Mike Beresford, and sharing experiences. Foxy shuffled towards him in his old carpet slippers. His scarred face sagged and was weirdly contoured in the artificial light like tide-washed sand. Josh suppressed a shudder, somehow glad that Andy had died, not been left limbless and disfigured for a punishing lifetime. As he came near he patted his arm, gripped it and said, 'I'm glad you came. Take care of yourself.'

Josh hated to be touched but controlled his aversion. *Not long now, you'll be out of here. Remember what you did to Gran, don't pull away.*

He remembered Andy's medal in his jacket pocket. 'I've got something for you, Foxy. It's Andy's medal, he was awarded it posthumously. I know he'd have wanted you to have it.' He went to hand it to him, but the old man pulled away. Angry, his face twisted and ugly.

'I don't want it. You keep it. Won't bring him back, will it?' he kept shaking his head and muttering.

Josh stood there helpless. 'What am I supposed to do with it?'

'Keep it. Or sell it, give the money to charity.' Foxy moved back towards him. 'Where's my keys?' All friendliness had gone from his voice.

'They're here.' Josh held them out.

You better lock yourself out and put 'em through the letterbox.'

Josh was confused, hurt, angered. He'd come all this way to tell him about Andy and give him the medal. Even went out to get him sodding bread and milk *and* nearly got knifed in the process.

'No! *You* lock me out. And thanks for nothing!' The anger rose above his hurt and confusion, blinding him to an old man's struggle with a dark hallway and awkward security-gate fastenings.

Foxy immediately became contrite. 'I'm sorry, son. Didn't put that very well, did I? I *am* grateful you came to see me, to tell me about Andy. Wouldn't have known otherwise, would I? Sorry.'

He made an effort to calm down. 'Seriously mate, I've gotta go. Meeting someone up at the pub. An old army buddy,' he lied. 'Now,' pause, 'D'you want Andy's medal?'

The old man gave him a crooked, grotesque smile. 'Yes please, it'll serve me to remember him, won't it?'

He made the mistake of touching Josh's arm, pulling him towards him to shake his hand. Josh's mind went blank, falling into a well of blindness, where everything was black, like being in a thick-walled, windowless and doorless room. In the next moments there was nothing but blinding white light, an aridity dry as a desert. He was stumbling in this searing heat with no hat and staring up at a merciless sun that was trying to cut his eyes in half. He raised his hands to his face, trying desperately to shut out the sun. Nothing could take away the uproar that was going on about him. It was impossible to identify, just unbearable noises. He heard screaming, but guttural, not ear piercing; the groans of someone else in pain. Not him, it wasn't him.

He clutched metal in both hands, gripping and ungripping, without knowing what each hand held, but he didn't release either. For a moment his mind cleared sufficiently for him to realise that in one hand he held two keys and in the other, a circular object like an engraved coin on the end of a piece of ribbed material. Andy's medal. He stuffed it into his jacket pocket. When his sight returned, he stared at the keys. They belonged to the old man, didn't they? Andy's friend from his childhood, Foxy with the scarred face. But where was he?

'Hey, are you there?' he called into the room where there was light, aware that he was standing in the hallway. Further along were the doors that locked and unlocked with these keys.

The old man did not answer. Josh rubbed his hands on the wall until he found a light switch, pressed it and illuminated the narrow corridor that would lead to the doors, the wooden front door and the grated-iron gate that held you prisoner and kept out the enemy at the same time. A voice inside his head told him, 'Josh, you've gotta get out of here. It's not safe anymore.'

Why? Where would I go? He was confused. It was as if the blinding white light had returned, burning his eyes like the relentless desert sun. He stumbled along Foxy's hallway towards a bundle of clothes, a lifeless bundle. It was him, blocking Josh's exit. He shuddered, knowing he would have to touch the old man, pull him to one side so he might get through to the front door.

Foxy was still warm to his touch: he slid his hands under his armpits to drag him away from the door. Foxy's head lolled onto his shoulder like a rag doll with no neck bones, leaving him lifeless, face exposed and betraying the ugly scars.

Josh wanted to throw up, like when Andy died and he could not find enough pieces to make up his friend's body. Instead he swallowed the bile. *Best get on with it. But what is it? What do I have to get on with? Round and round in terrifying giddy circles of the mind, like that song Dad used to sing along to on the car radio when he washed his motor on the driveway.*

Josh fitted a key in the door, turned it and heard the click as it prepared to give him his freedom. *Turn the light off, Josh, you don't want to be seen by any nosy neighbours. What, here in London? You gotta be having a laugh!* He unlocked the metal gate and winced as it creaked noisily open. He shut the street door, locked it, leaving the inert figure of Foxy on the other side. Looking around outside in the dark he saw no-one. The glazed front door of the house opposite was in darkness. He shut and locked the metal gate as quietly as possible, pushed the two keys through Foxy's letter box, waiting for the clunk as they hit the floor inside. No sound. Why? Had they landed on him? Can't have done, hadn't he dragged him away from the door, along some, so's he could let himself out? What was going on? Panic set in and he legged it, not up towards St Pauls Road, but left and around the corner opposite the park, which was now in darkness and totally deserted. He turned right again into the back end of the square, where it met the Overground Railway fence, and began to walk towards St Pauls Road, then left towards the pub, The Railway Arms.

When he reached it, he could hear music playing through an open door. A blade of light hit the pavement in front of him. He heard laughter with the music. Someone having an early party? He looked at his watch-face as he passed under a street lamp. Six thirty-five. Christ! Where had the time gone? He remembered the guy, what was his name? Oh yeah, Mike Beresford: said he'd have a pint waiting for him. How long ago was that? Would he still be there?

9

Coming in from the fresh air outside, Josh could smell the beer as he looked around the room. They were a mixed bunch of drinkers: saints and sinners, Gran would have said. Old men in smart long overcoats with velvet collars: straight from the days of the Kray twins. He smiled briefly, his face softening for the first time that day.

'Josh,' someone called from the crowded bar. Mike Beresford.

'Gotta pint for you here, mate.'

He negotiated standing bodies and filled tables before he reached the bar, careful not to push and shove. Wouldn't do in London.

'Cheers,' he said. Took a grateful gulp of the foamy liquid and swallowed deeply.

'Looks like you needed that.'

He nodded. 'You could say that.'

'How was your visit? What kept you?'

Josh's head shot up. 'How d'you mean?'

'You know, to the old man, Foxy... mmm, Hollander I think his name is?'

Josh looked into his beer. 'Yeah, OK, fine. We chatted for a while... about Andy. He was asleep when I left him,' he added.

There was a short silence between them. Josh knew he was being examined. He fidgeted and played with his glass, sliding it slightly sideways and back on the bar counter. His drinking partner remained silent for a minute or so. Then, 'Daft question, but how was Afghanistan, or wherever you were?'

'Hot, dry, filthy, and bloody cold at night.'

Mike grinned, 'Sounds about right. Did a stint there myself. But that was after I left the mob. Went out there with one of our bigwigs: close protection work. Did you say you lost your mate out there?'

'Yeah, Andy. Got blown to bits, IED, side of the road. Bastards.' He spat the word out and shut up. Mike stayed silent too. Then. 'Want another?'

'No, it's my shout. What are they?'

'Kings. Local brew, not bad. Less shite in it than most on tap.'

Josh liked the way this guy spoke: no fancy toff words, more like one of the boys, one of us. Pretty street-wise he considered, especially the way he handled 'tracksuit' today.

'Same again then?' He held up a ten-pound note: hoped it was sufficient. You never knew in some of these London pubs. Needed a mortgage sometimes, for a round.

One of the old geezers with a velvet collar coat joined them.

'Ullo sonny,' he said to Mike in a deep, gravelly voice. 'Ow's it going?'

'Yeah, good, thanks Harry. This is a mate of mine, Josh. He's just back from a stint overseas. Josh, this is Harry.' Mike omitted surnames. The two men shook hands, briefly.

Harry's face resembled a road map on one side. He had a major scar running from his left eye, curving round to the bottom of his ear lobe. The centipede legs of stitches (like side roads) led back to the black patch that covered the offending eye. Josh tried hard not to stare. Harry smiled. 'Got it in Korea,' he said. 'Bastards tossed a grenade down into our bunker. My mate caught it and tried to throw it back out. Reached ground level before it exploded. Took out all my mates and left me with this.' He touched his face but not the eye patch. 'The QVH, Queen Victoria's Hospital at East

Grinstead, did me proud. My old Dad was a tailor,' he grinned. 'Doubt if he could've made a better job.'

Strange, thought Josh, how both he and Foxy were scarred. Harry through his war and Foxy through his. *I hope you're not dead, Foxy. Please don't be dead.*

'Like a drink, Harry? I'm just getting them in.' He put away the tenner and fished out a twenty.

'On me, lad. Proud to buy Her Maj's men a drink.' He called over to the barmaid. 'Mary, give these gentlemen drinks on the house. Whatever they want.'

'All right, boss.' She smiled and shimmied over to them. 'Same again, lads?'

Josh nodded. 'That old geezer own this pub?' he asked her, when Harry returned to his mates.

'And three other ones, dotted about the East End.' She cranked the pump handle and filled their glasses, careful to place them down on a bar mat. Josh and Mike raised their glasses in Harry's direction and he acknowledged them with a nod and a lop-sided smile.

'I'm impressed,' said Josh, when the barmaid had moved away from them. 'Looks more like a gangster than a publican.' This was said in a whisper. Didn't do to get overheard in such an establishment. 'What's he into, d'you reckon?'

'Dunno mate. Down here you don't ask. But knowing Harry,' Mike added, 'probably not drugs. His generation don't approve. Bit of money lending maybe, or hostesses in clubs. That sort of thing.'

They sank another three beers apiece, but made the barmaid take their money.

'You'll get me shot,' she said. 'Boss said to give you drinks all evening.'

'Well, put it in your pocket for later then.' Mike insisted she take his cash, while Josh got drunk and was out of it.

'Best crash out at my place for a few hours,' said Mike as

Josh turned a groggy face towards him.

'Wouldn't mind,' he slurred. 'Just for a little while. Gotta get back to Kent soon as. Gran's on her own, been burgled. Cat's gotta be let out.' He closed his eyes and fell forward. Mike grabbed him before he hit the floor...

10

It was daylight when Josh opened his eyes. He didn't know where the hell he was. His mouth felt like it was full of sandpaper and his head throbbed behind his eyes. Laying quietly, his memory went into reverse. Pub, beers, the guy. On cue, he heard tuneless whistling and Mike came into view carrying a mug of coffee and a plate of toast. Both smelled better than Josh's breath judging by the rancid taste in his mouth. This must be Mike's pad. No way could he have gotten home to Kent.

'Thanks.' He was not quite sure how to address him, so omitted a name, title, whatever. 'What time is it?'

'Eleven forty-five.' Mike set the coffee and toast on a low table by the sofa-bed.

'Bloody Hell!' Josh sat up too quickly, winced at the pain in his head.

Mike grinned. 'It was a good night last night... you enjoyed yourself, anyway.'

Josh shut his eyes, blinked and opened them again. He puffed through half-open lips. 'Don't remember much of it. Didn't make a c... – an idiot of myself, did I?'

'No, you were fine. Anyway,' he added briskly. 'I gotta go out in half an hour, business meeting. You want a shower? It's through there.' He pointed across the hallway. 'Bog's there too.'

It was then Josh noticed his host was clad in just a towel, his hair still damp. He felt guilty, drank the coffee down in three gulps. *Ignore the scalding. Eat the toast, jostle up your liver.*

His bladder filled as he came properly awake and he climbed swiftly out of bed. 'Thanks,' Josh called through the open door. Gratefully he emptied his bladder, ignored the beer odour wafting up. He stepped into the shower, savouring the needles of hot water beating down on his body. Five minutes later he was dry, dressed and had a moderately clean-tasting mouth. Another ten minutes on, he said goodbye to his host and made his way out into the street, not really knowing where he was. Looking right he saw the small park, and left, St Pauls Road. He remembered Foxy. Oh Christ...

The main road was busy, traffic everywhere, including cyclists on the pavements and in the bus lanes. People pushed and shoved. There was half a dozen of them who did the same to him, all together. Bad news: what goes on? He recognised one of them. Tracksuit. He'd found some friends and now they've found him. Sod it.

They pushed and shoved him into a small alleyway. He hadn't noticed it yesterday. They crowded him. He felt a blow to the kidneys and his knees being kicked from behind, making him fall to the ground, but not before someone else had kicked him in the crotch. The combined pain was unbearable. He wanted to be sick but they never gave him time to vomit. They flooded him with punches to face and body, drowning him in his own blood. After a lifetime, his, they stopped. 'Got that loose change now, my friend?' said 'tracksuit'. He rummaged in Josh's pockets. Found the wad of notes in his jeans pocket, a look of greedy pleasure on his face. One more kick and they left him groaning alone in the unfamiliar alley. He lay there for some time until he felt strong enough to stand up. Dizzy, in pain. Punishment for what he'd done to Foxy? To Gran? What goes around comes around. Another one of Gran's sayings.

He felt in his inside jacket pocket. They'd left his wallet. Good. He had cards in there, and his return ticket to

Westgate. He fished in another pocket for a handkerchief and wiped his face, carefully. It had blood on it and grime from the dirty street. He licked the cloth and wiped his face again. Less blood but he could feel his eyes swelling. *Bet I look a pretty sight. Like I've been in the ring with Tyson Fury.* He wanted desperately to be home...

11

By the time he reached Victoria Station, the only immediate train to Westgate was the slow one, stopping at every station en route. It would have to do: he couldn't trust his legs to stand much longer. People eyed him, avoided him, or at least avoided eye contact. A BR policeman asked him if he was ok. He mumbled 'yes', through bruised lips, and limped onto the platform. No-one else bothered him and there were few other passengers. Good, maybe he'd get a four-seater with table to himself. Once aboard he fell into an uneasy sleep and was blissfully unaware of the journey until he reached Herne Bay. Two more stations and he'd be home. Mum and Dad would be in Portugal now. Bugger, he'd forgotten the cat: hoped it had let itself out through the cat-flap. What about Gran? How was she? Oh boy, his head hurt, and his face, as if it had been used for practice in the Premier league. If he looked as yellow as he felt, chances were his kidneys had suffered badly in the attack as well. He was tempted to get off at Birchington, go to Gran's and get cleaned up. Decided against it, better to be in his own home.

A tinny voice announced the train's arrival at Westgate. Soon now he'd be home and then he could assess his injuries, lick his wounds.

The cat had been locked in the front room, unable to get to its food, drink or the cat flap. The smell was overpowering. He threw up right there, in the room with the imprisoned cat. It snarled when he kicked it and made an odd, screeching sound at the second kick before escaping through the open door. He hoped it had found the flap. What a mess, his vomit and the cat's faeces. It had tried to do them in one of Mother's pot plants on the window shelf, so there was earth and shit mixed together. Only him to clear it up. He felt more like dying than cleaning but it had to be done.

In the kitchen, under the sink, he found bleach, some kind of cream cleaner, a room freshener that informed him it smelled of cinnamon and other delicious spices. He'd just have to believe it. Bucket, cleaning cloths, hot water. *Get on with it before you're sick again, before hairy moggy returns and needs feeding.* The thoughts of opening a tin of cat food made him want to vomit again. He scrubbed the soiled carpet, grabbed lumps of cat shit and earth in kitchen roll. Likewise, the contents of his stomach. After a seriously long half hour, the place looked clean again. Opening the windows had chased away the disgusting smells and he combined the fresh sea air with the cinnamon-smelling aerosol. The offending plant pot he flung into the garden. He could always buy Mum another one. It would do... would have to. He was near to collapse; bed was the only answer for the time being.

The phone ringing downstairs in the hallway roused him from an uncomfortable sleep. His mouth felt clogged with blood and vomit and something equally revolting. Last night's beer probably. Who the hell was ringing now? Didn't they know that Mum and Dad were away at the music thing? Maybe they were sitting on a beach now, or beside a hotel pool drinking poncy cocktails. Why they went to these things he had no idea. Maybe it was some kind of charity do? It didn't answer the phone though. By the time he had reached the bloody thing, after limping downstairs and along the hallway it had rung off: typical. He traced the call number, thought he recognised it but was not sure. He put the phone back in its cradle, stood on his good leg and chewed his bottom lip, wondering if it might ring again. The sudden jangling made him jump and, acutely conscious of bruised muscles around his stomach, he picked up the phone.

'Hello?'

'Josh?'

'Yeah.'

'It's Sue.'

'Sue.' *Sue who?*

'Sue Wainrose. Remember me? The girl you slept with two nights ago.'

Oh, that Sue, the one with the gorgeous body and handleable tits, the one I shagged too quickly and ejaculated almost immediately. She's obviously forgiven me, hence the phone call. 'Oh, hi Sue. Sorry I haven't called. Been down in London, visiting an old friend of my mate Andy.'

'Right.' Pause. 'How long've you been back?'

He looked at the clock through the kitchen door. 'About three hours. I stayed the night with an old army pal.'

'Fancy a meet up then?'

It was the last thing he wanted, but life has to go on. Maybe not for old Foxy, but best not dwell on that. 'Yeah, great. Fancy dinner?'

'That would be good. Meet you at The Blue Elephant and we'll go on from there?'

'OK. Give me about an hour.' He looked at the time again. Christ, six-thirty! Another day gone.

'Seven-thirty it is then. See you later, byeeee.'

Yeah, byeeee to you, babe. And hello too. He made for the bathroom: a nice stinging hot shower was what he needed right now, followed by a juicy steak in The Blue Elephant, a few beers, then bring the chick back here to smooth away the last of his aches and pains. He got an erection just thinking about it. *Down boy...*

He showered. Again and again, let the sting of hot water help to heal his physical pain. Towel-dried, he padded to his bedroom. From the chest of drawers, he fished out clean boxers, socks, and handkerchief; and from the wardrobe a dark-blue shirt, slacks, no tie, and his navy jacket.

Downstairs he fed the cat, and shut it in the kitchen where the cat flap was. No shitting or pissing, he mouthed at it. Smiled grimly when the animal hissed at him. Nodded at it and passed his finger across his throat, to confirm a warning, and was about to leave the house through the front door when the phone rang again... Sue. *Now what does she want?*

It was sunny but cold. Should he go back for a sweater? The wind was blowing in from the sea, a north-easterly. It wouldn't be sunny for long, he guessed.

Sue had reneged on him last night. 'Josh, I'm so sorry,' she had said to him on her mobile. 'Something's come up.' She didn't explain. 'Can we meet tomorrow instead? Same place? I'll buy you lunch,' she had added.

He was angry at first. Then secretly relieved. His body was still battered. Another night's sleep would see him over the worst. Maybe some of the bruising would subside. He strode into the wind. Felt the icy bite of oncoming winter. Not as bad as Afghanistan, or the north of England, like wild Catterick, but cold enough. He walked swiftly to the bus stop just as one approached. *That was good timing, Josh.* Not all things were bad. He paid the driver, took his ticket and settled near the front of the bus. A few old dears with their shopping trolleys, and ridiculous hats on crimped hair, reminded him of Gran. Guilt-ridden thoughts. He pushed them away and thought of Sue instead. Lunch and then what? Taxi back to here? Cosy afternoon in bed? He got an erection again just thinking about it. Apart from the other night, over too quickly (his fault), how long had it been since he'd last shagged a chick? Must be six months or more.

Except for that young girl he'd rescued from the Taliban bombs. All alone in the near-demolished house and her shivering with fear. Parents and siblings nowhere to be seen. He'd presumed they had been killed in the bombing, and had put an arm around her to comfort her. Spoke soothing words to her until she stopped shivering. Then when she had looked up at him in a hesitant trust and gratitude, with those big brown eyes and beautiful long black lashes, something had snapped. He had thrown her roughly onto the mattress, ripped off her robes. Raped her until he had his climax. All the time she had not uttered a sound. Only afterwards she keened and rocked her body, covered her tiny breasts with her scratched arms. It was through kindness he killed her, quickly – hands about her throat, knowing her life would not be worth living once her people discovered what had happened. He had dressed her lifeless body as best he could. Then rocked her, gently, backwards and forwards in his arms as he sat on the shattered floor of her bomb-pocked house. He crooned as if he was rocking a baby, telling her to 'hush little girl'. She made no sound. She was dead.

The reality made him drop her lifeless body and get out of there. Back at the unit, he gave them some muttered explanation. Was told he was a mindless idiot, end of. Next day, Andy had been killed: blown to smithereens. Two lives cut short inside twenty-four hours. And he had been with both of them... Why had he done it to her? Why kill her afterwards? Kindness? Be bollocks. Yet he still, at odd times, regretted it. Apart from killing rag-heads in battle, Josh had never killed anyone. Never wanted to... not for real. Not even like the 'bang, bang you're dead' war games you played as a kid.

There was little time to reflect or regret, duty was forever. He was glad he hadn't told Andy, though. His mate would have gone ballistic if he knew what Josh had done.

He got out at the seafront and watched the wind whipping up the sand like a desert storm. He looked over to the Blue Elephant. There she was, sitting in the window, waving at him and mouthing words. As if he could hear her, daft cow. *Be nice Josh, you might be getting your leg over this afternoon, and lunch thrown in.* He'd offer to buy the wine, a nice full-bodied red to go with a juicy steak, followed by her nice juicy body in his bed.

She stood up when he reached the table. 'What's happened to your face?'

'I walked into a hoodie... and his six mates.'

He liked it when she showed her concern, the way she stroked his bruises then gave him a deep-tongue kiss. *Promise of things to come? You bet.* He went to the bar, ordered a white-wine spritzer for her and a beer for himself.

'Do us a favour darling,' he said to the barmaid. 'Uncork a nice bottle of red for us and we'll have it with our steaks. Table seven, in the window.' He nodded in Sue's direction. She was still studying the menu. *Looking for a dessert already? I've got a nice one for you but not in here. Back at my place, and I promise not to rush things today.'* He smiled when she looked up. Slowly, slowly, he told himself. He was thinking only of pleasure: no bombs, no violence, no injured old men or old ladies, and no young ones either.

He liked Sue, she was easy to get on with. Not clinging, unlike some girls he'd known in the past. She enjoyed a good time, no strings or rings, no wanting to be told 'I love you' a million times. His kind of woman. Bring it on...

12

Now she was dead, tangled up in bloodied sheets on the floor by the side of the bed. Her eyes staring without seeing him or anything else: her face a contortion of the fear and degradation his viciousness had caused her. She had a crooked twist to her mouth where she had gurgled out that last sound before she died. Something like 'Why?' *But she'd said more than that, hadn't she Josh? Remember? How she fought you, tried to scratch your face and push you away? It was her, wasn't it, who kept screaming 'No, no' and 'Stop it, you're hurting me.'*

He wasn't sure. Uncertain whether these things had been said or not said. He only remembered the before, and saw what had happened, what he'd done, afterwards: after his world had turned black. His bed, not big enough to be called a double, more like a large single, but they'd managed comfortably on it. And he had held back until they were both suitably pleasured. Afterwards he wanted to lie back and chill out. But she wanted to crawl under his arm, lay her head on his shoulder. Only he failed to recognise what she wanted. As she pulled his arm, tried to wrap it around her, the blackness washed over him like a discoloured sea mist. He was lost in it, floundering, suffocating, overtaken by some irrational fear, some alien-being attacking him. And in the blackness, the all-engulfing dark vacuum, he lost time. He lost the now of his life, the yesterday and tomorrow. He was not conscious, yet was not insentient, just lost, lost, lost.

How long for, he had no idea. Even now, when he looked at her mangled body with the staring eyes, he could hardly believe she had died at his hands. But who else was there to blame? He remembered something else she said, or did she? Was it again part of the nightmarish dream or for real? *'You're insane. Let me go...'* Panic set in. It was like she had just spoken, that dead, mangled body with those staring eyes had just accused him of insanity. He put his fist to her lips, ground it into them until they were silent, until they stopped their accusation. He muttered to himself. 'Gotta get out, Josh; gotta move her... move it.'

What the hell was he to do? He paced the room, refused to look at the mess. 'Think, man. What must you do?' One thing was sure, he could not leave a dead body in his parents' house. 'Come on, you can do it. Think straight.'

Who had seen them arrive? The taxi driver for sure: he didn't speak to them, Josh remembered, only to say 'Fife poonds' for the fare. His car radio was playing ethnic music but from where Josh was unsure, could be eastern European, could be Pakistani, Afghan or anywhere. Maybe he would keep his mouth shut if questioned; he might even be an illegal.

He remembered the Blue Elephant had been busy, staff scurrying from kitchen to tables with barely a glance at the customers, only a mechanical 'Enjoy your meal'. The houses either side of this one were owned by people who went out to work all day, so no curtain-twitching neighbours. The knowledge gave Josh a slight relief, but he still had to get rid of her. How? Where? *Don't panic man, think. Steal a car? No. Hire one? No again. You might leave traces of blood on it. There goes the phone again. Fuck it, who's calling. Can't be Sue this time, she's there on the floor and very dead.*

'Hello Josh, is that you?' *Gran. Course it's me, who do you think it is, the cat?*

'Hello, Gran. You all right?'

'Well, yes dear, but I've run out of milk...' He smiled despite his irritation. The trivia of her life. Major drama over an empty milk carton. But it reminded him of Foxy. *Careful Josh, you've enough on your plate with her upstairs.*

'OK, Gran. I'll go to the shops and pop some round for you. Anything else you're short of?' *Like another £400?*

'No, that's all dear. I'm very grateful to you.'

She rang off. He went back upstairs. Sue had not moved. Well she wouldn't, would she? Then he remembered. Granddad had had a car. He wondered if it was still in Gran's garage, or had she sold it when the old man died: passed away, as she would put it. *Dead is dead, you're not passing anywhere, only to the crem or the graveyard when they bury you.* He finished dressing, grabbed a jacket, and legged it round to the shops. As well as the milk, he bought Gran a bunch of flowers. Best to sweeten her if he was going to borrow the car.

13

Amazingly, the car started first turn of the ignition. 'I just want to go into Canterbury,' he had told his grandmother. 'And the buses are not the greatest at the moment: winter hours and all that.'

'Of course, you're welcome to use it, dear. Don't know if there's any petrol in it. Your mother used it not so long back, when theirs was in for servicing.'

He noted the way she put on her serious face, at the mention of Mum, and that flat, cold voice. She clearly did not like her daughter-in-law. As if Josh cared. He wasn't that fond of his mother himself, or Dad.. They were two different people. Dad had accused him of being gung-ho when he joined up. Josh thought of his father as a bit of a wet, only enthusiastic in his boring daytime job with Thanet council or his weekend games of bowls. But Mum borrowing the car would explain why it started so easily: all to Josh's favour.

'All right if I bring it back tomorrow, Gran?'

'Keep it as long as you like, dear. I don't need it and your mother's away...' She let the sentence hang.

It was getting dark by the time Josh returned to his parents' house. Still no lights either side. Good. He was feeling more confident now, knew what had to be done. He drove the car, unseen, into the garage and shut down the door. The cat was back in the kitchen, still hissing, still unfriendly. He snarled at it, and grinned when it flew through the cat flap. *Watch it Moggy, else you'll be next.* Was he getting a taste for death? He shuddered. *No. No, no. It was all their faults. Why don't they just leave me alone?*

Her body lay as he had left it, still entangled in the bed sheet. The blood was now dry and going black. He got hold of her feet, noticed how cold they were and their stiffness. He dragged her slightly towards the door. That's good, no blood on the carpet. None on the bed either, he noted. Next thing, 'Operation Remove It': the body to the car. He no longer wanted to use her name. She was not a person anymore, just a corpse. He still had no plan for disposal. But it would come. No hurry now. Nobody home, except for himself, for at least another week: car hidden in the garage, and Gran happy with her milk and flowers. God's in his heaven, all's well with the world, except he did not believe in all that religious crap. When you're dead, you're dead. No heaven, no hell, except on a battlefield, maybe. He dismissed the thought. War was a long way away. That war anyway. This battle inside his head was different. It had no country, no war-hungry politicians sending young men and women to do their dirty work while they sat in their over-priced designer offices. No time for that now, best get on with it...

He zipped Sue's body up in a full-sized garment carrier from the back of his wardrobe, the one he used for his dress uniform. Not the easiest thing to do, but he managed to, kind of, fold her inside it. Nobody would miss it, the 'body bag'. Not Mum or Dad anyway. He doubted if they had looked inside his wardrobe for years, not since he had joined up for sure. It was easy to bump her downstairs in it, and to drag her out, via the kitchen door, to the garage. He struggled to get her into the boot. Next, he went out to the back garden to where, he knew, there was a pile of bricks. Left-overs from the raised garden bed Dad had built last summer. He added four to the garment bag. Now he had an idea of where to dump the body: burial at sea. Yeah.

He was beginning to panic. He had driven round and through Margate, Cliftonville, then out to Herne Bay: even as far as Whitstable. There was nowhere within or without these places where he felt he could dump her body. It was well dark, and blowing a gale. Not the sort of night that would produce witnesses to what he wanted to do. Yet still he had not found the ideal place. Then he remembered the place where Granddad used to occasionally take him fishing when he was a kid, where the Wantsum flowed out to sea at ebb tide.

The area was in complete darkness: such a small community did not merit street lighting. Mostly farming folk, such as there were, they were in their beds before eleven and up again with the first signs of daylight. The road, leading to the river mouth where it met the sea, was long and straight, almost like a mini runway but much narrower. Swirling leaves from trees lining the road caught at the windscreen wipers, like skeletal fingers trying to impede him on his journey, trying to pierce the glass. *Ignore them, Josh. Get rid of the burden.* His lifeless cargo bumped slightly in the back as he hit a pothole. Josh cursed, then felt relief: there was no-one around to hear the car as it groaned over the hole. One pothole followed another, as did his curses. He didn't remember there being so many.

He panicked again when he saw the little bridge looming up before him in the midnight gloom. Hell's teeth. He'd forgotten that. End of the road. Now what? *Think man, think.* He sighed, slumped back in his seat for a moment. Nothing for it, he'd have to drag the body bag over the bridge on foot. He killed the engine and sat for sixty seconds, piercing the darkness, window down to listen for sounds. Only the gulls screeched out there in the darkness, and small creatures shuffled in the undergrowth and hedgerows. *Don't they ever sleep?* No human sound, thank Christ, or dogs barking: just the gulls, the unseen animals and the wind. Meant the tide was still in, a good sign. Meant he would not have far to go to dump it, his load. It was no longer human, no longer called Sue, just an inanimate consignment, to be rid of ASAP.

He insinuated himself out of the car, crept round to the boot and opened it in silence. The bag seemed to have grown heavier and needed plenty of exertion, on his part, to lift it out and lower it to the ground. He remembered the bricks. No need for them now, the lighter the better for the bag to be sucked out to sea. The gulls wheeled around. Food? He growled them away. *Not yet, you morons. Let me get it in the water first.* The wind blew in his face bringing with it the smell of the sea that he could now hear as it battled with the out-flowing river water. Like a clash of Titans, he thought. He lugged the bag nearer to where the waters met, waited to hear a different sound as the tide changed and gurgled in the sandy mud, dragging the Wantsum into the sea. He knew, in daylight the waters would interchange and change colour. Black river-water would become brown silt and mix with the blue-green seawater. They would have a last tussle before going their separate ways, yet each was joined to the other in perpetuity.

Josh remembered, as a boy, tasting river water and seawater, one muddy and one saline. But where they conjoined at high tide both tasted salty. Both tasted foul to a twelve-year-old boy. No way would he want to try that experiment again. Best to dismiss it: there were much more important things to do now. He bequeathed the bag and its gruesome contents to the sea and the screeching, wheeling gulls. He did not watch for it in the gloomy night: no need, he knew the power of the tide at this point. Soon it would join the Channel: that is, if the gulls didn't have their greedy fill first.

Josh drove back slowly along the single track, no lights switched on, trying to remember the exact places of all the potholes. He clunked over them again and the car bucked like a frenzied wild horse, throwing him everywhere.

Relief finally, though it seemed to take forever to reach the main road, especially with no headlights to guide him. At last he saw the serpentine street lamps ahead and knew he would soon be there. He flicked on the car lights and accelerated slightly, looked from side to side for any tell-tale lights of houses and folk awake in them. There were none. When he reached the main road, there were no cars going in either direction. Home and dry. Well almost. Was that a cop car on the roundabout? Would they stop him? Relief again, they were too busy to notice him, apparently: communicating with their station by the looks of it. He could hear the crackle of their radio phones in the otherwise silent night.

Carefully, he negotiated the roundabout back towards Birchington and on to Westgate, leaving the late-night police to their vigil. Birchington was quiet as he drove through it, pubs shut and people behind closed curtains and doors. Most of them in their beds, he opined. He took the car back to his own house, not wanting to disturb Gran at this time of night. There was still the matter of cleaning out the car and the house before he went anywhere else. *Hope you don't need me in the night, Gran.* Once inside the garage doors, he flashed them shut, eased out of the car, flashed that too, then went slowly indoors. His body felt lead-weight: enough excitement for one night. All he wanted was to put his head down and sleep.

The bed was as he left it, tousled and without a top sheet. Little did he care. He undressed down to his boxers, conscious still of his bruised body, too weary to be bothered. He fell onto the bed and was asleep in minutes. His last thought was almost a prayer. *No nightmares tonight. Please.*

But Josh's prayers are callously ignored. He moans in sleep and tries, ineffectively, to wave away the horrors with his useless injured arms. All sorts of aberrations appear before his tortured vision, limbless beings with half their heads blown away: maggots feeding on the barely dead, and those whose life is bleeding out of them. In vain, he struggles against creatures clawing him with long-nailed talons where hands should be. He screams and screams. Then the music comes, not the kind he wants to hear; a cacophony of sound, loud and clanging symbols followed by a whining, like a call to prayer. A fierce banging of drums makes him clutch his ears as he tries to shut out the noise. Someone is screaming. 'SHUDDUP,' he yells, not realising it's his own voice that's screaming. Then comes a mantle of blackness, a silence that weirdly hurts his eardrums. In a strange way he welcomes it, anything that shuts out light and sound and the dreams assailing his tormented mind.

14

Josh awoke to an exhausted calm, both down there in the street and inside his own mind. It was like both had been purged from the evil of the night. He was first conscious of it being daylight outside, a watery beam invading his bedroom. And secondly, an awareness of diminishing pain in both mind and body. This thought gave him a quiet satisfaction that he was healing. Consideration of Sue and what he had done were way down on the list of memory and awareness. Even further down the guilt road.

The phone rang, once again invading his privacy. Well it couldn't be her this time; she wouldn't be ringing him, or anyone else, ever again. He smiled a grim smile and ignored the phone. It was probably Gran again. Well she can't be needing milk, he thought. *Besides, I'll be going round there later on to take the car back. Don't need it any more.* The thought passed his mind that he might go back to the Wantsum and make sure all was ok. But he decided to resist that urge. Like they used to say in books and things, the murderer always returns to the scene of his crime. Still, if he did go back, it wasn't exactly 'the scene of crime', not unless you counted dumping the body there as 'the scene of...' *Shut up, Josh. Leave it. Get up, get dressed, go and see Gran. Wonder if her memory will ever come back? Take the car back, then go for a nice long walk along the seafront and clear your stupid head of all these stupid thoughts.*

He put the car away in Granddad's garage and walked through the back way into Gran's conservatory sitting-room.

It was full of sunshine, high-rise chairs, artificial out-of-season flowers on small tables, and Gran on the phone to someone. Josh plonked himself down into a chair, squinted against the watery sunlight, and waited for his grandmother to finish her conversation.

'Yes, that's right, one of your "yellow" posies and my message, "Get well soon, much love, Eleanor Swales." My card number? Surely you have it in your records? After all, I always use you for my bouquets, Mrs Bouquet that's me.' An old lady's giggle, followed by faint wheezing. 'Yes, that's right, Visa card number 4974...'

Josh closed his eyes while she droned on, to whoever was at the end of the line, mildly surprised at her using her full name. He'd forgotten that Ellie was Eleanor. Sounded a bit grand for his gran. At last, she said her thank you and goodbye, put down the phone and smiled at him.

'Hello pet, sorry about that. I was just arranging for some flowers to be sent to my friend Millie in the care home. She's not too well, poor thing.'

He gave a half smile, at least – spread his closed lips sideways; it didn't reach his eyes. 'S'ok, Gran. I've just brought Granddad's car back. It's in the garage.'

'Thank you dear. There was no hurry, you could've kept it for a few days.'

'No, you're all right. I don't plan on going far again too soon. Thanks anyway.' He stood up. 'Would you like a cuppa while I'm here? Tea? Coffee?'

'Ooh, a cup of coffee would be nice. It's such a lovely morning, I got the carer to serve my breakfast in here today. Nice girl, Kayleigh her name is. She's a black girl, probably African I'd say.'

Probably born and bred in bloody Margate or Ramsgate.

'Coffee it is then. Got any cake or biscuits, Gran?'

'Plenty dear. Help yourself. None for me though, not long

since I've had breakfast... Kayleigh,' she said it almost to herself, digesting it. 'Pretty name isn't it?'

'Yeah, very pretty.' *Doesn't sound very African though, you silly old biddy.*

'Actually, she's a very pretty girl, for an African,' she finished.

What would you know? When did you last go to bloody Africa? Besides which, it's a continent with diverse peoples, all shapes, colours, and sizes. Not too many called Kayleigh either, I should think.

Josh went through to the kitchen, passed the front door and noted two sets of keys on the side-table. He pocketed one. *Don't suppose they'll be missed too soon. I'll get a spare set cut for me.* He whistled as he made coffee for them both, nibbled on a chocolate digestive and cut a generous wedge of fruit cake, put it on a small floral tea plate, then poured boiling water over the coffee granules. He was glad that Gran liked good instant coffee. Not like Mum bought, cheap instant and decaf at that: just cos she didn't drink it... only tea. He sniffed appreciatively: smelt just like fresh. Job done. He took the mugs and the cake back through to the conservatory and placed them on a small table next to Ellie.

'Just what the doctor ordered,' she beamed, her wrinkled face in multi-coloured rivulets of shadow and light. Would make an interesting portrait, he thought, except he was no artist.

He suffered another twenty minutes of aged chitchat before saying his goodbye. 'Gotta go, Gran, I'm meeting a mate in Margate at twelve. Thanks for the loan of the car.' He kissed her cheek and let himself out by the French windows. 'See ya.' He smiled and waved. *Old ladies like you to wave to them. And little kids. Wonder why?*

15

Josh decided to walk into Margate along the seafront. Gulls wheeled and screamed all around him. He ignored them. Stupid birds, scavenging idiots. He wondered briefly if any of them had managed a meal out of *her* contents before they sank. Or maybe the fish had most? He dismissed all thoughts of the Sue situation and enjoyed a fluffy breeze from seawards as he climbed up, towards the main road, away from the cliffs.

He passed by the Nayland Rock, once Margate's most elite hotel. Like so much of the town, it showed signs of decay. Not his problem. He glanced over at the Blue Elephant and looked away again. That place will be a no-no for a while, he thought. He wandered on, not really sure where he was going. There wasn't a mate to meet up with: that had just been his excuse to get away from Gran. But he did come face to face with someone he knew from the past, Mr Arnold: Parri as in Harry Arnold, his old English teacher. They never knew what the Parri stood for until their last term at the Ramsgate School. Mr Arnold then signed their references as Pargiter Arnold BA (Hons) Eng. Lit. His parting remark, on Josh's final report, read 'Josh is a pleasant young man who could go far if he applies himself with the diligence I know he is capable of.'
Well, I did go far: fucking Iraq and Afghanistan. Fat lot of good they did me.

Mr Arnold recognised Josh at the same time as Josh recognised him. They nodded, paused and, hesitantly, shook hands.

'Josh Swales. How are you, my boy?'

He hasn't changed much, Josh thought. Pargiter Arnold, English teacher *extraordinaire*. The man who dragged us all up by the seat of our pants and instilled – if not a love – a respect and an interest in the English language. He fleetingly remembered how Arnold used to snag his tongue on words like vicissitudes or disquietude or complicities, and burn his tongue on incandescence. But nevertheless, the rough and not so rough of the seaside town's comprehensive pupils, all scraped their way through English GCSE, literature and language. Not many A grades, but D was at least a pass.

He noted, as they shook hands, that the old boy still wore unconventional clothes for such a school. More suited for an Oxbridge college. His jacket was olive green and velvet, his trousers corduroy, both at least twenty years old, judging by their fading colours. And, in contrast, he sported a red and white spotted bow tie. Jaunty. Definitely a one-off individual.

'Mr Arnold, how are you, sir?' The sir came quite naturally. Josh was back all those years ago, remembering this foppish geezer who also managed, more than once, to show a hint of capable brutality: an unerring shot with the chalk, if you spoke when he was talking.

'I'm fine, Josh. A little older than when we last met,' he laughed. 'But still got most of my faculties. And you?' He examined his former pupil's face, apart from fading bruising, noting faint lines of anxiety and a stress-related tic.

Josh shrugged. 'I'm ok, yeah I'm good. Not long back from Helmand, as it happens. R&R for a couple of weeks, then probably a stint in Catterick or Germany.'

Arnold nodded, looked his former pupil up and down, assessing how good was 'I'm good' and decided Josh would cope.

'Are you still teaching, sir?'

'Good lord, no. I retired ten years ago. Best day of my life.' He laughed again, displaying a mouthful of dentures. 'I still see some of the old staff from time to time, at least the ones that haven't popped off.'

Josh recalled Mr Arnold's deputy teacher, English: Miss Hedges. Poor hopeless, helpless, Miss Hedges. She should never have been a teacher, certainly not in a just-about-average seaside comprehensive. She might have coped in some pleasant, rural primary school. Just... maybe.

For an average sized female, she had huge feet. They nicknamed her 'shrimp boats' because of her large, ugly shoes and they whistled an old tune, 'Shrimp boats are a-coming,' whenever she entered their class. (Gran had taught Josh the song when he was little and it kind of stuck in his memory). Her lips were full, with tiny pimples, like baby nipples, covering them. Rice pudding lips. And she wore unflattering, out-dated spectacles.

Plain would be the kindest description for her. Actually, Josh supposed, she was quite ugly, in a pathetic sort of way. She had no charisma and no class-control technique whatsoever. Josh remembered how their behaviour, their lack of any good manners, would send her scurrying out into the corridor, obviously in tears. Then they would all feel guilty, go quiet, sit still and await her return, hoping she would not be accompanied by Mr Arnold. That could mean death to them all.

Mr Arnold broke into Josh's remembrance. 'Fancy going for a coffee or something?' Be nice to talk over the old days.' He winced. 'Fancy me using the dreaded word nice.'

They had been forbidden to use it when writing English essays, Josh recalled. Parri Arnold used to bark at them, 'Nice? Nice? There are a hundred different ways of describing someone or something. A pleasant day, a good time, delicious food, a pretty girl. And so on and so on. Never NICE.'

Josh grinned. He was glad to have encountered the old boy. Always one of his more favourite teachers. 'Yeah, coffee would be good. Where's a decent place to go around here, now?'

'The Blue Elephant serves pretty fair coffee. About the best nearby, anyway.'

Josh cringed. Would yesterday's waitress be on duty again today? Anyone in there who might recognise him? *Take a chance. They were probably all too busy to click your face onto their memories, anyway.*

'Right then, the Blue Elephant it is.'

Unlike yesterday, the place was practically empty. Too early for the lunchtime crowd. Only a few window seats were taken, by people with an average age of eighty, Josh thought, examining the occupants.

'I'll get them,' he offered. 'What sort d'you like: cappuccino, latte, espresso?'

'Oh, just black coffee with a little cold milk, thank you Josh.'

'American then.'

He lay down the gauntlet, marched up to the counter and stared straight into the eyes of yesterday's waitress. 'One latte and one black with cold milk, please love.' He proffered a five-pound note and looked at her name badge, Sue. Coincidence. He spread his lips across his face, a suggestion of a smile but not an eye smile. He didn't do those too often.

'Ta love.' She took his five-pound note and gave him one pound fifty change. Cheap in here, he thought: the coffee.

'Do you want to wait for it, or shall I bring it over to the table?'

'The table's fine,' he said, and nodded in the direction of his ex-schoolteacher.

'Number sixteen. No probs, it won't be long.' She turned to the coffee machine, clunked a double helping of coffee into it, pressed a button and put two cups underneath. Josh left to the sound of whishing milk as he walked over to the table. She had not recognised him. Good, now he could relax.

'Up and running,' he said to his old friend. 'Be ready in a couple of minutes.'

They settled into their seats. Josh noticed the old boy fidgeting with his jacket pocket. He took out an ancient pipe and put it away again.

'Can't get used to this no smoking ban,' he smiled. Josh smiled back, relieved that he had never picked up the habit, and remembered that Andy had smoked. Went quiet.

'So, tell me Josh, what have you been up to all these years?'

'This and that,' he shrugged. 'I joined up soon after leaving school. Mostly it's been good. Except my mate Andy caught it last tour. Blown to frigging pieces he was.'

His old teacher wore a look of genuine sympathy. 'So sad.'

'Anyway,' Josh smiled, a sincere smile. 'Fill me in on all the teachers. Who's gone and who's still around?'

'Beaumont's retired; moved up north to be with his sister, I believe.' Roger Beaumont, Maths and Technical Drawing. 'Poor old Miss Black died last year. Coming up to eighty, I believe she was.'

Josh remembered the history teacher well: the purple lady. Bizarre in her colour co-ordination: jaw-dropping, every possible item was purple. Twinsets, skirts, blouses (probably knickers as well), amethyst necklace and matching dangly ear-rings, stockings and shoes: handbag, yes handbag as well. Her coats and jackets, all purple, even her books and folders were covered in a kind of purple foil, and her pens and pencils, (did she paint them?) deep lavender. Apart from this mad colour assembly and her contradiction of a name, Miss Black was a quite ordinary-looking, late middle-aged lady; grey hair worn a little too long for her years. The pony-tail would have been more suited to a younger woman (even Miss Hedges). It was – of course – tied back with a purple ribbon, cleverly plaited through the grey strands. Her voice had a slight lilt to it, Irish maybe, or somewhere way up north like Newcastle. If she had introduced herself to the class as Lilac Purple and not Miss Black, they would have believed her...

'No way! I didn't realise she was that old.' He did not dare ask if she had a purple funeral. As if guessing his thoughts, Mr Arnold said, 'Quite an odd funeral really. Her brother organised it and asked us if we would all wear something purple, his sister's favourite colour.'

Josh grinned. He was enjoying this. 'What did you wear, sir?'

'Please, call me Parri. You're not a schoolboy anymore. As a matter of fact,' he grinned, 'I happen to own a purple velvet suit. Used to wear it when we went to Covent Garden.'

'No way!' Josh wondered who the 'we' were.

'I felt it was appropriate for the occasion.'

'Awesome.'

'The coffin, draped in purple of course, was carried through town on a white carriage pulled by white horses, whose livery was purple.'

'Would like to have seen that. Many there?'

'Oh yes, a fair amount of former staff and pupils. It created quite a stir in the town, that day.'

'I bet.'

The coffee arrived and they fiddled with the wrapping on two small biscuits. They must have chatted for the best part of an hour, Josh catching up with the news and Mr Arnold telling him who was dead or retired or of any still teaching at his old school.

'I married Frances Hedges, you know.'

'No, I didn't. When?'

'Must be thirteen years ago now, not long after you left school. She was a lot younger than me, but we got on. Rather well actually; it was a good marriage. No children, sadly. But then our lives were all about children. You lot were such rogues to her, forever causing her to come running to me in tears. I should have walloped you all, except they brought in that stupid rule of no corporal punishment. I expect you've had worse than that, since joining up?'

'For sure. Can't help noticing,' he added, 'you talk in the past. Did the marriage fail or something?'

His companion did not answer for a few moments, lost somewhere in his private world.

'My lovely Frances died, two years ago. Cancer of the ovaries.'

Josh did not know what to say. All he remembered was a pathetic, ugly teacher who could not control a class of boisterous teenagers; who ran out of the classroom and cried in the arms of this man opposite him, the now lonely widower.

As he glanced around the bar, he noticed the tables beginning to fill and the bar counter accommodating the noisy lunchtime crowd, all jostling for first place in the queues. Time to go, Josh thought. He stood up and put out his hand.

'Good to see you again... Parri.' He hesitated to use the older man's first name. Didn't seem right really.

'You too, Josh. Take care now, and keep in touch.' He gave his former pupil a small card upon which were his name, address and telephone number. Josh noted there was no email address. Strange, he thought Parri Arnold would have been into computers in his retirement.

'No email?'

'Well, yes, I do have an email address: just never had it added to these cards. It's p.arnold@btinternet.com. All lowercase. Do you still use your parents' address?'

'Yeah. Don't have an email of my own but you can send me a message any time on my Dad's email; his address is p.swales123@yahoo.co.uk. He'll pass on any message to me.'

They said their goodbyes, Josh watching his elderly ex-teacher making his way through the now-crowded bar. He decided to stay for a beer, just one, and moved onto a queue at the counter. Standing behind the suited and the booted, he listened to their affected conversations; their bragging about spending two hours at the gym 'working out'. He thought a puff of that sea breeze outside would probably knock them flying. Prats.

The waitress called Sue served him again. She looked at him, examined his face. 'Don't I know you?' she said.

'Don't think so love. I don't come from Margate.' He failed to mention about being here, with Sue, only yesterday.

'Right.' She poured his pint and passed it over. 'Two pound fifteen,' she said. He gave her three and waited for his change, then stuck it in the charity box that was chained to the counter, RNLI. 'Thanks,' she said and smiled. 'I'm still sure I know you from somewhere.'

Josh paused, chewed his lip. 'We all have a doppelganger.'

'Dopple what?'

'Doesn't matter.' He walked away and stood by a high table watching the passers-by outside. The wind had got up, attacking coats and scarves, sending them flapping around their legs and faces. The sun was still shining but outside, it looked cold. Josh drank up, hunched into his jacket and went outside. *Where to now? Round to Gran's. What for? Dunno, just something to do, somewhere to go.* He knew his leave was beginning to lose its attraction. He wanted to get back, among familiar army surroundings, among men who he understood, and who understood him. This world was alien to him; he didn't belong among these people. Even his own parents were distant, not his kind, not of him or even for him. Only Gran understood. She had always been there for him. Which made him feel ten times worse about the burglary, the fake burglary. Even worse, the fact that she had been injured because of him. *Please don't remember, Gran, ever.*

He caught a bus back to Birchington that dropped him at the top of his grandmother's road. It had begun to rain: that chill, icy rain of winter-on-sea. He rang the bell, pushed on the door, peered through the letter box and called out 'Gran, you there?' No response from bell, door or letter box. *Doesn't matter, I got a key. Do I risk it?*

Josh let himself in, wondering where Gran could possibly be. She rarely went out, only to the doctor's or the bank; sometimes shopping with Mum or one of her carers. But Mum was away. He hoped Gran was ok, not fallen again or anything. Not dead, he hoped. *Seen enough dead bodies lately.* But the bungalow was empty. In the kitchen, he found washing up on the drainer, a cereal bowl, cup and saucer, plate and cutlery for one. In the bedroom, the silky throw-over was pulled up neatly to the pillows and no clothes invaded the bedroom chair or the floor. There was the same tidiness in the front room, except on the windowsill: next to Gran's high-rise chair was a letter from her optician to remind her of a pending eye test. Mystery solved. He read the time of the appointment. One-thirty. He looked at his watch, one-fifteen. Plenty of time for him to mooch around, delve into her personal life. *Wonder if she's left any money, her 'slush fund', in her drawer there?*

Josh pulled it open, his jaw dropped. There was something unbelievable about the side-table drawer, something that caught his eye more than the usual or unusual items would have done, such as a quarter bottle of gin, a gun, a secret diary or a spare set of Gran's dentures or her hearing aid. The unbelievable was nothing, well something, obviously. It was confetti, not real confetti, not the coloured variety you throw over a bride and groom when they emerge from the church. Neither was it the ticker-tape variety so famously strewn by Americans during big-time celebrations. This 'confetti' was made from the simple task of ripping out pages from a ring-bound notebook: probably more than one page at a time and leaving behind tiny scraps of crenelated paper, self-shredded by the violence of the tear, and scattered on the drawer bottom, the otherwise empty drawer...This was so weird. What the bloody hell was she up to, daft old biddy? Or was one of her carers robbing her? They'd better not be. She paid them enough already for their two short sessions a day. Or at least the care firm that supplied the carers. Josh felt a momentary anger against these people, even as he shut the drawer that did not belong to him. But he had to solve the mystery of this confetti. What had Gran done with the money, her cheque book in its ridiculous fluffy lavender cover, all the odds and sods of paperwork she kept in this drawer?

He glanced at his watch again, thirteen-thirty (back in military mode). Fine, she wouldn't be back for at least half an hour, the very least. Probably nearer to an hour, but he wouldn't take that long. He soft-soled through to her bedroom, noted again the floral throw-over with its matching silky pillowcases all tidy and in place. On one side of her bed was the triple-mirrored dressing table with a glass tray of bling necklaces, brooches and bracelets, hairbrush, lacy mats, and her pills. On the other side of the bed, under the window, her old-fashioned bureau, probably 1930's. He pulled at the lid, it wasn't locked. And looked inside. There, problem solved: a dish of coins, mostly one and two pounds, and fifty pences, two neat piles of notes, tens and twenties and her cheque book, the old one with just the stubs left in it. *Yeah, she would have the new one with her if she was getting new specs. Spend it, Gran: spend, spend, spend. Spend the kids' inheritance. Just leave some for me in my old age. That's if I ever reach it.*

He made to leave the tidy room that smelled faintly of lavender, suddenly aware that both bedside cabinets had gone. More changes. Who was influencing her? Who was taking over her life? He had a feeling of resentment. Jealousy, like a kid being introduced to its new baby brother or sister. He shook his head. Stupid thoughts. Ludicrous. Time to go.

He looked up, through the lace-curtained bedroom window. Bloody hell. Who's that? Bloody gardener, that's who. His mind raced. Did he have enough time to get out of the front door without being seen by the old boy? Gotta chance it. He guessed the old boy would go into the garage to fetch the mower. Best leg it. Quietly close and lock the door. Ten seconds, eight, five, three, one... He heard the wrought-iron gate clang and the growl as Reg (that was his name, Josh remembered) dragged the lawn mower through onto the small drive and take it towards the front lawn. By this time, Josh was on the pavement, but he knew he had been spotted. He did a swift reverse, made it look as if he was just arriving, not going.

'Hello, young Josh. How's it going?'

'OK, thanks mate. Thought I'd pop round to see Gran.'

'Well, you're unlucky, son. She's gone to the optician with one of her care ladies. Don't s'pose she'll be back for an hour or two. Just in time for our tea and cake,' he grinned. He pulled out a silver Hunter watch from the top pocket of his overalls. 'Mm, a quarter to two now. Yes, she'll probably be back at half-three or near enough.'

'I'll come back later then. Thanks Reg, see you.'

He sloped off towards the main road, hands deep in his pockets. Getting cold now. *That was lucky timing. Don't think the old boy suspected anything.*

16

Ellie Swales had her eyes closed, although she wasn't really asleep. She sat in the waiting room with Lorna, her carer, until it was her turn to see the optician. She had talked herself dry of small talk with Lorna, so feigned sleep. That way, she could think without the girl's inane interruption. The thinking bit meant she was getting stronger mentally, more determined to get back to normality, to live life as *she* wanted to. Not in constant fear of Josh, or of him discovering that she had not really lost her memory on that dreadful day. Pity about her crumbling body, the bones that refused to be healed any more. The price of being eighty-five, she supposed. Was it better than being painless dead? She nodded inwardly, yes it was. Did she still love her grandson? Yes, she did. *Not sure if I still like you though, Josh. But I can't abandon you. I've been there forever for you, more than Paul and Pat: no, Paul and Trisha. They never really wanted you, did they? Ben and I suspected they were thinking of aborting you, that's why your Granddad gave them the money to put down on a house, get jobs down here, save you. Let you be born. I wonder, after all that has happened, all that is happening, were we right, Josh?*

She had read in the local paper, and heard it on Radio Kent this morning, about a body being washed up in Kingsgate Bay. So far, the police hadn't said whether it was male or female. Why should she associate it with Josh? Why indeed. Gut feeling? Not a pleasant one and she hoped she could dismiss such thoughts as ridiculous.

Another coincidence: also on the national news program this morning. That bit about an old man discovered in his London flat. They think he has been dead for some time. Won't know until they do a full autopsy on him. The police say (that's how the announcer put it) that they are regarding his death as unexplained. Which means they don't really think it is down to natural causes. Unexplained... *You were up in London, weren't you Josh? Went to see your friend Andy's old man, the one he knew from childhood? You came back bruised and battered. Walked into a tree my foot!*

'Mrs Swales, Ellie Swales?'

'That's you dear.'

I know it's me, Lorna: silly girl.

Ellie struggled very slowly to her feet, grabbed one arm of her carer, and both walking sticks with her other hand.

'Yes, I'm coming,' she called out.

The young Indian optician peeped around a blue-curtained examination room. He smiled and moved towards her, displaying a perfect set of brilliant white teeth and a white shirt dressed with a purple and silver striped tie. Ellie nodded in approval. Nice young man, and very good at his job. She remembered him from before.

He showed patience as she hobbled very slowly towards him. She reminded him of his grandmother at home: old, disabled through age and a previous poor diet in her childhood. She was well looked after now, his grandmother, now she was in England, cared for by his mother and all the family and the National Health Service.

'How are you, Mrs Swales?'

'Oh, ticking over: you know.'

Yes, he knew. It's what the elderly did, ticked on like a clock, until one day...

When she had finished at the optician's, and chosen new specs, she asked Lorna to take her to the Auction House, just off the main road, in Cliftonville. It had been a long time since Ellie had attended one of their sales.

Lorna pushed Ellie through the already-filling room towards the front. The Auctioneer greeted her personally.

'Lovely to see you, Ellie. It's been some time.'

'Too long, Robert, but I'm here now. I've come to see the drum-table, number fifty-five in the catalogue.' She waved a copy in front of him, noting his tweed jacket, checked shirt and plain woollen tie. He still scrubs up well, she thought, as they say nowadays.

'Yes, it's a nice little number. Not too far down the lots either. I think we have four hundred in today.'

Ellie laughed, 'I don't think we'll be staying till the end, Lorna, my carer, has to be back before seven to get my dinner and then go on to her next old lady. She introduced the two of them then turned to greet one of the porters in his light brown overall.

'Hello Len, how are you?'

''Ello Mrs Swales, nice to see you. Yes, I'm fine thanks.'

'How's your boy coming on?'

'Great, he works here full time now. Mr Fullerton's gonna train him up to be an assistant auctioneer; thinks he's good enough.'

She could hear the pride in his voice. 'Well done that lad.'

Len removed a wooden chair from the front row to make way for her wheelchair, nodded to Lorna and left them to begin his work.

'You'll love it,' she told Lorna.

'I bet I will: never been to an auction before. Seen them on the telly though. You planning on buying anything else, Mrs Swales?'

'No, just the little drum-table. You have to bid for it first. Just watch and listen, you'll get the hang of it. But don't bid,' she warned, 'unless you can afford to pay for whatever you bid. Once the hammer goes down, you're committed.' She showed Lorna her numbered wooden paddle. 'This is what you hold up when you want to bid.'

Lorna giggled. 'It reminds me when they give you those wooden spoons in the Jolly Maltster, when you order your food at the bar. Anyway,' she added, 'I won't be buying today, didn't bring any cash or cards with me.'

Ellie nodded. 'Ssh, they're about to begin.'

Robert Fullerton mounted the rostrum, his small hammer nestling comfortably in his large hand. 'Good afternoon, everyone.' The crowd murmured, shifting their feet, rustling their catalogues. One or two coughs came from the smokers, or the nervous.

'Right then, let's make a start. Lot number one.'

He turned towards Len, his senior porter, who held up one of two chairs.

'A pair of Edwardian bedroom chairs. Fifty pounds? Thirty then? Ok,' he said to the silent room, 'Start me at ten pounds. Ten I'm bid, twelve,' and he waved his hand at someone in the back of the room. 'Fifteen, eighteen, twenty, twenty-five. You, sir, at the back, do you want twenty-eight? No?'

A new bid came from somewhere in the middle of the room. Finally, the bedroom chairs went for thirty pounds. Very quickly, Robert Fullerton went through the lots until he came to lot fifty-five.

'Here we have a very nice drum-table with cupboards *and* drawers. I have bids of forty-five, fifty, fifty-five,' and he pointed towards a sheet in front of him. Sixty was offered in the room: the auctioneer turned his hand back to his paper, did a nose-dive down with his forefinger. 'Sixty-five.' Someone in the room offered seventy pounds. Ellie did not raise her paddle until there was a brief lull in the bidding.

'Do I hear one hundred? New bid at the front.' He looked down at Ellie. She nodded.

'One hundred pounds, the lady in the front row.'

Ellie could sense eyes turning towards her. Another pause. The old excitement took over her; butterflies fluttering in her stomach, adrenalin flowing. There was just herself and an unseen bidder now, towards the back of the room, and his bids were coming in after significant pauses. She willed no more bids. She wanted that table; such a pretty piece of furniture, to replace the old one she and Lorna had emptied that morning. The one that Josh had 'robbed'.

'I'm going to sell at five hundred pounds. Going once, twice,' and he brought the hammer down on his desk. 'Sold to bidder number twenty-five,' he said to his assistant who was busily writing down the details.

Ellie knew she could not stay till the end of the auction. It would be dark by then and much colder. Besides, Lorna had to be with her next client at seven-thirty. She wheeled Ellie round to the paying booth and gave the girl, behind the glass window, Ellie's bidding paddle.

'Hello Mrs Swales, how're you?' Tamsin was Robert Fullerton's daughter, his cashier and secretary.

'I'm fine, Tamsin. Would love to have stayed till the end, but well, you know...'

Tamsin smiled. 'That'll be £560 including commission and VAT. If you just sign it,' she indicated Ellie's chequebook, 'I'll fill it in for you.'

'Thank you dear.' Ellie, rested the cheque book on her lap, signed her spidery signature and passed her chequebook over the counter. She saw, out of the corner of her eye, Lorna's wince, probably at the final amount for the purchase of a drum table that you couldn't even sit around. Ellie gave a secret smile.

Tamsin showed her the completed cheque. 'Would you like me to fill in the stub as well?'

'Thank you, dear, that's kind of you.'

'No problem.'

Everyone says that nowadays, 'no problem'. Used to be 'that's all right', or 'you're very welcome'. Now it's 'no problem'. Mmm.

Ellie was glad to get back to Lorna's car and even more relieved when they arrived home.

'I'll put the kettle on, Mrs S. I think we can both do with a cuppa after such a busy day. Very exciting though. When will they deliver your new table?'

'Probably late tomorrow morning, around noon. They usually make me one of their first drops after loading the van.' She yawned. 'Yes, it has been quite a day. Think I'll be early to bed tonight.'

17

Ellie could not settle. Lorna had left an hour ago after preparing her evening meal. A light one, of scrambled egg on toast with a fruit yoghurt to follow and a final cup of tea. Then the two of them, carer and client, teased and jollied the old lady out of her day clothes and into a nightie with the minimum amount of pain. Finally, the carer tucked up her charge in bed, kissed her on the cheek and said, 'Night, night, sleep tight and don't let the buggers bite.' She said this every time she put Ellie to bed but it still made the old lady giggle. Lorna said her goodbye and Ellie heard her shut the front door behind her, lock it, and the chink as she dropped the keys into their outside safe with its four-figure combination numbers, ready for the morning carer.

But sleep would not come; she was uneasy. Josh had been here, she knew. She had picked up signs that Lorna would not have seen or been aware of, a barely visible imprint of a desert boot on the carpet in front of her bureau, the faint aroma of deodorant, man perfume. And when she had sat in the lounge, with her supper tray on her lap, she had noted one or two scraps of paper on the floor that had definitely come from her side-table drawer. She felt invaded, vulnerable, not master or mistress of her own destiny. It was vexing enough having to rely on a team of carers to feed, wash and dress her: which meant she'd had to relinquish much of her independence and her privacy, and most of her dignity. But to think that Josh was coming and going in her home both frightened and angered her. *You have no proof, Ellie. The footprint could have been there on a previous visit. No, it couldn't, Julie's been here since then, cleaned the whole place and vacuumed the carpet. Mmm. What about the paper scraps in the front room? Don't know, maybe Lorna or I dropped them when we cleared out the drawer this morning. How d'you get in, Josh? Got keys, have you?*

She decided to get out of bed and go through to the front room. *Might as well watch a bit of telly.* It took the best part of ten minutes to put her feet to the floor, feel her way painfully into her slippers, and drape a soft fleece dressing gown around her shoulders: every movement agony but necessary. For a moment, she felt independent again and smiled to herself. *Go Ellie, go.*

A further ten minutes took her into the hallway, past the bathroom that was now a wet-room. All mod comforts here, she thought; until she was level with the front door in one direction and the lounge opposite. Ellie saw a piece of paper peeking through the inner lid of the letterbox. Not like Lorna to miss that, she thought, unless it had been pushed through later, maybe from one of her neighbours. She hobbled towards the front door, dark on the outside and only a dim light in the hallway. She retrieved the scrap of paper and took it slowly through to the front room. The curtains were closed but there was sufficient light to guide her to her chair and the touch lamp next to it. After tucking herself into a chenille throw-over, she put on her specs and unravelled the note. It was from Reg, the gardener. 'Thanks for tenner (found in the garage). Have given the front lawn what should be its last mow of the year, and tidied up the back garden some. By the way, your grandson called while I was here, said he would call back later. See you next week, Reg.

So, she was right, Josh had been here. *How did he get indoors? He <u>must</u> have a key. Means I'll have to get the locks changed again. Damn you, Josh.*

Ellie switched on the TV. Might as well watch something to take her mind off the problem. 'Who Do You Think You

114

Are?' was just about to start. That would do, although she knew who she was. It's the other buggers. She resorted to swearing, something she rarely did, but had to admit it was happening more recently. Perhaps that's what dishonest grandsons made you do, she thought. The program turned out to be a disappointment; an emotional second-grade actress crying her crocodile tears for a long-dead ancestor. Didn't she know all the poor suffered in those days? Not like some of the so-called poor today, with their many ear and body piercings and multiple tattoos and fifty-two inch televisions invading their living space.

She nodded off in her mute disapproval and woke at something past midnight, got up slowly and hobbled painfully back to bed. It was gone twelve-thirty when she eventually turned out the light. Sleep overcame her almost immediately. Yes, it really had been a long day.

Ellie was relieved that today's carer, Tessa, arrived early and had her up, dressed and breakfasted by nine o'clock. She wanted to be ready for Len, Robert Fullerton's porter, when he delivered her table.

'That's right, dear,' she said to Tessa. 'Just put that table,' (indicating the one she was replacing) 'over by the door, then we'll put the new one there in its place.'

Tessa grinned. 'You're really looking forward to your delivery, aren't you, Mrs S?'

'Oo yes, a bit like Christmas, don't you think?'

'Absolutely. Right,' and she lifted out the table with ease. 'Off with the old and in with the new is what I say.'

'Quite so. Er, is that a van drawn up outside?'

Tessa looked out of the window. 'Yes, a massive one. It says Fullerton's Auctions on the side. There you go,' she added. 'You must be their first delivery.'

Ellie watched as two men in their light-brown overalls jumped nimbly out of the furniture van, walked round to the back, unfastened the two doors and clipped them to the side with a noisy clang. They wound down a large, wide step and the slightly younger porter, that Ellie recognised as Buckingham Norman, jumped inside and presently emerged with the drum table she had successfully bid for yesterday afternoon. He carried it up the garden path, and around to her front door, followed by Len. Tessa was there with the door open, ready to let them in. She pointed through to the front room. 'In there, guys,' she instructed them.

Ellie gave the two men a welcoming smile. 'Splendid,' she said. 'I knew you'd be early, but you've exceeded yourselves. Well done.'

Len gave a mock bow, 'All part of the service, Mrs Swales. Besides, you're our favourite customer.'

Norman nodded, grinning his agreement. 'Sure are, ma'am.'

Tessa called out from the kitchen, 'Would you guys like a brew before I go?'

'Please love,' said Len. 'And a wedge of Mrs S's lovely cake. She's bound to have one, always does.'

Ellie wagged a finger at him, 'Still as cheeky as ever, young Len.'

'I like the young bit: wish I was.'

She noted his greying hair, the stoop to his thin body, no doubt caused through years of lifting heavy furniture and the like. Yes, she thought, portering for an auction house was definitely more suited to younger, fitter men. Norman, though not much younger than Len, was built more stockily. He used to be a cattle drover in Buckinghamshire (hence his nickname): took the beasts, as he called them, to various markets in and around his native county. When the work dried up, he moved to Kent and was soon employed by Robert Fullerton.

'Lovely cuppa, girl,' Len said to Tessa. 'Shall we christen the new table, Mrs S?' and he hovered over it with his plate containing a generous slice of fruitcake.

'Don't you dare, Leonard Cousins! Stick your plate on the mantelpiece.' But she laughed, saying 'Course you can.'

Ellie liked the table even more now she could see it at such close range. Yes, she thought, it will suit me well. *My only problem now is Josh.*

When everyone had gone, she could think about the Josh problem. She decided to ring Reg: not only her gardener but a good, general handyman. 'What I can't do,' he often said to her, 'I know someone who can.' This was always said with a laugh. Reg was of the age when he found amusement in his own jokes and Ellie would always laugh with him. Reg was a trusted friend. She picked up the large-numeral phone and slowly dialled his number.

'He...hello, is that you, Reg?'

'It is, Ellie. Are you all right?

'Yes, I'm fine. Just want a bit of advice.'

'What about?'

She hesitated, wondering how much to tell him, about the 'burglary', about Josh.

'Tell you what,' Reg broke into her thoughts. 'I've got a spare few hours, why don't I come round?'

'Ooh. That would be lovely. You don't mind?'

'Course not. Anything for you, Mrs S. I'll be round in half an hour. I'll bring your bedside tables with me; they're both fixed now.'

Ellie thanked him, rang off, and sat back in her chair. Relieved now she had made a decision. Get the locks changed, get them to work for her with some kind of remote control: maybe a speaker system so she could identify the caller. Yes, give her the power...

18

Josh returned to his parents' home frustrated, thwarted. Twice he'd been to Gran's house and twice she hadn't returned. He daren't risk letting himself in a second time; she'd surely be back and know he had a key. Tiredness took over. Not the sort from overwork, more from troubled sleep: Josh was getting plenty of that.

The cat did its usual mewling and growling at the sight of him. He snarled at it and the cat hissed back. God, how he hated that animal. *No food for you, mate, not until you learn some manners. No drink either.* He had noticed the cat's drinking bowl was empty. It mewled at him again, a feline plea for food and drink no doubt. Tough.

Josh wandered through the empty house and climbed the stairs. He sniffed. An unpleasant smell, worse – a putrid smell. Sue come back to haunt him? He frowned, then smiled. Yeah right. The smell got worse in his bedroom, made him feel uneasy. No such thing as ghosts, or haunting. *Leastwise, not in my book.* He found the source of the smell, cat piss and shite on his clean throw over. Bastard! He took the stairs like a toboggan, reached the kitchen.

'Oi, moggy. What's wrong with using your bloody flap instead of my bed?'

He grabbed it by the tail, ignored the scratching and biting, then shoved its head towards the cat flap in the kitchen door. Only it would not go through. Somehow the flap had jammed, self-locked. He felt the cat's head crunch with the force of it hitting the immobile flap. It snarled like it had never done before, wriggled like a maddened viper and sank its sharp teeth into his arm, drawing blood immediately.

There is music in Josh's ears; but not the kind of music he wants to hear: a cacophony of sound. Loud and clanging symbols one moment, then a whining, mournful Muslim-like call to prayer. Followed by ferocious banging of drums, or bombs or guns. He clutches his ears, tries to force out the noise. He falls on to his knees, crouches, still holding his ears. Someone is screaming, 'SHUDDUP.' Not realising that it's himself who screams. His own voice.

Then comes a mantle of blackness; a silence that stills the pain of his eardrums. He welcomes it, anything that shuts out light and sound. Anything that hushes the thinking of a tormented mind.

It is like a muffled sleep, when your head as well as your body is wrapped inside the bedclothes, shutting out the world beyond. There is no world, only this cocooned darkness, nothingness, numbness. An embryonic state of floating in pre-birth waters. There is no pain, no memory, no consciousness, not even the id state of being.

Josh has no drugs in his system, no alcohol; nothing that could be said to have induced this black void. When he comes to, he sees the cat spread-eagled on the kitchen floor. Its mouth is open showing traces of blood, and something else that Josh does not care to identify. Its body seems to have no bones to shape it, more like the floppy, empty pyjama case he had when he was a boy, only that was a tiger that Gran had bought him.

The cat was clearly dead, had met a violent death. Josh shook his head. How? When? Why? *You must have done it, Josh. No-one else here.* He had no memory of doing anything. He rubbed his chin, saw the blood and abrasions on his hands, cat scratches. Bastard! He moved to the kitchen sink and washed his hands under near-scalding water, rubbing them in liquid detergent until all traces of blood disappeared. He dried them on a tea towel.

The cat was still dead, had not moved. Well it wouldn't, would it? Not till he got rid of it. Easier than Sue, anyway; straight into a bin bag and outside to the wheelie-bin. The dustmen were due tomorrow he thought: Mum and Dad another week's time. Bit of luck that.

What to do now? Then he remembered the bedclothes. He ran up the stairs, tore into his bedroom, and ripped off the disgusting bedclothes, folding them into each other, even the pillows. He stripped the bed bare, opened the window to get rid of the nauseating odour and took the offensive linen downstairs, pushed it into two bin bags and dragged it out to the wheelie bin to join the remains of the vicious, now dead, moggy.

He went back indoors, shivered as the sea winds followed him in. He only had slacks and a short-sleeved shirt on. The house was warm, central heating on, but he was sure the smell lingered. He found a fresh-air spray under the kitchen sink. Lilies of the valley; that would do. He went upstairs, sprayed his room, the upstairs hallway, then down the stairs and back into the kitchen, emptying the canister. He watched the tiny droplets cascade around him, sniffed the floral smell and nodded. He was satisfied. Now what? Best put fresh linen on his bed. There would be plenty in the linen cupboard upstairs; Mum always made sure she had plenty of sheets, towels, duvet covers. Just in case of... what? Unexpected guests? Josh smirked at the thought. When did they ever have anyone to stay? Used to have Andy occasionally, when they came home on leave together. Won't be doing that any more.

He found a fresh duvet-cover, sheet and pillowcases. Scowled. He'd thrown away the duvet and the pillows along with the shite-infested bed linen. He searched the cupboard for pillows. Yes, there were two and a duvet, a double. That would do. Just have to swap the single cover and sheet for doubles... he shivered again, remembered the open window. He looked out onto the back yard, saw lights on in the windows opposite. As he shut the window against the cruel breeze, he saw a girl, beyond the back yards, at a window the same level as his. Bloody hell! She was undressing, sweater off over her head. *Nice head of hair, long, blonde.* She bent double. *Must be taking off her trousers.* The thought made his pulse race: he stiffened inside his slacks. She stood up again and took off her bra, then down again. *Panties this time?* Josh drew his breath in, stuck a hand down his trousers and felt his swelling. She must have suddenly realised she was doing a strip show in front of her uncurtained window, looked straight at him, or so it seemed. She was not close enough for him to see whether she blushed, but she pulled her drapes across, almost viciously. *Spoilsport, I was just enjoying the view. Nice tits, lady.* Maybe she didn't see me, he thought. He still had the light off.

After finishing making up the bed, Josh went downstairs for a beer. The smell had left the kitchen but the cat's bowls were still on the floor. He picked them up and shoved them in the swingbin. Won't be needing them anymore. He thought about what he would say to his parents when they returned. *Sorry Mum, but I killed the cat, bashed his head against the locked cat flap. That's what must have happened, wasn't it?*

There was still a four-pack of lager in the fridge, a mouthful of cheese and a mouldy tomato. He pulled out a can of lager from its cardboard wrapping, and the cheese, ignoring the mouldy tomato. Enough housework for one day, without having to clean the fridge. He glanced at the kitchen clock: bloody hell, five o'clock and gone. Almost dark outside. Street lights were on anyway, bringing the darkness even closer. He paced up and down the kitchen, beer in one hand and wedge of cheddar in the other. He was restless, what to do next? Go out? Where? See Gran? *She's bound to be in and having her tea; cardboard sandwich and an iced fancy or something.* Josh still felt hungry but did not relish the idea of eating on his own in the house. Nothing left anyway, apart from the rotten tomato, or made-up meals in the freezer. He could pick up a chicken and salad wrap or something at the deli on the way, eat it en route. He nodded, bit into his bottom lip. Yeah, that's what he'd do...

19

He shrugged on a jacket, looped a scarf round his neck, unconsciously copying the guy in London, Mike; thought about gloves even, but had no idea where there were any. He shut the front door behind him, head down against the wind, and turned left towards the next road and the bus stop. It was only a couple of stops to Gran's but he didn't relish the walk tonight. As he turned the corner towards the deli and the bus stop, he noticed a girl in front of him, recognised the head of hair, about the only thing left to recognise as the rest of her was wrapped, similarly to himself, against the cold. It was the girl who had stripped at the window opposite his bedroom. Interesting, he thought, and quickened his pace, wanting to keep up with her. *Wonder if she'll know who I am?*

She went into the deli in front of him.

'Hi Luigi, can I have two of your chicken panini, please?'

She had a pleasant voice, slightly deep, good diction. *Nice bum, squeezable, very.*

'Pronto, signorina. E insalata?'

'Just tomatoes and lettuce thanks.'

Josh watched while the Italian shopkeeper deftly sliced the warmed bread and the tomatoes. Razor-sharp knives, he thought: could do a lot of damage with them.

'And a bottle of Pinot Grigio di Veneto, please. Have you got one chilled?' she added and looked round at Josh as if suddenly aware of his presence. She gave a half smile, but not one of recognition. *Good, could mean he was in with a chance.* He risked a jokey remark.

'Sounds like a pleasant start to the evening. Party night?'

The smile wavered, did not become a full one, the voice not quite so pleasant.

'Not really. Supper at my brother's actually.' *In other words, mind your own damned business.*

Luigi placed the filled paninis and the bottle into one of his green, white and red paper bags, smilingly took her money, said 'Grazie signorina', and turned to Josh. 'Signore?'

Reluctantly, Josh looked away from the girl. *Try another time.*

'Yeah, I'll have... erm... one of what she had?' He turned to look at her again but she was already leaving the shop, pulling open the door which pinged as she went through. No backward glance, just a wave and 'Ciao, Luigi'.

The shopkeeper grinned at him. 'Bella, aye?'

Josh nodded and grinned. His smile widened when Luigi put his right hand into his left elbow-joint and pulled up his left hand in a lewd gesture.

'Yeah, that as well...'

He watched while the Italian sliced the tomato, the bread and the chicken: admired the slightly-dramatic movement of his hands as he put the panini sandwich together, placed it in a paper bag and swept it into a tri-coloured carrier.

'Something else, signore? Some wine perhaps, or Peroni beer?'

Josh looked at his watch; nearly six thirty, bit late to go round Gran's now. The carer was probably there, getting the old girl ready for bed. Maybe he'd ring her, make sure she was ok. Maybe he would, maybe he wouldn't. He scowled in his head.

'Give me six Peroni's, please mate.'

'They come in a four pack: do you want four or eight?'

Decisions, decisions... 'Eight sounds good.'

He paid, took his bag of goodies, pinged the door and

walked out into the biting wind. So much for living by the sea. He shivered, anxious now to get back to the house. He'd go out tomorrow night. As he walked back to the corner, he saw the girl step into the bus, go up to the driver and pay her fare. *Wonder where your brother lives, darling? Wonder if he'd mind another guest tonight? Perhaps not.*

20

Josh was home, in bed; not his own. Even with clean linen and the air polluted with fresh-air spray smelling of lilies of the valley, his room felt anything but right. He was in his parents' king-sized bed, with its crisp, white Egyptian-cotton linen. He sat up, leaned against three of the four pillows, sipping his father's best malt. Downstairs in the kitchen were crumbs from his panini sandwich and eight empty Peroni bottles.

He let his thoughts drift, vaguely heard the sounds of seagulls outside, ghosts of the night; waves splashing, crashing against the impenetrable seawall. An occasional car going by, its lights briefly illuminating the room, first in one window, then the other before disappearing into the night. He could tell which direction each car was going by which window caught the light first. He wriggled on the pillows, scratching an itch in the middle of his back, till he found a second one, a third. He thought, funny how one itch leads to the next. He remembered, years ago, either Mum or Gran had had this long bamboo handle with carved fingers on the end, a back scratcher; how they had used it to reach the unreachable places on their back, a look of almost ecstasy on their faces when the itch was scratched: of moving the long-handled fingers to a fresh spot to alleviate a second or third itch. It made him think of something Parri Arnold used to quote. 'The moving finger writes, and having writ, moves on.' From the Rubaiyat of Omar Khayam, he recalled.

Another car briefly illuminated the room then left it again in darkness. Josh switched on the side-table lamp. He looked around, kind of resenting his parents for having this room, large, airy and facing the sea with its ever-changing maritime vista. And his room, that stupid back room with only a small garden and the backs of other houses for a view. Dead boring. Except for the girl who stripped in front of her window.

He was glad they were away, on one of their stupid exotic holidays; his mother probably having one of her pampering sessions while his father drank downstairs at the hotel bar with whoever's ear he could bend. Except, Josh knew, Paul was not the most interesting raconteur, not like Gran.. Hadn't he overheard someone in one of the locals say he was a boring old fart? The man had then looked sheepish when he realised Paul Swales' son was in the room, had heard his remarks. Not that Josh cared. He didn't think much of his dad's drinking buddies, especially those from the operatic society his parents belonged to. Stupid prats.

He wished his parents would never come home. Then this could be his bed, his bedroom, for always. The house too, he supposed. Downstairs he heard the cat flap. *That can go for sure. F---ing dirty animal. But he's dead now, so why the flapping?* He realised it was probably the wind. Tide's in, by the sound of the crashing waves.

Of course, there would have to be changes. Redecorate for a start. The red cherry wallpaper would defo go; replace it with boring magnolia emulsion. He liked magnolia, simple, uncomplicated, neutral. It's what he needed every now and then, especially now: neutrality, anonymity, quiet in the head.

He wondered how Gran was and her 'retrograde amnesia'. How long would it remain retro? What will happen when her memory returns? Will he have to really kill her? Chrissakes! No way does he want to do that; he loves the old biddy, her crimped hair, her clacking dentures, and her stories that she used to weave inside her head for him when he was a boy.

No, Gran has to live; he'll get round her memory returning, somehow. He still has her money. Untouched. Hidden in his wardrobe. *I'll get it back to you, Gran. Promise.* He would sooner kill the parents, at least wish them dead. Maybe their plane will crash. Now he thinks about it, he really wants them dead, sitting up in their bed, drinking his father's expensive whisky, listening to the waves, the occasional gull as it wheels and screeches out there. All he can do is wish... He swallows, tastes his own bad breath from eight Peronis, a drunken sleep and then the malt. He glances at the bedside clock, bloody hell! Twenty-two-thirty? How long has he been asleep? Another day gone and not much to show for it, except two fruitless visits to Gran's and watching a girl strip through his bedroom window. Even that was only a part show. Yeah, he saw her tits but precious little else. He wondered if she was back from her brother's. Or did she stay the night?

He climbed out of bed, scrunched his feet on the carpet, and rubbed his sole along its pile, getting rid of another itch. He padded through to the back of the house, shivered, clad only as he was, in T shirt and boxers. The central heating was off, timed for some ridiculous hour: ten o'clock probably. The meanness of his father. Oh yes, he could spend hundreds on his hobby and the like but the central heating has to go off at ten to save on the fuel bills. Mad.

He did not bother switching on any lights in the hall or his bedroom. He was used to the dark of the desert. He looked through his window, saw some lights on in the rear houses, but not one in her room. He opened the window slightly, still imagining the smell of cat; chewed his lip, rubbed his nose on knuckles. Might as well go back to bed, bloody freezing out there and in here come to think of it. By the time he got dressed, if he bothered, the pubs would be closed and he didn't have membership for any clubs that might be going on longer. He shut the window and returned to his parents' bedroom. At least he could watch a late-night movie... and have another glass of his father's best malt...

21

Marilyn Innes lived at number twelve, Acacia Crescent, with her widowed mother, Laura. She knew Mrs Swales, who lived at number twenty-five, slightly, through Mum. In the past, when she and Mum used to go shopping together, before Laura slipped and damaged her hip, they occasionally bumped into Mrs Swales and her daughter-in-law, Pat. They would pass the time of day, and Laura calling Mrs Swales Ellie. Marilyn addressed her as Mrs Swales out of respect. To Pat she would just nod her head. Laura did not like the daughter-in-law much; called her selfish and neglectful of her mother-in-law. Marilyn did not question her mum's judgement, neither added to the criticism nor took any away. Privately, she was not that interested in Pat Swales: thought her a bit stuck up, above herself.

Marilyn had her own family; china dolls, those with the staring eyes and shining artificial hair that clung electrically to your fingers. Sometimes it came off on your clothes, if you brushed it too hard. She loved the way it shimmered in the light like a rainbow spider's web.

Her dolls were all girl dolls; Tara, Betty, Christine, Ella and so on. There were thirty of them and she knew each one by name. They were her children, and what mother does not know the names of her offspring?

Her boys were all teddy bears; large and small ones, middle-sized and some in between. The biggest and eldest was called Robert (Bobby), then came John (Jon-Jon), Samuel (Sammy) and on. There were thirty of them as well. What a lucky Mummy, Marilyn often thought, to have an equal number of boys and girls.

Laura was eighty-four and spritely. She still did all the cooking for herself and her daughter. Marilyn shopped for the food, daily, after the breakfast that Mum had prepared under the watchful eyes of the teddies and the dolls. Every morning she and Marilyn enjoyed a dish of tinned prunes, toast with lime marmalade, and PG Tips tea with milk and one sugar. Then Laura would clear away and wash up before settling down again, to read the Daily Mail that was delivered at eight o'clock sharp. Marilyn would get herself ready to go to the shops, kiss her mother on the cheek and say 'Goodbye, Mum, won't be long.' She would step through the front door with her 'bags for life', her shoulder purse looped around her and door keys that would be dropped into her coat pocket.

Marilyn wore a different outfit every day: always beautifully co-ordinated, no mis-matching, and the ribbon in her long, grey, plaited hair matched the colour of her shoes and tights, and everything in between.

She would hum a little tune as she walked towards the bus stop. It helped her pass by the other bungalows where the enemies, called neighbours, lived. Marilyn did not find them very neighbourly. Oh yes, they would say 'Good morning' or 'Good afternoon' if they were out on their front drives washing their cars; or in their front gardens tending their flowerbeds and tiny lawns. But she was suspicious of them, all of them, except, of course, old Mrs Swales who lived on her own.

Sammy and Bobby and Jon-Jon often warned her about the neighbours, especially the ones either side of Mum's bungalow. So did Tara and Betty and Ella. How did they know? Simple. When Marilyn sat them outside on good summer days in their special-sized chairs, to have afternoon tea in the garden, the glassy eyes took in everything, and the porcelain or furry ears could hear a distance away. Oh yes, her little family warned her about the enemy...

Marilyn liked to shop in Birchington, not Westgate or Margate: Margate was becoming scruffy and foreign. Lots of people skulking around, speaking in strange languages or English with foreign accents. Today she decided to catch the bus. It was only three or four stops to the village centre, and most often she walked it. But today the sky was overcast, grumpy, with the wind rumbling in from the sea. Also, she did not want to leave Mum alone for too long. Or her family. She knew Mum shifted the dolls and teddies, away from the kitchen table, when she read the paper and did the puzzles in the centre pages. She never put them back in the same place. It irritated Marilyn but she did not mention her irritation to Mum. After all, it was still her mother's bungalow. When Dad died, ten years ago, he had left the home and thirty thousand pounds to Mum and ten thousand pounds to Marilyn, plus his war medals. She had pinned them onto Bobby, as he was the biggest and the eldest teddy: he wore them proudly, she could tell, as he sat so upright in his chair..

Sometimes Mum sighed when she looked around her home. Was it because she missed Dad? Probably. But Marilyn suspected she was a mite tired of sharing every room with Marilyn's little family. Everywhere except the bathroom and her own bedroom, that is. She drew the line there.

'Enough, Marilyn,' she said. 'My room is my room and you certainly cannot put these things in the bathroom. Definitely not.'

She was hurt by Mum calling them 'these things'. They were her *family*, the children she had never borne. Her womb was unblemished, as were her genitals. She had never known a man, not in that way: didn't even know if she could bear it, knowing a man in *that way*. She almost blushed at her intimate thoughts.

'Good morning, Miss Innes,' said the butcher, 'What can I get for you today?'

'Oh, hello Mr James. Sorry, I was miles away.'

She daren't tell him where she had been, not something she felt she could ever discuss, leastwise with Mr James. She had also been just three bus stops away, back at the bungalow, irritated with Mum and her attitude. Mum was old, did not understand her daughter's needs. Plus, all this trouble lately, with her water tablets.

'I'll have half a pound of lamb's liver and half a pound of best back rashers today, please.'

He ignored her use of avoir du pois and weighed a little under 250 grams each. Near enough.

'How's your mother, Miss Innes?'

'She's fine, a little slower than she was, but considering her age...'

'Give her my regards,' he said as he wrapped the bloodied meat and popped it into a polythene bag that he sealed on his special machine. He did likewise with the rashers of bacon and handed them over the counter to her. Marilyn put both items into one of her bags for life, said goodbye and crossed the road to the greengrocer. The butcher watched her through his shop window. Funny old dear, he thought, real old maid. She waddles too, like a duck, not that she's overweight or anything, just waddles. He went back to his wooden block and chopped up a loin of pork into thick pork chops.

At the greengrocer's, Marilyn was again greeted as Miss Innes and again asked what the shopkeeper could get for her. She looked around at his colourful array; pyramids of fruit and vegetables of every shape and size; plastic bowls of tomatoes, kiwi fruit, and mushrooms, that he sold at 70p a bowl. Not the bowl of course, he refilled them for the next customer.

'I'll have two pounds of Charlotte potatoes, a small white cabbage, and some of those nice sprouts: enough for two. Oh, and two oranges, two pears and one apple.'

Mum did not eat apples anymore, said they made her choke and made her dentures wobble.

After Mr Downing's shop, Marilyn went to the baker's; bought a small Hovis loaf, still warm, and two chocolate cream éclairs. A treat for her and Mum with their afternoon tea. Her final stop was the chemist, to pick up Mum's prescription for her water tablets. Secretly, she wished mother would stop taking them. Twice this week Mum had wet the bed upon waking. She was a proud woman who hated to do anything that was remotely undignified, but the doctor prescribed them. 'To keep your blood pressure down, Mrs Innes,' he told her. So, it was not up to Marilyn to argue with that, but it was annoying to have to change her routine and put a wash in more than twice a week. It spoiled the schedule.

Marilyn caught the bus back and arrived home in good time for Mum to prepare lunch. She let herself in and called out, 'I'm home.'

There was no answer. She called again, 'Mum, you there?' Still silence. She went through to the kitchen. Mum was on the floor surrounded by dolls and teddies. Her eyes were closed as if she was asleep. Marilyn quickly put down the shopping bags, knelt down and placed her face next to her mother, 'Mum?' Laura did not answer, could not. She gave no response, was she dead? It looked as if she had fallen over her daughter's 'family', hit her head on the corner of the table and the shock was enough to take away her last breath.

Marilyn felt tears welling. Again, she whimpered, 'Mum'. She touched Laura's hand. It wasn't exactly cold, but neither could you say it was warm. She got up from her knees; put the dolls and teddies back on their chairs and told them in a whisper to be good. The paper lay open on the table; only half the crossword done and just two of the Sudoku puzzles. Mum had usually completed all the puzzles by the time Marilyn arrived home. She knelt by her mother, took her hand again.

What to do? She let go of Mum's hand and it dropped. Lifeless, onto the cold, tiled kitchen floor with a dull thump. The dolls and teddies stared, unfeeling, into space. For once, Marilyn almost disliked them, all of them. They were being no help, showing no sympathy. She limped through to the small sitting room that faced the road, next to Mum's bedroom. Through her tears and the open door she saw the bed was still stripped and a small stain was visible on the mattress.

'I should have put clean linen on there,' she whispered to herself. 'Sorry, Mum, I'll do it in a minute.' But Mum could not hear, Marilyn wondered, would she ever hear her again?

She looked out of the window onto the row of bungalows opposite. They seemed as lifeless as her poor mother, net curtains a barrier against friendliness and help. She bent her neck, peered upwards to where Acacia met the main road. A man had turned the corner and was walking towards her. She recognised Mrs Swales' grandson: Josh, she thought his name was. She ran to the front door, fiddled it unlocked and opened it just before Josh was about to walk up his grandmother's driveway.

'He... hello,' she called out.

He looked up, pointed at his own chest. 'You talking to me, love?'

Marilyn nodded, unable for a moment to answer, tears welling again. 'I need help.'

Josh saw the tears and the woman's crumpled face.

'What's wrong?'

'It's my Mum,' she whimpered. 'I think she's dead. I found her like it when I got back from shopping. On the floor. All cold like.' She ran out of breath, out of words.

What was it with dead bodies? They seemed to be following him around. He couldn't leave the old dear though, she seemed in a bad way.

He crossed the road, prepared to walk up the drive, noticed curtains twitching in at least two of the adjoining bungalows. Nosey buggers. Why didn't they come out to help? He hoped Gran hadn't seen him from her sitting room window, it might cause her to worry and wonder why he had gone by. He followed the woman inside, noted the golden-leaf design of the hallway carpet; an autumn, the fashion of twenty or thirty years ago.

He sniffed discreetly: pee, not cat pee, human pee from someone who had recently drunk tea. There didn't seem to be a wet patch on the carpet, but that was understandable given the intensity of the autumnal pattern.

'In here,' said the woman. She pointed towards the kitchen at the back of the house. Not like Gran's opposite, whose kitchen faced the road.

'Oh no!'

'What's wrong love?'

'She's not here. I left her there,' she pointed downwards. 'On the floor, right by the table.' There was genuine shock in the woman's voice. Josh took in the scene, where the woman was pointing, with mild surprise. It resembled a bizarre teddy bears' picnic with their friends, the china dolls, going along for the trip. Shelves, that normally would hold plates and things, were filled with the furry creatures, and on work surfaces sat china dolls, their eyes staring lifelessly into space. Some of both were seated at the table which was covered with an opened tabloid. He read 'Daily Mail' upside down. Two chairs were unoccupied, for mother and the Baby Jane daughter he supposed. He saw a damp patch on the floor beside one of the chairs. *Must be where the old lady fell. Where is she?*

'She was right there,' her daughter wailed, and pointed in

the direction of the damp patch. He patted her arm, hoped she would not do that back to him.

'Maybe she's gone to the bathroom?'

'How could she? She was dead,' sobbed the woman. 'At least, she had her eyes shut. And she wasn't moving. And I touched her and she was cold.'

Josh could do without the hysterics. 'What's your name love? I'm Josh.'

'Yes, I know you are, you're Mrs Swales' grandson. I'm Marilyn, Marilyn Innes and my Mum is Laura Innes.'

At least the introductions stopped her hysterics... They heard a soft moan across the hallway.

'Marilyn love, I'm in here.'

'Marilyn love' rushed across the hall. 'Mum, how did you get there? I thought you were...' she didn't finish the sentence.

'I've wet myself love,' and, 'my head hurts.'

Josh followed Marilyn, heard what the old lady said, noted the blood smeared forehead. He took control.

'Marilyn, go and ring for an ambulance.' To the old woman, who still wore the trousers that betrayed a wet stain, 'Come on love, let's see if you can stand up. Here, hold my hand.' He put one arm around her tiny back and under her arm; with the other he held her hand, gently coaxed her to her feet.

'I feel a bit dizzy,' her voice was shaky. 'I think I'm going to be...' She didn't get the last word out; instead vomited on the floor and over him. The smell was disgusting, pervading the lavender-scented bathroom and his clothes

Thanks, he thought, aware he'd put on everything fresh this morning.

'Mum!' her daughter stood in the doorway, ashamed of what was happening. Josh spoke sharply to her. 'Go and ring for an ambulance. Now.'

He sat the old woman down on the toilet, reached over to

the basin and turned on the hot tap. He rinsed a flannel under it, squeezed out surplus water and gently wiped her mouth free of vomit.

'I'm so sorry,' she said.

'It's ok, love.'

He rinsed the flannel again, this time softly wiping her head wound, noted a large bump formed and bruising under the bloodied wounds. He could hear Marilyn jabbering away frantically on the hall phone. Not to worry, they would deal with it the other end. They were used to it, knew how to calm the caller.

'It was the dolls,' Laura whispered. 'They were on the floor and I tripped over them. Hit my head on the stove. I must have fainted.'

He nodded, understood; more than slightly relieved he was not dealing with another dead body.

'When I came to, I realised I'd wet myself. Didn't want Marilyn to deal with it. She gets annoyed when I do it. Can't help it,' she added. 'It's the water tablets.'

He continued to bathe her face, gently, with sympathy, like he might be bathing Andy, Gran, the little Afghan girl, Foxy, Sue... But not the cat.

'They're coming,' Marilyn stood at the doorway, snivelling into a bit of lace hankie; her eyes were blotched and swollen. He thought how ugly she looked. And that stupid grey plait going halfway down her back. Then he heard the ambulance outside. Blimey, that was quick!

He explained to the paramedics who he was and what he thought had happened. Better he did it than her stupid snivelling daughter. Old though she was, she still acted like a grey-haired kid. As it happened the paramedics recognised him.

'We came out to your gran not long back,' one of them said. 'How is she?'

'Oh, she's fine now,' he told them. 'Still can't remember

what happened that day, but other than that, she's perky as always.'

Laura didn't want to go in the ambulance but they insisted, as did her daughter.

'Best get that head looked at,' they persuaded. 'You'll probably only be in overnight. Your daughter can come with you in the ambulance.' And to Marilyn, 'Do you want to sort some toiletries and a nightie and dressing gown for your Mum? Some slippers?'

Marilyn dithered. Josh thought, God, you're so pathetic. He told her to hurry else they wouldn't wait. Laura looked distressed and pleaded with her daughter to go and get her things.

Glad I didn't have any kids, especially if they grew up like you, you idiotic woman. Josh barely disguised his contempt.

Ten minutes later (seemed like two hours), mother and daughter were gently bundled into the ambulance. Josh saluted the paramedics goodbye and went back to see Gran. As expected, she was bursting at the seams to know what was going on.

'Go on, son, put the kettle on, and then fill me in with what's happened.'

'Got any cakes, Gran, I'm starving?' he called from the kitchen

'In the cupboard, next to the kettle. There's a chocolate sponge or some little coconut cakes. Help yourself.'

He brought the tea and cakes through on a tray and set them down on the drum table. 'That's new. A present to yourself?'

'Yes, one of my carers took me to Fullerton's, the auction rooms in Cliftonville. Haven't been there for ages. We had a great time.' She finished. 'Oh, we went to the optician's first.'

No wonder you weren't around when I called.

He sat opposite her. 'These cakes are good; d'you make 'em?'

'Don't be silly,' she laughed. I couldn't even mix the ingredients now, let alone get them ready for the oven.'

'Only joking.'

'Anyway, what was wrong with Laura, Mrs Innes?' She leaned forward in her chair, crumbs escaping from the side of her mouth. Her button eyes gleamed.

Gran's better, he thought, much more like her old self. It was a relief. *So long as she doesn't regain her memory.*

"So, what happened at number twelve? Why the ambulance? Is Laura ok?'

'That's three questions, Gran,' Josh laughed as he answered her. Really, he was annoyed: he resented being rushed into giving explanations. 'Right, what happened was, the old girl tripped over some china dolls.' He paused. 'Can you believe that house? Ever been in there?'

'Yes, I have. Beggars belief, doesn't it?'

'Anyway, she hit her head and must have conked out. Her daughter – what a weirdo she is – found her on the floor, thought she was dead, came out into the street and grabbed me.'

'So Laura's not dead then?'

'No, she was just stunned, then pissed...sorry, wet herself and crawled towards the bathroom: which is where we found her.'

He bit into another cake and took a swig of his tea. 'Bugger, that was hot. It's burnt my lip.' He put a finger to his mouth, licked the injured part, and finished off the rest of his cake.

'Then what happened?'

Josh was conscious of his grandmother's heightened enthusiasm. *Not a pathetic old thing with memory loss, are you?* He would have to tread on egg shells from now on.

'Not a lot. I called the ambulance, calmed down Baby

Jane and washed the old lady's face. Poor crow vomited up her breakfast, some of it over me.' He pointed to the wet patch on his sweater.

'Go and get one of your granddad's. There's some in the big wardrobe.'

He stared at her. What is it with old people? Are they for real? Now why would he want to wear one of his dead grandfather's sweaters? Josh was getting tired of Ellie. Bored. Time to go.

'No, you're all right, Gran. I gotta get back and feed the cat,' he lied.

'Thought you told me that Tiddles was missing?'

'Well it was. It's back now.'

He bent towards her to give a dutiful kiss, and almost shuddered at the texture of her wrinkled skin. He decided he did not like OLD. 'I'll pop round tomorrow,' he promised.

'Maybe you could call in to Mrs Innes's. See how she is.'

'Oh, ok. Tomorrow then.' And he was gone.

Ellie awoke from her afternoon nap and was conscious it was dark, both outside and in. *Another day gone and what to show for it?* She got up slowly, painfully from her chair, struggled to get hold of her two sticks. She badly needed the bathroom. *Don't wet yourself again. Doing it a lot lately, aren't you?*

She switched on her side lamp, hobbled towards the door and into the bathroom. *Made it.* On the way back she made herself a mug of tea and carried it through to the lounge. Almost six o'clock. Time for the news.

She settled in her chair, worked the remote control just as Huw Edwards' face appeared. Good, she liked him; liked the soft, Welsh lilt to his voice. He looked straight at her through the TV screen. She nodded her acknowledgement. 'Tonight's headlines,' he told her.

'Once again the government has won by a narrow

margin.'

She missed what it was for as she took her first sip of tea. Never mind, she knew it would be fully explained in a moment. Next there was more trouble in an African country, one of those that changed its name when it became independent. Likewise, there was conflict in a Middle Eastern country. Neither of these subjects held much interest for her. She sipped her tea then sat up quickly, upon hearing the next item.

'A man's body, found three days ago in his Highbury flat, has now been formally identified as seventy-eight-year-old John Hollander. His body was discovered in the hallway after neighbours called the police, concerned he had not been seen for several days. His neck was broken. The police are treating the death as unexplained.'

Ellie thought back to a week ago. Josh went to London to see an old man. The newscaster continued. 'They also wish to trace a man, possibly in his thirties, who was seen knocking at Mr Hollander's door several days ago. He is described as 'white male, approximately five feet eleven, slim build with mid-brown short hair. He was dressed in dark jacket and jeans. Mr Hollander lived alone, and the police are anxious to trace any relatives.'

The description of the man wanted for questioning bore an uncomfortable similarity to her grandson. Ellie felt sick. *Was it you, Josh? What's happening to you?* These worrisome thoughts stayed with her, long after her carer had put her to bed.

22

Rob Stevens drove slowly along the single-track road until he reached the small gravelled car park adjoining the bank of the River Wantsum. He listened through the open window as the car crunched tiny stones under his tyres. He loved that sound. Didn't know why.

Today was proving to be one of those rare winter days when the sun shone and the winds blew elsewhere, far from this north Kent coast where the mouth of the Wantsum gently spewed its waters out to the North Sea. There, where it met the last of the Thames Estuary, the warmth was almost spring-like.

Rob knew how to pick the right time of day, had checked in the local paper when the tide would be out and the tiny river at its calmest. He was dressed warmly, a hand-knitted sweater over thermal vest and long-johns. His thickly-stockinged feet were pushed into waders and he wore a waterproof jacket over his sweater. No sense in taking risks at his age; you never knew when the weather would turn.

He stopped the car and noted with satisfaction he was the only angler there. Good, he could choose his favourite spot, near the reeds where carp lurked and, maybe, that pike his mate had caught back in the summer. He might use a roach rod, stretch it across to the other bank with a bit of light line on it. Or ledger upstream for carp, but what he really wanted was to catch that pike. Rob grinned, remembering when his mate had caught it last; kept his hand away from the bugger's mouth too, as he cut the line.

He lugged his fishing gear from the back of the car; his

box, three rods, bait and his own food and drink – bacon
sarnies and a flask of hot coffee. It was ten o'clock, late for
Rob to be setting up but winter was not kind to early
morning anglers. Rob, at seventy, had been retired for five
years. No need to rise early, unless he wanted to.

Josh is restless as he looks out onto the bright sunny day.
For once, he has had a good sleep. No dreams, no
nightmares, no blackouts or black moments. He sits at the
breakfast table, eating toast and marmalade. What to do
today? Does not fancy another trip into Margate, or to visit
Gran. He decides to go for a long walk along the front, west,
towards Herne Bay. He tips his plate and mug into the sink.
They can be washed up later. He climbs the stairs, goes into
his bedroom. *No smell there now.* From the wardrobe, he
chooses a thick sweater and a pair of combat trousers. He
pulls on warm socks and folds a scarf round his neck. That'll
do, no need for a jacket.

He clatters downstairs, sees there is post sticking through
the letterbox in the hallway. Looks like a postcard, from
Mum he expects. He pulls it through, while pushing his feet
into walking boots. Holds the postcard in his teeth while
lacing them up. At least it has arrived before they're back.
Makes a change.

'Hi son, lovely place, super hotel. We're enjoying the
music festival, and both getting nicely tanned.' *Bully for you
two...* 'Don't forget to feed the cat, ha-ha! See you Monday
week, from Mum and Dad.' There were several views of a
little fishing village, a harbour, and the five-star hotel within
walking distance of it. No wish you were here. No line of
kisses. Ah well.

He tossed the postcard into the bin, changed his mind
and stuck it on the dresser, above several hanging mugs. He
thought about Mrs Innes's kitchen and its occupants, stuffed
bears and china dolls. He shuddered. Perish the thought...

time to go.

It was not the best of Rob Stevens' fishing days. All he had caught were two small roach and he'd played with a carp that had twisted his line around the reeds, finally taking off with the hook still in its mouth. He reeled in the line, attached another hook and more weights, and threaded three maggots onto the size-ten hook. The river was not still anymore. Tide's coming in, he reckoned. He added a ledger weight onto his rod and cast it to his right, among the reeds on the opposite bank. It might attract another carp. He laid the rod securely across two rests. Time for a sarnie and some coffee.

Josh had walked farther than he intended. Deep in thought, he ignored the freshening wind playing with his scarf, but was aware of the screaming gulls overhead. Maybe their noise had triggered a memory. Whatever... He wondered how far Sue's body had been dragged out to sea. Who had had the lion's share of her, the fish or the gulls? The thought intrigued him. What would it look like now, her body? Any flesh left on it, or just bones that swayed gently, back and forth, in their underwater grave?

He changed direction, veered away from the coastline and followed the mouth of the Wantsum, over the bridge and down towards the gravel car park where he had driven a few nights before. How many nights? Three? Four? Not that it mattered. He surprised upon the lone angler, eating his bacon sandwich. It smelled good in the fresh air, made Josh's mouth water. The coffee smelled good as well. He nodded to the old man.

'All right mate? Any luck?'

Rob cleared his mouth of food with a swig of coffee.

'Not bad. A couple of small roach, and the proverbial carp that got away. Trying for a pike now, over there.' He indicated the reeds to his right.

Josh smiled. 'Plenty of those, aye? The ones that get away. Had a few of them when I was a kid.'

'Did you used to fish here?'

'Yeah, years ago with my grandfather.'

Suddenly the line tugged. Rob dropped his sandwich and coffee mug. He leapt towards his rod. 'This feels more like it.' He flicked the line upwards, to snare whatever was on the end of his line, then began to reel in. Josh looked on, interested.

'Not much fight to it, aye?'

'You're right son; maybe I've caught a branch.' The old man laughed until he reeled in the non-fish. Not a branch but a severed arm, devoid of much flesh and two fingers.

'Jesus Christ! What the...?'

The old man stood up, still reeling in his horrific catch. He slipped and Josh caught him before he hit the ground. The man shuddered, struggled with his collar trying to loosen it. He fought to say something but the words choked in his throat. His staring eyes pleaded with Josh. *Do something. Do something.* But Josh did not know what to do, could not understand what the old man was trying to say. He looked down at the severed arm, mesmerised, and almost ignored the struggling angler. *Was it Sue's? No, not possible, not here.* He had no inclination to examine it close up; what was left of it. He could see white bone in between gnawed pieces of flesh. That too was white, bleached by its time in the salt water.

His attention returned to the man. His face now was blue, contorted. It seemed he could only suck air in, not let any out. His eyes bulged like giant marbles and his tongue looked swollen, too big for his mouth to hold. Through the darkening lips, Josh could see the old man's dentures had detached themselves. He knew he should remove them before the man swallowed them, or inhaled them down into his lungs.

Nothing worked on Josh. He was still as a statue but with seeing eyes. He stared at the bizarre scene unfolding. Man dying, a severed arm, the smell of bacon and coffee and gulls screaming for their share. One got close enough to take a daring peck at the arm. Josh chased it off and came out of his trance; turned his attention back to the old man. One look told him he was too late. He stared at the bulging eyes, blue lips, and teeth half in and half out of a gaping mouth. The man had slipped backward off his fishing stool, one leg awkwardly caught under the other, his body lying on top of both. His arms were flung out, making his body look like a short, squat cross.

What if he pumped the chest? Gave mouth to mouth? Didn't fancy that with those dentures blocking the way. He struggled to pull the man's legs from beneath his body, then began to push down on his chest. Rhythmically one, two, three, four, pause. And again: one, two, three, four, pause. No response. The angler was one dead angler. As dead as the arm that lay there on the slippery, muddied bank. The fishing hook still bit into a piece of flesh. And there were maggots. Josh watched, mesmerised for a few seconds as they wriggled onto the severed arm. He shuddered. Best to get rid of them and toss the arm back among the reeds. Chances were, the pike Rob Stevens failed to catch would finish it off, swallow it whole. The pike would dine today; the old man would not even finish his bacon sandwich, let alone eat another dinner.

Josh found some scissors in the box, cut the line, wound a little around his hand and slung it with the severed arm attached into the opposite reeds. He watched the bubbles where it sank. Once more he looked at the old man. Nothing to be done there. He poured himself some coffee and ate the remaining sandwich. Daft to waste it.

23

Josh used his mobile to call the police and an ambulance. They would need one to take away the body. He explained where he was, told them about the old man, saying he thought he was dead. He told the policeman, over the phone, that the old man had slipped, probably had a heart attack or something.

'Don't touch anything, sir. We'll be along in a few minutes. What did you say your name was, sir?'

Josh closed down his mobile. *I didn't say what my name was. You'll know soon enough.*

He wiped the scissors on his sweater and replaced them in the man's fishing box. Best the police didn't find his finger-prints on anything. He wiped the cup too, the side he had drunk from, and screwed the paper sandwich bag between the dead man's fingers, to make it look like he'd finished his own sandwiches. Josh noted the man's fingers were already stiffening. He let go when he heard approaching vehicles. Stood there putting on a concerned and worried face, as any caring citizen might do in the same situation.

He recognised the police officers as soon as they climbed out of the car. Same ones who had come to Gran's. What were their names? Dave and Kelly, or Katie? Not today though.

'I'm PS D Rawson and this is WPC K Tiptree.' He paused. 'Don't we know you, sir?'

'Yeah, you came to my Gran's last week, when she was burgled. I'm Josh Swales.'

'Got it. Yes, Josh Swales: on leave from the army, right?'

'Yeah, a month's R&R after my tour in the Middle East'

Just as well to remind them you're as good as them. Else they treat you like shite...'

'So, what happened here?'

'Dunno really. Think maybe the old boy had a heart attack. Perhaps he caught the big one and died of shock.' Josh grinned. Realised, too late, it was not quite the emotion he should be showing. He drew his cheeks in, tightened his lips.

'Was he still alive when you arrived here? Come to think of it, why *are* you here?'

Josh chose to ignore the last question. What's it to do with them anyway was his thought. 'I came across him while he had stopped fishing. He was eating his sandwiches and drinking his coffee. I asked him,' he continued, 'if he'd had much luck.'

'Then what?'

'His line went taut, he jumped up to grab his rod and sort of slipped. I reached out to help him. That's when his face went all funny; sort of blue and constricted.'

'How soon did he lose consciousness?' This from the paramedics, who had come on the scene and were busying themselves, trying to resuscitate the angler.

'Erm... quite quickly, I think. I tried massaging his heart, didn't fancy trying mouth to mouth as his dentures had dislodged themselves.'

Finally, the paramedics stood up. 'No chance. Poor chap. Relative of yours?'

'No, no. I just happened to be walking down this way, chatted to him, then – this.' He pointed to the body.

'Any reason you walked this far?' asked the policeman. 'Bit of a long way from where you live, isn't it?'

'No reason,' said Josh. 'It was just a nice day, sunny for a change. Didn't realise how far I'd walked, to be honest.'

'Hmm.' The policeman was non-committal.

'His name's Rob Stevens, sarge.' Said the policewoman. She had been rifling through his fishing box and held up his angler's licence. 'He lives in Birchington, Rutland Gardens it says here.'

'Any phone number with it?'

'No sarge, but there's a mobile phone in the box here.'

'Let's have a look at his contacts, see if there's a Mrs Stevens.'

'I'd better go,' said Josh. 'That's if you don't want me anymore. Ought to call in on my gran.'

'Just a minute. We'd like you to come to the station and make a statement.'

'What, now? Can't it wait till later?' Josh resented the way he was being ordered about. Wasn't his fault the geezer had died.

'We really need a statement as soon as possible, sir.' The police sergeant changed his approach. Chances were the old boy had died of natural causes: no sense in getting the younger man's back up. 'Perhaps you could call in tomorrow morning?'

Josh thought. 'Yeah, I suppose that'll be ok.' He watched the paramedics load the body onto a stretcher and lift it into the back of the ambulance. He really wanted to be away now. What was it with these old people? Did they wait for him, then get ill or injured and die? First Gran, then Foxy, Mrs Innes and now this Rob Stevens. *Sue and Andy and the little Afghan girl weren't old, were they? And they had died. Perhaps I'm a jinx on people?*

The last thing he wanted was to dwell on Sue and the young Afghan girl, they weren't his finest moments.

The wind was picking up and the sun had disappeared behind pillows of ominous clouds. Back to winter in two short hours. It meant the beach was pretty deserted, no dog walkers, no beach casters, just himself and the gulls: always the gulls.

He was passing Birchington and heading towards Westgate, along the concrete promenade that adjoined the chalk cliffs. The tide was in displaying a grey swell, apart from the rusty coloured foam that crashed against the sea wall. One large wave splashed all over him, and he was soaked: not pleased. Why did he have to go walking in the first place? Could easily have stayed in, picked up a six pack and DVD, and chilled out for the day. Instead, he had added another notch to his list of bodies *and* got wet into the bargain.

He was tempted then to go back and stop off at Gran's: her bungalow was always warm and yes, he could swap his wet clothes for some of Granddad's old ones. Besides, Gran was bound to have more cakes. A hot cuppa, and a plate of her specials, would go down well now. Yeah, that's what he'd do.

He turned around and quickened his pace, as he passed the old wartime coastguard's ruin that was now home to a concoction of pigeons. Years ago, white doves had eloped from their domesticated dovecotes and flown into the embraces of wild pigeons. The resulting crossbreeds were interesting, a kaleidoscope of colours: some white and brown, some speckled blue, with white or grey. They all cooed at him in a territorial way, daring him – it seemed – to come any closer to their domain.

Josh shivered from cold and a certain trepidation. He didn't like pigeons any more than he liked gulls. Something about them he found sinister.

'All yours,' he shouted up at them as they stared down at him. He strode past their glorified dovecote, stuck up two fingers in salute, and then felt foolish. What would they know? As he rounded a bend in the cliffs he saw a group of guys coming towards him, shaven headed, wearing sleeveless T shirts that revealed multi-tattooed, muscular arms. They were swaying, pushing into each other. They belched and farted, laughed as they did it. Schoolboy humour. Well gone, he thought. He glanced at his watch, not much past one-thirty. He shrugged. Not his business. Nevertheless, he opted to give them a wide berth. As they approached, one of them gobbed on the walkway, grinned at his mates.

'Wish that was fanny juice, aye?'

They saw Josh, nudged each other. He clenched his fists, smelling trouble as well as their beery breaths.

'All right mate?' said one of them.

'Yeah, great,' Josh replied.

'You local?'

'Yeah.'

'Don't recall seeing you around these parts.' It was almost an accusation.

'Maybe 'cos I've been away.'

'Oh yeah, inside?'

Josh looked at the gobshite. 'No. Afghanistan, as it happens.'

'Right.' They gave him looks of almost respect.

'Good on you mate, hope you gave them rag-heads what they deserve.'

He chose not to answer. No sense in getting into a political debate with these no-hopers. Up close, he could see the studs and tattoos, LOVE and HATE knuckles that clutched beer bottles, hands that had never handled a military weapon in their lives: a few baseball bats, maybe. They passed either side of him. He half expected them to jostle him but, probably, the word Afghanistan had given him some clout.

'See ya,' one of them shouted after him.

'Not if I can help it,' he mumbled under his breath, grateful to be on his way without further confrontation. He guessed they were Margate boys. He knew there were several gangs now that roamed the streets. None of them congenial. He resisted the urge to hurry, even though he felt like breaking into a run. *Come on, man, you could knock skittles out of them with one hand tied behind your back. Yeah right.*

24

What a morning. First the old boy pegging it in front of him, now this lot. He almost wished he was back in Helmand with his mates, especially Andy. This leave was turning out to be a nightmare. Didn't matter which way he turned, trouble seemed to follow him, more like stare him in the face. What was happening to him? It was like he'd been cursed or something. *Don't be daft, no such thing.* For the first time in years he felt alone and lonely, vulnerable. It was not a nice feeling. He wanted to go somewhere, but where? Who was there left for him to meet? Gran was a no-no after his stupid mistake; Sue, well, Sue was no more. Andy's friend, Foxy, was probably dead as well, so that part of London was a no-go area. Shame, he quite enjoyed the evening with Mike whatever his name was. Beresford, that's his name. His kind of person, even though he's an ex-officer. Seems the kind of guy with no side. Not a snob, that's for sure.

Josh thought back to a couple of days ago when he caught up with his old teacher, Parri Arnold. Maybe he could walk into Margate after all: see if the old boy was around again. Then he remembered Parri had given him his address and his email. Could always go round there. Bet the old boy wouldn't mind. Probably enjoy the company. He might be out, might have gone away to stay with friends or relatives. *Well you won't bloody know, will you, unless you get in touch?*

The salty tang of the sea refreshed his nostrils, made him lick his lips and taste the salt on them. And the gulls, always the gulls, wheeling and diving: screeching for food, for airspace or because they could. They forced their way into his consciousness and he ducked as they dived close to him. He wanted to shout at them, tell them to piss off and leave him alone. *Steady, Josh, you're losing it.*

He had walked beyond Westgate and home automatically, on towards Margate. The wind had all but dried his sweater. Maybe he could go further, Cliftonville, North Foreland, and Broadstairs. Walking, walking, keep on walking. Go down the cliffs to the chalky beach, walk into the sea.

'Hello Josh, good to see you again.'

He stared at the face, at the mouth where the voice came from. A familiar face. He blinked. 'Hello, sir.'

'Parri, Josh. Remember? Call me Parri.'

Josh allowed himself a smile, relieved to be part of the real world again.

'Hi Parri, good to see you as well. How's it going?'

'Not bad, son, not bad. Bit of rheumatism, that's all, nothing I can't cope with. Anyway,' he added. 'What brings you to Margate today?'

Josh shrugged. 'Nothing in particular. Had a bit of an experience this morning.'

'Oh?'

'Went for a walk towards Herne Bay, as far as the Wantsum. Some old bloke, fishing there, died on me.'

'He did what?'

'He hooked this big fish on his line... told me he'd hardly had a bite all morning. Think the shock of catching such a monster killed him, gave him a heart attack.'

'How dreadful. Such a shock for you.'

'Yeah, had to call the police and an ambulance. Time I'd finished explaining to them what happened, I started to walk back, and just, sort of, carried on walking.

He thought about the severed arm, the whiteness of it, the half-eaten flesh barely covering the bone. He shuddered, did not mention the arm to Parri Arnold, same as he had neglected to tell the police about it: hoped by now the pike had enjoyed it for its midday meal.

His old schoolteacher looked at him with sympathy. 'Come on lad, join me for a spot of lunch in the Blue Elephant?'

Josh recovered and brightened. 'Sounds good. Come to think of it,' he stroked his flat stomach. 'Could do with a bite to eat.'

'Good, let's get out of this wind.' The old man's sparse hair blew into his eyes. He stooped into the doorway and brushed his hair back off his face. 'That's better. Now, what're you having to drink?'

'Pint of bitter'd be great thanks.'

'Right. Pint of bitter coming up. You go find us a table and I'll get the beers.'

Josh located a table, overlooking the road and the beach beyond. Not many cars hiding the sea view at this time of year. No holiday makers, that was for sure. Except up at Cliftonville, you always got the odd coach load of pensioners staying there, summer and winter. Just as well for the struggling hoteliers, now that so many went abroad. Didn't understand their mentality: two weeks in a foreign resort, often getting second-rate food and a dangerous suntan. Crowded plane. Not for him, sooner go for a week in Cornwall or Devon, or good old Brighton, long as you watched your rear end there.

He looked over at Parri, the same barmaid was serving him. Damn. He felt sure one of these days she would work out where she knew him from: here, with Sue. He almost regretted coming in here today. Suppose she came to clear their plates once they'd eaten. So? Make conversation with her, brazen it out. She hasn't got much brain anyway. Daft little tart.

Parri came back with the drinks, slightly spilling them. 'Blasted shakes,' he complained.

'Heavy night last night?' Josh grinned.

'I wish. No, unfortunately I'm in the early stages of Parkinson's. Not so easy to get rid of as a hangover.'

Josh was silent, bit his lip and nodded in sympathy. What could he say that wasn't a platitude? He took a generous swig from his glass and licked froth from his upper lip. 'Bit of a bugger, that.' He added, meaning the Parkinson's. 'Man, this tastes good.'

He picked up one of the menus and quickly scanned its laminated columns. Soup of the day, plus garlic-stuffed mushrooms and chilli chicken wings, followed by the usual fish dishes, scampi or cod. Same old, same old. The other choice of main-course dishes was also predictable, steaks or gammon with fried egg or pineapple. Chips with everything, and mushy peas or garden peas. Chef's Special held more promise: steak and ale pie served with fresh veg and winter-boiled potatoes.

'What's the difference between winter- and summer-boiled potatoes?'

'No idea,' laughed his ex-schoolteacher. 'Perhaps they sprinkle them with chilli flakes?'

'In that case, I'll settle for the pie.'

'Me too.'

The old man approached the bar and placed their order. The barmaid glanced over to their table, raised her eyebrows and smiled at Josh. He neglected to return the smile. He turned away and gazed out of the window at the sparse traffic, and the clouds coming in over a robust sea that crashed against the harbour wall. He wished she would find another job, in another town, hundreds of miles away.

'Now, young Josh, apart from that unfortunate incident this morning, how are things with you? How's the family?'

'Mum and Dad are away – again,' he emphasised the word again. Gran's ok, apart from her arthritis. She's pretty spritely in her mind.'

'Good, that's good to hear.' He smiled. 'Your parents remind me of my own, forever away they were. Spent most of my boyhood holidays with my Grandfather.'

'Me too,' said Josh. 'Mostly with Gran. Granddad was away quite a lot in the summer months; used to go back up North at harvest time to help his sister on the farm.'

'My Grandfather,' the old man said, 'lived in a house in the forest. Both are long gone and to this day,' he continued, 'I don't know its name. We only referred to it as the forest, and the house as Grandfather's house.'

Josh was quite happy to let his old teacher ramble on. Sounded like an interesting tale would emerge from the memories.

'It was a magical place in a little clearing, where rabbits played in the early morning sun and foxes barked in the still of the night. They say Grandfather built the house himself, from stone found nearby, with a Welsh slate roof to keep out the winter storms and spring rains. Downstairs was one large room, with nooks and crannies that separated the kitchen and dining area, and a place to sit cosily, around the wood stove for warmth, on chilly nights.'

Josh liked the old man's voice, his gentle Welsh lilt that became more noticeable when he talked about his boyhood days, spent in the Welsh hills and valleys.

'There were two wooden settles made by Grandfather, with hand-stitched cushions that Grandmother had made in her day. A handmade rug, also made by her, on the floor in front of the fire. I liked to sprawl there and Grandfather would tell me stories of his boyhood. He sat in a rocker chair, smoking an ancient Meerschaum pipe and gazed into the open door of the wood stove, his eyes reflecting the flames.

'Grandmother had died before I was born, and her photo was set on the mantelshelf, along with his spare pipe and a curious lighter. It was a metal tube with a wheel that you flicked with your thumb, to produce a spark and light the petrol-soaked wick. I was eight,' he laughed, 'before I could master the action and produce a flame. Grandfather patted me on the head and told me I was a good boy.'

'I can just imagine your delight,' said Josh. 'What an achievement for an eight-year-old.'

'Quite,' said the old man. He continued with his little tale. 'I used to stay with Grandfather every summer while my parents went away. Never knew where. I thought they went off somewhere to work. I didn't care, staying with him was a magical interlude between two school terms.' He took a swig of beer, licked his lips. 'Sure I'm not boring you, Josh?'

'No, not at all, I'm enjoying it.' He failed to say that the gentle storytelling was easing his own troubled mind, like a warm, soft cloth, gently wiping away his tortuous memories.

'Each morning, we'd go out into the forest and examine the traps that Grandfather had set the night before. Sometimes there would be a rabbit, occasionally a wild pheasant and often a long-eared hare. If I cried or complained, Grandfather would say, "We only kill to eat, Parri. There are plenty that get away to live their lives." We collected wild berries, herbs and garlic, to flavour the stews he made. Delicious they were, too, with potatoes dug from a small plot near the house, that he called his allotment, and crusty bread to dip in the gravy.

'We'd walk into town every few days, along the forest path that was too narrow for a car, barely wide enough for a pony and cart. Grandfather had neither. We enjoyed the walk, listening to birdsong or the bleating of sheep up in the mountains beyond the forest. It was not far, maybe two miles there and two back. The town was hardly a town. Apart from a few houses and cottages, it boasted three shops, an inn, a church and a hall where the people met, once in a while, to discuss important matters.

'We bought bread, butter and eggs, tea and coffee, sugar

and a tin of dried milk for when Grandfather's tethered goat failed to give milk. It was all we needed really. Grandfather grew his own vegetables in season and ate the fruits of the forest. But he would buy me apples, large red ones that he rubbed on his jacket sleeve to make them shine. I was convinced they tasted better because he polished them so vigorously.' His eyes twinkled as they remembered these pleasant interludes. 'After shopping we would visit the inn, sit in a corner at a large round table with some of Grandfather's old friends. They drank frothy beer out of pewter tankards and licked the froth from their beards and moustaches. I was given lemonade and crisps, the ones with the little blue salt sachet to sprinkle over.

'The men liked to play dominoes which they held in one hand like a fan of cards, banging a matching one down on the wooden table. I always jumped.' He smiled at the memory. The winner bought the next round and a lemonade for me if I had drained my glass. Later we'd take our shopping back to the house in the forest with Grandfather hiccupping most of the way.

'One summer he whittled a horse for me from a fallen tree. And a little handcart that I could pull to the shops and carry our purchases home. He gave me one of his old knives, taught me how to carve simple things. He told me to only use the knife to create things, never as a weapon. Enough knives and guns have been used to destroy lives is what he said.'

'Your Grandfather was a wise man,' said Josh.

'Yes, that was my Grandfather.'

'Sounds like you had a great childhood.'

'Only the summers mind, I expect the winters weren't quite so idyllic.'

The food arriving interrupted their conversation. The same barmaid served them, busying herself with wrapped knives and forks and a small square dish filled with sachets of pepper, salt and various sauces.

'Anything else I can get you?' She looked at Josh. They both shook their heads and told her no thanks. 'Enjoy your meal then,' she said, and returned to the bar, giving Josh a backward glance that unsettled him.

Parri put a forkful into his mouth. 'Mm, this is good.' Josh noticed he wiped his mouth on a serviette after almost every mouthful even though no bits of food were sticking to his clean-shaven face.

'My wife, Miss Hedges as you knew her, was a wonderful cook. Another thing I regret in her passing.' He paused. 'Yours all right, Josh?'

'Yeah, yes it's fine. Sorry I was miles away,' he lied. He stopped pushing the food around his plate, took a forkful. 'You're right, the pie's as good as my Gran used to make. Can't do it now, bless her, has to rely on ready-mades nowadays.'

'How old is she now?'

'Eighty-five. Had her birthday a couple of weeks ago.'

'My, that's a good age. I imagine she has some tales to tell.'

Josh grinned. His mood lightened. 'She used to keep me enthralled for hours when I was a kid. All her stories about her childhood up north.'

'A fine raconteur, was she?'

'The best.'

They ate some more between their conversation and the barmaid came over when they were halfway through their meal.

'Everything all right guys?

'Fine,' said Josh.

'Excellent,' said Parri. Which Josh thought was a slight exaggeration. He shrugged his shoulders: the old man's palate, not his.

'Can you bring us another beer each, love?'

'Sure. Two Master Brew, isn't it?'

'Spot on. Thanks darling, you're an angel.'

She dimpled and took away their empty glasses.

'Pretty girl,' said the old man watching her walk back to the bar.

'Yeah, knows how to wiggle.' Not as pretty as Sue, Josh thought.

They carried on eating. The old man glanced out of the window. 'Traffic's building up. Wonder why?'

'Maybe there's been an accident out Cliftonville way.'

'Mmm, could be. Ah, here comes the lovely lady with our drinks.'

Josh went to pay, pulling a ten-pound note from a roll.

'No, no, dear boy. I said the treat's on me today. Put it on my tab, will you, young lady?'

'Certainly sir.' She dimpled again then glanced at Josh. 'Got it. Now I know where I've seen you. It *was* here. You came in with Sue, Sue Wainrose. Last week, wasn't it?' Haven't seen her around since then. You got rid of her?' She laughed.

The last mouthful stuck in Josh's throat. He wanted to throw up but forced himself to smile instead.

'No. Matter of fact I haven't seen her either. Think she might have gone away: work or something.'

He hoped it sounded casual enough, more offhand than he was feeling.

Parri Arnold joined in. 'Did you say Sue Wainrose? She was in the year below you, Josh.'

He was feeling hemmed in, wished they would both stop talking about bloody Sue. The pub manager came to his rescue: he called the girl back to the bar to serve some more customers. Josh excused himself, told the old man that he needed the gents. It was busy in there too, loud voices and cliquey behaviour from half a dozen knobs. He zipped up and left, returning to a once-again busy bar. In his temporary absence, it had filled with a coach-load of pensioners, all wanting halves and all wanting to order and pay individually. The girl, he thought, would be kept busy now for half an hour.

Their plates had been collected and Parri sat fingering his pipe.

'Do you want to go out onto the terrace? You can smoke there.'

'Good idea, Josh. Is that all right with you?'

'Sure. Could do with a bit of fresh air. Bit crowded in here now.'

'Let me just settle up.' He looked over to the bar. 'Think I can spot a gap in the queue.'

Josh forced himself to calm the shivers inside. *Better make this my last visit here.* He could hardly contain himself, desperate to get out of the place. It felt as if all eyes were accusing him, demanding him to answer. 'Where is Sue?' He shook himself. *Don't be so stupid. There's only one person likely to stare, and that's the stupid bitch over there.*

Parri returned to the table clutching the flimsy slip of his receipt.

'Shall we go?'

Josh nodded. 'Yeah, sure.' Relieved. He didn't look over to the bar, as they made their way through the crowded tables and out to the terrace. He guessed she would be staring after him. A mouthful of undigested pie forced its way up to his throat. He swallowed it: pure acid. Once outside, he breathed cold air deeply into his lungs.

'Thanks, Parri,' he said. 'That was really good.'

'You're welcome.'

They sat at a table facing the beach. A few diehards were walking on the sand from where the tide was receding: a few waves still splashed against the harbour wall. The old man decided not to light his pipe. 'Don't fancy battling against this wind. Fancy a stroll along the front? Help our lunch go

163

down?'

Josh hesitated. Torn. He didn't particularly want his own company, but he'd had enough of the old man now.

'Would love to, Parri, but I promised Gran I'd look in on her this afternoon.'

He saw the look of disappointment on the old man's face. *Christ, what am I? Caretaker to the aged?* Josh almost changed his mind... though only almost.

'Right then, I'll be on my way. Good to see you again, Josh.' They shook hands. 'Think I might spend an hour in the library. Keep in touch, you know where I live,'

The younger man nodded. 'Of course, sir, and thanks again for lunch: my treat next time.'

They set off in opposite directions. Josh looked back once, to see his old schoolteacher walk slowly towards the town centre and be swallowed by the shoppers. He turned towards Westgate. Two choices, left past the front of the Nayland Rock Hotel's entrance, or right, behind it and along the seafront walk. He chose the sea front. About half a mile along it, he wished he had chosen the main road: past the three-and-four storey houses, that had, at one time, been guest houses in Margate's short summer season. Now, they're more likely to accommodate students, DSS or migrants. Not the pleasant walk it used to be, with shops interspersed between the houses. Shops where you could buy anything from flowers to motor-cycle parts, maps and postcards to fish and chips. Dull or not, busy with cars or not, it would have been the safest route. The seafront wasn't. Between the cliffs and the grey splashing waves, his path threatened to be blocked: by six shaven-haired, tattooed, and very drunk, Margate Boys.

25

They were the same bunch he had passed earlier. Somehow, he didn't think they'd be so friendly this time round. He clenched his fists, thoughts racing as to how he could outwit them if they turned nasty. Soldier he might be, but the six-to-one odds were not in his favour. Diplomacy would have to be the order of the day: even a bit of boot-licking, if it saved him from a beating.

As they drew nearer, they grew louder: every other word a 'fuck' or 'bastard'. Bet they weren't taught by Parri Arnold, he thought.

'Well, whaddya know, it's the soldier boy.'

Not a good start. Josh nods at them. 'Fellas.'

They walk six abreast and part as they reach him, hemming him in between them. *Don't touch me, you prats.* They press nearer. What do they want to do? Squash him? *Leave it out, fellas. I don't want trouble.* Josh feels himself freeze, tense up. His breath becomes shallow, quickens up. He is beginning to panic, not through fear, not through being afraid of the six-pack around him. The fear is irrational. He cannot explain it, even if he was asked. He can feel the darkness descend upon him, hear the noise of the bombs, the screams. Someone pulls his arm, it's the last thing he remembers.

When daylight returns, he can hardly believe the carnage around him; bodies everywhere, blood, knives, groans of pain. He examines himself. No blood, no cuts from any of the knives strewn about. One of the bodies sits up, his face has been reshaped and is bloodied. He spits a tooth out, looks around him at his mates and glares at Josh.

'What's with you, soldier boy? Or is it frigging Superman?'

The others begin to sit up, try to stand on distinctly shaky legs.

Josh looks bewildered. *Did I cause this carnage?*

He goes to speak, but can't think what to say. Amazingly, the six of them back off.

'Look mate, enough. We don't want trouble, know what I mean?' One of them holds out his hand. Josh is unsure of the gesture.

'It was only a bit of fun.'

'Yeah right: six against one doesn't seem like fun to me.'

'And you're like a fucking tornado. I pity those poor rag-heads if they came up against you. Bet they thought you were a bleedin' one-man army.'

They all stood up, backing slightly away from him, wary, but showing grudging admiration.

'No harm done, aye?' Again, they attempt to shake hands with him. Josh puts his hands up in a gesture of conciliation, doesn't try to take any of their offered hands.

'Gotta go,' is all he says.

'Yeah, see ya.'

Not if I see you first.

Ten minutes later, he reached Westgate and was walking towards his house. With a slight feeling of unease, he wondered what had happened between himself and the six-pack. His mind was blank, like he had lost his memory. Perhaps he had what Gran had, retrograde amnesia. He remembered the threat of the six, remembered them hemming him in. Then nothing, until his mind cleared and he saw them on the ground: the blood, the knives, and hearing their groans. He grinned to himself. Well, whatever had happened, he'd come off better than them. *Don't knock it, Josh.*

The house was cold. And empty. What next? He wandered the downstairs rooms, aware the daylight was already fading. Or was it because the sunshine had disappeared behind a grey cloudy sky? Whatever, he felt justified in switching on lights everywhere. The smell of cat had completely disappeared and a faint suggestion of lilies of the valley remained. A small thing, but it pleased him. He wandered upstairs. From now until the parents came back, he was definitely sleeping in their room. He would drink Dad's malt, watch telly, mull over life in general. There was still the view from his room, of the girl's bedroom. He could feast his eyes on her whenever she was around. It would be good to get to know her, but not to do to her what he had done to Sue. No more killing, accident or otherwise.

The phone rang, interrupting his thoughts. Gran? Could be. Best answer it.

'Hello?'

'Hello Josh, it's Gran. Can you come over? I've some news for you.'

'Can't you tell me on the phone?'

'Not really.'

He sighed. *Now what?* 'Ok, Gran, I'll be over shortly.' He put the phone back in its cradle and looked at his watch, sixteen hundred. Still in his outer clothes, he decided to change his jacket, which had a small tear from his encounter with the Margate Boys. Not bad, if that was his only 'injury'. He took the stairs two at a time, went into his bedroom, and without having to turn on the light, found another jacket. He could see well enough from a light at the back. Looking out of the window, he identified the source of light. It was coming from the girl's house, her bedroom, he thought. More stripping off for him? Another peep show? He ran his tongue slowly over his lips, a half-smile playing on them.

Yeah, there she was, jacket coming off, slinging it on the bed, he imagined. Bending down, that meant shoes or jeans or skirt, then she straightened up, walked to the window, and looked out to the darkening sky. Josh ducked back out of sight but he could still see her. She peeled off her sweater, struggling some with its winter weight. Next a T shirt. Oh, glory be, she's gotta be down to panties and bra, he thought. He felt his temperature going up a degree, and his penis hardening. *Oh, to be inside her... now that winter's here.*

The phone begins to ring. Now what? End of pleasurable feelings. *Bet it's Gran again. Thanks Gran.*

'Hello?'

'Josh, thank goodness I've caught you before you left.'

'What's up?'

'Nothing, dear. Can you pick me up a jar of coffee and a box of teabags? I seem to be low on both.'

'Yeah, course I will, Gran. Be round shortly.' He put the phone down. Considered going back upstairs to his room, decided against it. Better go get the tea and coffee for Gran. *Wonder if her memory's returned yet?* He hoped not.

'Come in,' she shouted to him, 'Door's open.'

Gran looked animated. Josh wondered what had happened to make her so excited. *You won on the lottery or something, Gran?* She had put the kettle on and had two cups ready, plus a sponge cake, already sliced, on her new drum table.

'If you can finish making tea and bring it in, I'll tell you all the latest news.'

Must be something juicy, he thought, to get her all fired up. He made the tea and brought two cups into the lounge. He noticed the birthday cards had been taken down. *Wonder if you'll make your eighty-sixth?* He didn't mention them. She was sitting in her riser chair, pleating her throwover. Fidgety.

'Ok, so what's new, Gran?'

'Laura Innes has died.'

'What?'

'The ambulance was there, first thing this morning. They brought her out on a stretcher. I couldn't see her face but Marilyn was crying. She went in the ambulance with her mother.'

'How d'you find out she died?'

'Well,' she paused, catching her breath. 'Marilyn came back from the hospital about lunchtime. My carer was here and let her in. She was in a terrible state, poor lass.'

Lass? She must be older than God.

'Apparently, Laura was all but dead when they took her in the ambulance. Died soon after. Septicaemia they told Marilyn.'

'How'd she get that?'

Ellie paused again, panted a little. Josh thought she had aged since last week. Wished he could turn back the clock.

'It appears that daft daughter of hers persuaded her to stop taking her water tablets. Said she was fed up with Laura wetting herself every five minutes. And this is the result.'

'Poor crow. I bet she's in bits, isn't she?'

'So she should be. Laura would still be alive if she hadn't told her to stop taking those tablets.'

Josh drank his tea, took a slice of cake and bit into it. 'This is tasty, Gran.'

'Home-made it is. Not by me,' she laughed. 'My carer's mum made it for me. Anyway,' she added, 'Marilyn has to go to the hospital and then on to the registrar at Ramsgate to register Laura's death. I wondered,' she paused, 'if you would take her, in Granddad's car?'

'Are you kidding?'

'Well, there's no one else she can ask. I'm the only person in the street she speaks to. Can hardly go myself, else I would.'

Thanks for volunteering me, Gran. As if I haven't had enough of death lately.

'OK, put like that, s'pose I'll have to.' He sighed, the pleasure of home-made cake and a brew gone. 'When is this supposed to happen?'

'Would tomorrow morning be convenient? If it is, I'll let her know.'

'Yeah, that should be all right. Just let me know what time.'

'You can take the car now, if you like. I won't be using it, will I?'

He brightened. Why not? 'Thanks Gran. I might go and look up some mates this evening, or something.'

'Have fun.' She dismissed him with fluttering eyelids. *Time for a nap before the early evening news*. She yawned. 'Marilyn wondered if you could pick her up at ten o'clock: she has to be at the hospital about a quarter-past.'

'Yeah, I'll do that.' He bent to kiss his grandmother goodbye, noticed the way she flinched slightly. Was she getting her memory back? He went cold to his stomach. Hoped it was not true. He was grimly aware there would be consequences, and unwilling to think what they might be.

She managed a smile. 'Bye, Josh. The car keys are hanging up in the hallway. See you tomorrow.' She took his kiss, mentally berating herself for almost showing her aversion to his proximity. Hoped he had not noticed. She feared the consequences if he had. A cat and mouse game, but who the cat and who the mouse? Surely, what she knew gave her a certain advantage? Then again, his physical strength over her body weakness made him the cat and her the mouse. She shivered, glad he was gone. She heard the car pull out of the garage, heard him clang the metal door down and drive away. The carer would be here soon, then she could lock herself in, both with the key and the new bolt her gardener had fitted that morning. It might keep her safe at night when she was most vulnerable, but she would have to get up before the morning carer was due, to slide back the bolt.

'Damn you, Josh,' she said for the umpteenth time. 'Damn you for taking away my freedom.' Ellie knew she would have to make a plan. She struggled to her feet, took painful steps into the bathroom. Her rheumy eyes circled the walls of the small room, took in the pottery mermaid and her faithful friend, the seahorse. How old were they, for goodness sake? She and Ben had bought them on a trip to Cornwall. So many years ago. She paused at the medicine cabinet... Mmm.

26

Josh took out his frustration on the A28 and the A299. He gunned the car towards the M2, taking it up to its rattling maximum of 100mph. He was careful to look for any traffic cops. The less he brushed with the law, the better. He'd had enough of them for one day. Someone flashed from behind. Cocky bugger. He glanced in his rear mirror, saw the red sports car. He was tempted to brake but decided Gran would not be pleased if he caused someone to bash into the back of Granddad's car. *What's with you, Lewis Hamilton?. I'm doing a ton. What's your hurry?*

The guy was obviously needled. He closed in on Josh, almost bumper to bumper. Saw an opening on the inside lane and accelerated past, undertaking him. He stuck up a finger as he passed. Josh was enraged... and frustrated: knew he could not catch up. He slowed down, went into the now-deserted inner lane, and took the Faversham turn-off before the road joined the motorway. As soon as he found a lay-by, he sat and fumed; then grinned to himself. *Far better things to think about than idiots in sports cars. The chick opposite his bedroom for example. Watching her undress was far more entertaining.*

He drove home, careful to keep within the speed limit. It was well after dark by the time he got back: street lights full on and most curtains drawn in the houses he drove by. *Hope yours aren't drawn, darling.*

He drove the car into the garage and went through to the kitchen. He was relieved there was no cat smell, no snarl to greet him. He switched on the light and looked at his watch.

Six-thirty. Hunger gnawed at his stomach, despite his big lunch with Parri Arnold, and Gran's cake. If he hurried, he'd catch the Italian deli before it closed. He let himself out of the front door and into the quiet road: except for the roar of the sea close by... and the gulls... of course. He quickened his pace, aware of the chill wind that carried with it a hint of rain.

As he turned the corner, he almost bumped into someone. 'Sorry, love.' It was the girl from the Blue Elephant.

'Hello again,' she said. 'Didn't realise you lived round here.'

'I don't,' he lied, his mind going into fast gear. 'Just been visiting my gran.'

She stared at him, at his face lit by the overhead street light. 'Right. So where do you live?'

He resented her question. *What's it to do with you, darling?* 'Up the road some, Birchington way.'

'Oh, I know Birchington quite well.'

So? he thought.

'Whereabouts?'

'Er, Rutland Gardens.' He remembered the old angler's address the policewoman had found.

'What number?'

He scowled. 'You wanna know a lot.'

Her face relaxed. 'Sorry, you must think I'm a right nosey old bag.'

Too right I do.

'You're all right.' He gave a half smile, wished she would go on her way.

'So, off home, are you?'

'Yeah.' He looked away. The last thing he wanted was eye contact.

'I'm just going to see a film.' She pointed to the cinema with a gloved hand. He had forgotten about the little picture

173

house, marvelled it was still going.

'Right then, enjoy.' He made to leave.

'Don't suppose you fancy joining me? It's supposed to be a good film. Missed it last time round.'

He had no intention of going with her; she was the last person on his wish list. 'What's the film?'

'*Skyfall*. Daniel Craig as James Bond.'

'Seen it. Anyway, gotta go.' He turned away then faced her again, briefly. 'Enjoy the film.'

She waved, no smile though. 'I will.'

He thought about Daniel Craig. Who was it he reminded him of? He racked his brain, went through the alphabet, a trick he'd learned from Gran when you wanted to remember something or someone. He got to M. That's it. The guy he met in London, Mike Beresford. Dead ringer for Dan Craig, a bit younger of course, but could be his younger brother.

He turned the corner towards the Deli. The guy was just about to close. Josh broke into a run. 'Hold it mate. Can I make a quick purchase?'

The shop owner paused, stopped winding up his blind. 'Sure, come in. What can I get you?'

Josh blew out his cheeks, relieved that he would not have to forgo supper. His eyes ranged the illuminated display counter. 'Er, I'll have some of that salami, some Parma ham and... a piece of cheese, that one with the black rind.'

'Good choice, signore, that's Montassio, where I come from, near Venice.' He paused. 'How much you like of each?'

'Erm, say a hundred and fifty grams of the meats and that piece of cheese,' he pointed into the display case.'

'Ok. Any beer tonight?' He began cutting the meat on the electric slicer, wrapped each separately in greaseproof and made a neat parcel of them. Did similar with the cheese, then hovered near the beer fridge.

'I'll take two four-packs of Peroni, thanks. How much do I owe you?'

174

'Twenty pounds and three pence. Call it twenty: I'm feeling generous.' They both laughed. Josh handed over a twenty-pound note and the shopkeeper passed over a carrier bag with the food and another with the four-packs.

'Oh, I forgot bread. Got any left?'

The Italian looked at the empty shelves and shook his head. 'Just a couple of rolls. You can have them, they only get thrown in the bin tomorrow.'

'Cheers mate, and thanks for staying open for me, you've saved my life!'

He bent into the chill wind as he left the shop, glad to be going home. Not much to stay out for anyway. There was bound to be a couple of DVD's that he hadn't seen. Bread, salami, cheese, and eight Peroni's, sorted. *Well, well, look who's just going home, the girl from the back. Doing anymore undressing, sweetheart?*

She hadn't seen him. He followed her, careful not to get too close. Didn't want to be labelled a stalker. He watched her turn into the road before his, waited till she was safely inside before walking up to identify her house number. Might call on her some time. Now to get home and out of this icy wind... settle down with his mini feast, and the beer. Maybe he could go up to the bedroom a couple of times to see if she might give him a strip show.

Once inside the house, he plated up the meat and cheese, buttered the two rolls, and lifted the cap off the first beer. The other seven he put in the fridge. He wandered through to the lounge, sorted through the parents' DVDs, and found a set of *Spooks*. Great, he'd enjoy those... had missed so many with his tours abroad.

27

What a wasted evening. Falling asleep watching Spooks, *beer all drunk, food all eaten and no strip show. Least, if there had've been, he'd missed it. What's the time? Midnight? Where did the day go? Might as well go to bed; gotta take that crazy woman to hospital tomorrow. And how crazy is she? That stupid long grey plait, the weird clothes and those dolls and teddies. She's gotta be sixty if she's a day, maybe more. Imagine having her for a mother? Perhaps not. What's her name? Oh yeah, Marilyn. Defo not Monroe. More like the mad Baby Jane in that old Bette Davis and Joan Crawford film. Better watch my step with her, she might have a knife in her bag, or a pair of scissors, razor sharp, to cut off my balls.*

Josh dragged himself upstairs, stripped, and fell into his parents' bed and into instant sleep. It was two in the morning before the alcohol left his body and the nightmares began. Dead bodies and mutilated body parts, all dancing before him, the faces on the whole persons screaming, laughing manically, threatening him. Bloodied hands clawed at him, tearing chunks of flesh from him and giving it to the dead to eat. They became bloated on his flesh and he screamed silent screams of terror, fought them off with flaying fists, grazing his knuckles. But no blood came from within his skin, only seeping pustules, green and yellow. He was in a bubble of death and violence, until the explosions came, assailing his ears and attacking him with even more disintegrated torsos and disembowelled bodies. He rolled around the bed in a tangle of sheets and fear-laden sweat.

Falling to the floor brought him a blessed awakening but scant relief. He stumbled to the bathroom, knelt before the lavatory and vomited up his supper and the beer. The smell and taste was revolting, but the relief of being awake kind of compensated. He shivered in his nakedness. *Something's gotta be done about this. Perhaps I ought to see a shrink? Excuse me sir, I keep blacking out and finding dead bodies when I wake up. Not only that but I'm having the most God-awful nightmares. Can't cope sir. Not anymore. Enough's enough. Can you do something about it? Yeah, I know, just kill me: I'm a waste of space.*

He took a shower, found clean boxers and a T shirt and climbed back into bed. He lay quietly, hardly daring to breathe let alone think. Exhaustion took over and Josh slept. No dreams disturbed him. He awoke at nine, to a bright, sunny day, and the phone ringing.

It had stopped before he came to, enough to answer it, but Gran's number showed up on the missed calls. He rang her back.

'Hi Gran. Sorry I didn't pick up. I was in the shower.' A lie.

'You haven't forgotten you're taking Marilyn this morning?'

'No, course I haven't. Just dressing now. I'll be round in twenty minutes.'

'That's fine, pet. Pop in and see me, if you can, before you take her.'

'I'll do my best.'

He rang off and finished dressing, adding a sweater and jeans, socks and black shoes. Best not wear desert boots or trainers today. He picked up a dark blazer from the downstairs hallway, shrugged into it and went through the kitchen door into the garage. He decided against breakfast. Even the thoughts of coffee nauseated him. He could get a swift one at Gran's if need be.

177

Marilyn-not-Monroe looked even worse than last time he saw her. Face blotched and swollen from a waterfall of tears, he reckoned. She was dressed from head to toe in black, with a black ribbon imprisoning her grey plait and low-heeled black shoes, with black bows, keeping her feet from contact with the pavement. Even her handkerchief was black. Josh marvelled at that, he'd never seen a black one before. Marilyn locked the front door of her bungalow with no less than three keys. *Fort Knox, or what?* She gave him a brief, sad smile and climbed into the front passenger seat, sniffing and saying, 'oh dear' every few seconds. Josh sent a brief wave over to Gran as he climbed into the driver's seat.

'Is that your granny you're waving to?'

No, stupid, it's the president of the United Bloody States. He nodded and switched on the ignition. 'QEQM hospital?' he asked.

'Yes, that's right. Mum will stay there until I make arrangements with the funeral directors. I'm not using the local one. Don't like them. They buried Dad for us,' she added.

Josh declined to comment, or ask why she didn't like them.

'Which one *are* you going to use?' he asked.

'Oh, there's a nice one in Margate, this end of the High Street. I'll go with them.'

He smiled inside. *You mean your Mum will go with them or through them, whatever.*

The mention of funeral arrangements brought about a fresh onslaught of tears. Josh kept silent, just drove. He thought she would run out of space on the black-lace handkerchief if she didn't stop blubbing. He hoped the morning would go by quickly; she was already doing his head in.

He was definitely not going to accompany her into the hospital morgue, thought he would be fine waiting outside.

But Marilyn gripped his hand so tightly, he was forced to go with her. Her mother was laid out on a raised bed, covered in a blue sheet, her face exposed. She looked tiny, white, pasty, and very, very dead. They saw her first, behind a plate glass window, until the nurse said, 'Would you like to go in and say goodbye to your mother? How about you sir, is she your Grandmother?'

Chrissakes!

'No, I'm no relation. Just giving the lady here a lift. She's my Gran's neighbour.'

'Oh, sorry. Would you like to go in with Miss Innes?'

'No, you're all right, I'll stay out here.' *Bad enough being this close to yet another dead body.* The nurse accompanied Marilyn into the room where her mother lay. Her face once more contorted in a fresh bout of crying. She bent over, her tears falling onto the inert form, and kissed what Josh knew would be an icy-cold face. He saw her shudder, bury her face in the nurse's uniform. He had to turn away, it wasn't a pretty sight. *Not as bad as when Andy died though. Nothing will ever be as bad as that again. Will it?*

After an indecent three minutes, the nurse persuaded Marilyn it was time to leave. He saw her glance at her brooch watch. Marilyn didn't notice. She seemed not to want to let go of her, clinging with those thin, birdlike fingers. The nurse almost hid her flinch, but not from him outside the glass window. He felt a brief moment's sympathy for her. He watched as the daughter once more touched her mother, which brought about more tears. *Christ, is there really that much water in your tear ducts? Come on, Baby Jane, let's get the hell outa here and go to the Registry Office. Some of us have a life.* Josh could have done with a drink; a tot of Dad's malt wouldn't have gone amiss.

It wasn't far from the hospital, less than four miles, and the streets were deserted. Josh parked up only yards away from the entrance to the Registry Office. He hoped, now there was business to see to, Marilyn would stop her constant crying. He could hardly tell her to 'man up'. They sat for a few minutes while she attempted to compose herself, wipe her swollen red nose, and dry her equally swollen, red eyes. What a sight. Made him shudder.

'Ready?' he said.

She nodded her head, attempted bravery through those watery eyes.

'Come on then, let's go.'

'I don't know what to do.'

'Don't worry, they will. You just hand them that letter from the hospital, they'll take care of the rest.'

He climbed out first and walked round to the passenger seat. He took her hand, gloved now in black. She looked like something out of a Victorian novel, the sort Gran used to like reading. *Wonder if she still does?* A short-skirted version of Queen Victoria in mourning, thinner than the old monarch, though.

Forty minutes later they were back on the road, Marilyn clutching several copies of the death certificate.

'Can we stop off at the funeral parlour, just before the bridge?'

He winced. Would this day never end? 'Sure love.'

Again, he was fortunate in the lack of traffic and finding a place to park, close to the undertakers.

'Will you come in with me?'

'Sure,' he said, and again he attempted a smile.

Her voice shuddered but, thankfully, no more tears. Baby Jane putting on a brave face? There were vases of white lilies in both windows of the double-fronted shop premises. Muted scenery of countryside behind. Or was it supposed to represent some kind of heaven? The vases rested on a shiny, purple material that was draped to look like waves. Someone, or something, being rowed over the River Styx?

Not really. Surely everyone who was buried by this lot went to Heaven not Hades?

They walked in to a deserted reception with lilac upholstered chairs, more highly scented lilies, and some kind of soft music playing: atmospheric and ghostly. A woman appeared, through a door behind the counter. She was middle-aged, Josh judged, and wore a black, well-fitting suit with a white blouse, opened by as much as three buttons from the neck. Enough to show a slight cleavage without being too revealing. And a smile: the sort of smile that displays welcome and sympathy together. Practised, Josh thought. She said, 'Good morning.' and waited for one of them to speak. He thought she was practised enough not to add 'What can I do for you?' *Pretty obvious what she could do, for whoever walked through these doors.*

Marilyn held out the certificate and a letter from the hospital. She could not hold back the tears and, from nowhere, a floral box of tissues appeared in the funeral director's hand. She pulled several out and handed them to Marilyn, with a soothing, hush-now sound. It worked. After a few minutes, Baby Jane calmed down enough to explain about 'Mum', the letter from the hospital, and the death certificate from the registrar.

Somewhere, he thought, she must have a discreet bell to ring, because a young guy, also dressed in black with pin-striped trousers and a crisp white shirt with a black tie, came through a rear door with a tray of tea.

'Thank you, Simon,' she said. He put the tray down on a small table in front of the upholstered chairs and disappeared, after acknowledging the lady's appreciation.

'My name's Muriel,' she offered. 'And you're Marilyn, and this is?' She pointed to Josh.

'Oh, his grandmother was Mum's friend...he's helping me with... today.'

'I'm Josh.'

She shook hands with both of them, poured tea while she chatted about the firm, and how 'we' like to do whatever is necessary and however 'you' want the arrangements to be. Marilyn nibbled on a biscuit, carefully wiping a crumb from the corner of her mouth like some old dowager from Downton Abbey: except dowagers don't use Kleenex tissues, or Josh didn't think so.

An expensive looking glossy was brought out from behind the counter, showing photographs of coffins and their conveyance for the final journey. Josh recalled Parri Arnold telling him about the purple and horse-drawn funeral of Miss Black. He didn't think Laura Innes' funeral would be quite as grand, or bizarre.

'I shall walk in front of the hearse when we leave your house and again before we reach the cemetery,' she told them.

'I didn't know women could do that,' marvelled Marilyn.

Muriel gave a thin smile. 'A few of us do, especially nowadays.'

Hasn't Baby Jane heard of Women's Lib?

They continued discussing the arrangements.

'Mum wants to go in with Dad. We bought a double plot for them, when Dad died.'

Josh marvelled at the way Muriel took on board the way Marilyn talked about her parents.

'That's absolutely fine. We'll arrange for her to stay here at our chapel of rest until her special day. Have you thought about what you would like her to wear?' she added.

'Oh, she's got a lovely lilac twinset. It's one of her favourites.'

'Ok. Any jewellery? Pearls maybe?'

'Yes, Dad bought her a string of pearls, the Christmas before he passed away. She wears... wore them a lot. They were her favourites.'

Muriel added pearls to her leather-bound notebook.

'Should I include underwear?'

'Of course,' said Muriel. 'Dignity, my dear. Respect. Even at the end, especially at the end.'

Josh squirmed. He really did not want to listen to this. He excused himself. 'Mind if I go outside for a bit? Just want to check on the car.'

Muriel sent him a look of empathy, nodded. 'We won't be long now Josh.'

Marilyn stared. 'You won't leave me, will you?'

'Course not love, just want a breather. I'll only be outside here, probably come back in before you're through.'

All good practice for when Gran snuffs it.

28

They drove home through quiet streets, past empty boarded-up shops, with very few potential shoppers had they have been open. Much to Josh's annoyance, Marilyn continued her snivelling. *Christ, I need a bloody medal after this morning, carting you about and listening to your incessant crying and 'oh dear, oh dear', a million times. Pity they don't put people like you down; one quick jab in the paw and curtains, no more Baby Jane.*

'I can't thank you enough, Josh. For taking me everywhere this morning.'

'S'all right love.' He didn't add 'it's a pleasure'. It had hardly been that. Anything but.

When he finally drew up outside her bungalow, she fumbled in her bag and pulled out some bars of chocolate.

'Here, take these.' She smiled and pushed the bars almost under his nose. *Is she for real? Do I look like some sort of chocoholic?*

'Oh, thanks,' he said, bemused. He thought Gran would enjoy them. 'I'd better go,' he said. 'Gran'll be wanting me to shop for her.' It was a lame excuse, simple enough for this mad old bat to understand though.

She climbed out of the passenger seat and put two feet firmly on the pavement: stood up, and once more thanked him, as she began to cry again. He almost shuddered at the sight of her ugly, swollen face, and the tears running down her wrinkles into the now-soaked, black-lace hankie. He averted his eyes instead and waited while she walked up to her front door, put all the keys into the locks to unfasten

'Fort Knox', and watched until she went inside. She turned to give him a final wave, a little girl's wave: not very regal or grown up. *Mad woman.* He ignored the twitching curtains either side.

'How did it all go?'

Josh was seated on one of Gran's multi-cushioned, high-rise chairs, drinking tea and munching on a sandwich.

'Nice ham, Gran. Yeah, it went ok, I s'pose. She cried plenty. Didn't think anyone had that much water inside their eyes.'

His grandmother sighed, looked out of her window to the bungalow opposite. She remembered her own grief when Ben had died: the aching loneliness in bed at night, without him by her side.

'She'll be very lonely now, I expect. Poor Marilyn, she's never been on her own all her life. Never married, and always lived with them, her Mum and Dad. I don't think,' she added. 'That she's ever really grown up.'

Josh laughed. 'You're right there. It's like a teddy bears' picnic in that house. And a dolls' shop. I've never seen so many outside of *Toys R Us*, wherever.'

'Mmm, strange girl.'

'Bit old for a girl. She must be getting on for seventy, if she's a day.'

'She's not, you know. I think she's only in her early fifties. About the same age as your mother.'

'Blimey! In that case Mum's wearing well. Dad must be doing something right.'

'She's a very lucky woman, having a good man like Paul by her side.'

Josh grinned and nodded. 'Yeah, I expect you're right.' Gran really didn't like his mother. He wondered why exactly.

'So, did she get everything done? The registrar, and so on?'

Josh yawned. 'Oh yeah. And the funeral's been arranged.

The undertakers near the bridge, as you come out of Margate. Nice lady in there. Apparently, *she* walks in front of the hearse nowadays. She took over the business from her father, so she told us. Seems funny though,' he laughed. 'Can't quite imagine a woman doing it.'

His grandmother agreed. 'No, it takes a bit of imagining. When is it, by the way? Laura's funeral?'

'Er, I think Muriel, that's the undertaker's name, said next Friday, ten o'clock. Mum and Dad will be home by then. Perhaps they'll take you, if you want to go.'

'I'd rather you did. Treat you to lunch after. Somewhere nice, wherever you want to go.'

'All right, you old biddy. You've tempted me.' Josh grinned at his grandmother, and felt a strange comfort that she had not died on that awful day. He hoped she would never regain memory of it. What would he do, if she did? What could he do?

He left soon after lunch, when Ellie began to nod off. Once her mouth fell open, and she started to snore and dribble, it was time for him to go. He kissed her forehead, whispered, 'Love you, Gran,' and quietly shut the front door behind him.

A chill wind threatened as he walked towards the car, ruffling his collar and sending shivers down his back. The curtains in the opposite bungalow twitched, must be Marilyn. Don't these old wrinklies have anything better to do? He resisted the urge to smile and wave: instead he shuddered and turned away. He had had enough of her for one day, one lifetime even. Regretted now that he'd agreed to take Gran to the old girl's funeral. Not the most pleasurable thing to be doing. And he'd have to suffer Baby Jane's tears again, that ugly, swollen red face and the all-black ensemble. *Wonder who else will go? Any relatives? Gran says she's an only child; some child.*

He flashed the car door open, got in and drove away,

dismissing both bungalows, anxious now to get home. Best to do some shopping first, he thought. The Italian deli again, why not? It was as good as any. Might even see the girl from the back window in there. He fancied the idea of taking her out for the evening, wine and dine, then back to his place for a nightcap and whatever might follow. He got hard just thinking about it. *Oh, please be in there...*

Amazingly, she was, cutely wrapped against the cold, with a white scarf and matching beanie hat. She wore a perfectly fitted, dark-blue coat, and tan leather boots to complete the ensemble. He smiled. The gods were good, sometimes. Only one drawback, the girl she was talking to was her from the Blue Elephant in Margate. They looked pretty pally, he thought. How come they knew each other? He stabbed an angry look at the barmaid. No chance of getting his end away tonight, not with the girl from the back-room window. Unless... maybe they'd like a threesome? Yeah – why not? The thought made his pulse race and Sir Percy to rise again.

Barmaid Sue's voice quickly dampened that eagerness. 'What are you doing here again?'

Backroom girl's eyes widened, a hint of a smile behind them. Great, he'd caught her in a good mood. He was about to say, 'I live here, don't I?' When he remembered telling the barmaid that he lived in Birchington. *That would go down well, getting caught in a stupid lie. Now what?*

'Been on a mercy mission,' he said. 'Friend of my Gran's died and I took the daughter into Margate and Ramsgate to do all the necessaries.'

Backroom girl turned to the counter. Luigi was ready to take her order.

'So... playing the knight in shining armour, are we?'

'Something like that.' He listened to backroom girl's order: two of everything, or enough for two. And a bottle of chilled white wine. Girlie night in by the sounds of it. Be nice to get an invite, but he doubted that would happen.

Purchases done, she turned around. God, she was beautiful.

'Right, that's my lot. I'm off now to Danny's.' *Her brother?* 'You getting anything?' she said to the barmaid.

'No, I don't think so. I'll have a bag of popcorn in the cinema.'

'I thought you went last night,' Josh said.

'Couldn't get in. It was packed. Going early tonight to make sure I get a seat.' As an afterthought, she said, 'Fancy joining me?'

His mind raced. If he said yes, he couldn't buy supper from the deli. If he said no it meant a lonely night in again.

'Tell you what,' he compromised. 'How about I meet you after? What time does the film end?'

'About ten, I think.'

'Ok, fancy going for a drink after?' He saw what he thought, what he hoped, was disappointment on backroom girl's face. *Yeah, I know, sweetie, better if it was you and me.*

'Ok,' said the barmaid. 'Where shall we meet?'

'I'll pick you up at ten, outside the cinema.'

'Right.'

The girls made to leave. He waved them off and turned back to the patient Luigi. 'Sorry mate.' He placed an order for home-cooked lasagne and a four pack of Peroni. No sense in getting lathered before the meet-up. The girls were still talking when he came out. He hoped they had not been discussing him, and where he lived. He had a thought.

'Can I drop you anywhere?' he asked backroom girl. 'Got wheels tonight.'

'Oh, erm,' she hesitated. 'Yes. That would be great. My brother lives in St Nick's. Are you sure?'

'Of course, it's not that far.' What a bonus, two girls in one night. Suddenly his evening looked full of promise. He turned to the barmaid. 'See you later?'

'Ok. Bye Suzie.'

They air-kissed each other as he opened the car door for backroom girl, or Suzie as he now knew. So many Sue's and her going to St Nick's as well. Seems like he was fated to keep going back there. They both waved to the barmaid. Suzie called out, 'See you Wednesday, Sue Ellen.'

Bloody hell, another Sue. Still, now he had both their names. He preferred Suzie.

'D'you want to put your bag in the back?'

'No, it's fine on my lap. Not that heavy.' She cuddled it like a big teddy bear. *Oh no, perish the thought. He'd seen enough of them at Baby Jane's.* He drove carefully through the now-darkened streets, out onto the main road through Birchington and onto the A28 towards St Nicholas at Wade.

'Whereabouts in St Nick's am I taking you?'

'Er, not into the village. My brother has a farm, out towards the Wantsum.'

He went cold. And silent.

'If you turn right at the roundabout and down the lane, it's not far from there. Danny generally picks me up at the bus stop, but I just rang him, to let him know I was getting a lift.'

Josh turned into the lane, thought of the angler and the other Sue. He drove carefully, thoughtfully, headlights full on.

'There,' she said and pointed to a three-bar farm gate. She touched his arm. 'Thanks a lot for the lift.'

His mind went blank as the blackness set in. He jammed on the brakes, and his passenger, who had undone her seat belt, almost hit the windscreen. She put her hands out onto the dashboard, yelled at him. 'Hey, are you all right?'

Josh blinked. His blackout lasted only seconds, not long enough for the bombs to explode or the bullets to fly. No screams. Someone was tapping on his side window. A guy with a torch and an angry face. Josh shook himself, killed the engine.

'Sorry,' he muttered. 'Don't know what happened there.'

'It's ok,' she said and called out to her brother. 'Hi Dan, it's me.'

He had already opened the driver's door; his anger was melting. 'You ok, mate?'

'Yeah, sorry about that. Suddenly got a searing pain in my head. Just back from Afghanistan,' he explained.

The farmer stood up. He was tall and powerful, with a farmer's ruddy complexion. 'Right.' Little sympathy in his voice.

'Ok, Suzie?'

'Yes, I'm fine,' she said and climbed out of her seat. The lights from the farm lit up the gate where they stood. She turned to Josh, 'Thanks for the lift. See you.'

Her brother examined Josh's face, his momentary anger gone. 'Sure, you're all right? D'you want to come in for a moment?'

Josh shook his head, attempted a smile. 'No, I'm fine. Gotta get back. See you around,' he said to the farmer's sister. She smiled and waved, now engulfed by several dogs. Her brother followed, controlling the dogs with a single word of command.

Josh decided to turn the car around in the little car park, further along the lane. Better than attempting a three-point turn in this narrow part. Briefly wondered why Danny Boy had not opened the gate for him to turn into the farm yard. Remembered the dogs. Maybe not such a good idea. He was surprised by blazing lights in the tiny car park. Saw familiar yellow and blue colours, identifying the cars as police vehicles. Now what? Another dead angler? He was forced to turn in there, nowhere else to go.

Two police with large torches stopped him.

'Excuse me sir,' always polite. 'Can we ask what you're doing here?'

'Just turning round. Road's too narrow and dark to risk a

three-point turn.'

'And where have you been?' The pedantic sods were insistent. He took in the scene beyond them. Men in white suits and police in high-viz jackets, and blue tape being tied across the car park. A hive of uncomfortable-looking industry.

He parried their question with a question. 'What's happening?'

'Some human remains have been found. Can you tell us where you've been?'

His mind raced. *That arm from yesterday*?

'I've just dropped a friend off, at her brother's farm back there. Decided it was easier to turn around here as it's dark.'

'So, you're familiar with this car park?'

'Used to come fishing here, with my grandfather, when I was a kid.'

'Right,' the policeman nearest him sighed. Smiled politely and said, 'Best be on your way then.'

Josh nodded, gave a half-smile, and reversed his grandfather's car away from the crime scene, before either policeman decided to ask him if he was the owner. Back home he put the car away and went through to the kitchen. He unwrapped the lasagne and put the foil tray into the oven, on a high temperature. The beers, he pushed into the freezer, among bags of crushed ice. They'd be ready by the time he had a shower and dressed. Was he looking forward to tonight? Not really. She was, after all, second best. He'd sooner have spent the evening with the delicious Suzie.

29

The shower was stinging hot: perfect after the chilly night out there. Hardly night time, but dark early now. He'd missed the English summer, being out in the Middle East. There, you suffered blistering heat during the day and mostly freezing nights. Both extremes took the skin off your bones. After ten minutes he towelled himself dry, and wandered naked through to the bedroom, to choose some fresh clothes. He glanced out of the window, into the darkness beyond. No light on in Suzie's window. Well there wouldn't be would there? She was at her brother's farm... and he was left with Sue Ellen, the barmaid. Ah well, can't win 'em all.

He ran downstairs, eager now to eat, and to enjoy a beer. The lasagne was slightly crisp at the edges, just how he liked it. He sprinkled Parmesan cheese over and added some chilli flakes, grabbed a knife and fork, and took it all on a tray through to the lounge, with his beer. The beer was pleasantly chilled. He liked that too. A forkful of lasagne burned his lips and the beer cooled it down.

Switching on the TV he was in time to catch the local news, amazed to find a top newscaster now relegated to Thanet. *Put you out to grass, have they? Happens to us all in time.*

'Human remains have been found in the River Wantsum. The police have not revealed details, but it is thought the remains are a leg or an arm. Forensics will give their result soon.'

Josh wondered if it was the same limb. Surely not. The

tide was definitely going out when he tossed it back, into the water, on the old man's fishing line. Surely the pike ate it? Maybe not, maybe it got stuck in the reeds. The newscaster droned on, mentioned more deaths, more doom and gloom. Josh barely listened until the newscaster's voice changed. 'Breaking news. A Margate man, Pargiter Arnold, retired teacher from a Ramsgate Comprehensive, was set upon, late this afternoon by a gang, as he walked home from the library. He was badly beaten, and suffered extensive cuts and bruising to his head and body. He was taken to Queen Elizabeth the Queen Mother hospital, where he received a total of fifty-one stitches. It is understood he is in a stable condition, though badly shocked by the attack, which police say was entirely random and brutal. They are following lines of enquiry and are confident of making arrests soon, particularly after the victim identified several of the gang from police photographs. A hospital spokesman says, "Mr Arnold will remain in hospital for the next few days."'

Josh put the TV on mute, stunned by the news. His old teacher being assaulted! *Bastards.* He guessed it might be the Margate Boys who had tried it on with him yesterday. *Complete morons. Drug and drink infested and no brains. I'll find them, Parri, and knock the crap out of them. They won't get away with it.* The ferocity of the attack took away his appetite and any thoughts of drinking. He took his supper back out to the kitchen, left it on the side and went through to the hall, where he grabbed his jacket. The car keys were still in his pocket. He went back into the kitchen, then out into the garage. He flashed the garage door open, likewise the car, then straight out onto a quiet and dimly-lit road. He could hear the sea on his left as he drove towards Margate and the QEQM hospital. Crashing angry waves matched his mood, his animosity directed at the mindless gang that could do this to an old man. For a split second, he thought of Foxy. *That was different. I hadn't meant to hurt him, if it was me. Same with Gran. She's the last person in the world I would harm.*

The hospital car park was almost empty. Josh drove as near as possible to the entrance, then remembered you had to get a pay-and-display ticket. *Even at this time of night?* He read the machine, which informed him tickets were required twenty-four seven, even for disabled drivers. *How tight can you get?* He hunched his shoulders against the strong tide's-in breeze, glad that he was only yards from the main entrance. A warm blast of air greeted him as he entered. He looked up to the information board, presumed Parri would be in Men's Surgical. He followed the signs round long winding corridors, hesitated outside the swing doors and peered through. The ward was well lit, with side doors leading off to offices and cupboards. A nurse came up behind him. 'Can I help you?'

'Yeah, er yes. I'm looking for Mr Arnold, Pargiter Arnold.'

'Are you a relative?'

'Not quite.' He smiled. 'He's my old teacher. We had lunch together yesterday. Must have been soon after,' he added. 'When those morons attacked him.'

'I know who you mean now. Bless him, he didn't deserve that beating. He's improving though. Bed 6a,' she informed him and pushed open the ward doors, indicating to Josh which side of the ward to go. He thanked her and crept towards a bed next to the window. Screens partially hid his old friend but the sight of him alarmed Josh, made his stomach churn. Parri's face was one huge bruise, putting Josh in mind of an over-sized aubergine. His left eye was almost closed and the right one looked bloodshot and swollen. There were stitches on his forehead, more on one cheek, and his arm was supported by a blue sling.

Parri tried to sit up when he saw Josh, attempted a painful smile. 'My boy,' he said through cut, swollen lips. 'Good to thee you.'

Josh moved quickly to his old friend's side. He took his uninjured hand and squeezed it gently. For a short moment, words failed him as he examined Parri's face. 'This is unbelievable, sir. How the hell could anyone do this? Why?'

His old teacher sighed. 'I don't know, Joth. I really don't know.'

Josh found a chair and placed it close to Parri's bed. 'Sorry,' he said. 'I haven't brought you any grapes.'

'Thath's fine, they'd only get under my plate. Denturth, not dinner.'

They laughed together. Chatted softly. After an hour or so Josh could see the old boy was wilting.

'I'd better go now, I'll come back tomorrow. No toffees or grapes,' he laughed. 'Maybe jelly babies or marshmallows.'

Pargiter patted his ex-pupil's hand. 'Thank you tho much for taking the trouble to vithit me.'

'No trouble at all. Just a shame,' he resisted the urge to swear, 'that I have to come at all.'

He whispered a goodbye, slid out of the screens and mouthed 'Goodbye'.

It was dark out in the car park, and cold. Quickly, he flashed the car door open, switched on the ignition and the lights on low beam. He sat there for a while, contemplating. Should he go to the police with his suspicions? Why not just ring them? Anonymously? They weren't his best buddies at the moment. Never would be, he knew. He switched on the car radio: it went straight to Thanet Radio and an aging DJ. 'The time is now nine fifty-five. Soon time for the news and local weather. Stay with us, guys.'

Josh could not believe where the time had gone and, at the same time, remembered his tentative date with the barmaid, Sue Ellen. She'd go ballistic if he was late. Well tough, he was going to be late. Nothing he could do about it. He gunned the car into first gear and made a speedy exit from the car park. Thankfully, the road was pretty deserted all the way to Westgate. He arrived at the cinema at ten minutes past ten. She stood there, shivering in skimpy clothing. Skirt too short for her plump thighs, and the bitter wind that played around them. Coat unbuttoned, and no scarf. He drew up beside her, leaned over and opened the passenger door. She bent down and hissed, 'You're late.'

'Yeah, sorry about that. Had to go and see an old friend of mine in QEQM. He got beaten up yesterday afternoon. By some moronic gang.'

She fidgeted on the spot. 'I'm frozen.' Not a word of sympathy for the old boy. Just a whinge about her being cold. He went completely off the idea of a night with her: thought how ugly she looked, when she was angry.

'I said I'm sorry, for Chrissakes. Being cold is nothing to what my old friend feels at the moment. Now,' he paused, trying to gain control of his temper, attempting to be nice to this unpleasant female sitting beside him. 'Do you want to go somewhere for a drink or what?'

She sat hunched, miserable, and sulky. 'Don't care. What d'you want to do?'

Not you, that's for sure, bitch.

'Depends. We can find somewhere to eat, or just go for a drink, or go clubbing if you want.' He really didn't care now, wasn't in the mood for socialising. Anyway, she was being nothing but a pain.

'I really don't know. Come to think of it, I just want to go home. Don't bother giving me a lift,' she added. 'I'll catch the last bus back to Margate. Maybe another time, eh?'

'Suits me.'

She got out of the car and walked off towards the bus stop. 'By the way,' she called back to him. 'I do remember you coming into the Blue Elephant, with Sue Wainrose. It *was* you.'

He watched her retreating back, thinking how ugly she really was, especially after that parting shot. Her too-short coat showed the backs of fat knees, with thick calves that were the same size down to her ankles. Two shapeless logs. She clomped along the pavement in wedge-heeled shoes, her shoulder bag bumping against her hip. He stared until she disappeared into the black hole of night, beyond the street lamps.

He sat there for some time, wondering what she meant by the last words she uttered, 'There's some I know who'll be interested – you being the last person who was seen with Sue.'

His eyes widened. How could she prove he was the last one to see her? And did she mean the police? He doubted that, relieved anyway that she didn't know where he lived. He looked at his watch: twenty past ten. Still time to go for a drink. He watched as people still coming away from the cinema, wandered into what looked like a café-bar. He didn't remember it being here on his last leave. Perhaps he'd take the car home first, then walk back. Or maybe not. He could always leave it here if he had too many. Chances of it being vandalised, around these parts, were pretty remote, he thought.

The café windows were all steamed up, but when he opened the door he felt a welcome in the warmth of the place and the noise of people chatting. There was a fairly small bar at the end of the room, a facsimile of a pub bar with colourful optics and rows of shining glasses on the shelves above.

'Yes, love?' The person who offered to serve him was colourful, wore eye make-up and was an aging male.

'Erm, pint of lager please, mate.'

'Don't do draft love, but I've got some great bottled beer.'

'Peroni?'

'Yep, can do. Glass or in the bottle?'

'Glass please.' Josh thought the congenial atmosphere warranted a glass.

He watched as his gay barman poured it with a flourish. Nodded an acknowledgement of his skill in producing the right frothy head and no spillage.

'Anything else, sir?' Gay boy's eyes twinkled.

Not with you, darling. 'No thanks, mate. How much do I owe you?'

'Three pounds fifty.' He took Josh's five-pound note, rang it in the till and palmed him his change. He smiled into Josh's eyes. 'Enjoy.' And turned to the next customer.

'Yes love?' This time 'love' was a woman and said with less enthusiasm.

Josh smiled to himself. *You can't win 'em all, sailor.*

He peered into the crowd. Not the usual pub clientele. Definitely not the Margate pubs. Trendy? Arty? He tried to identify the type, decided they were a mixed bunch, more a 40-50 than a 20-30 age group. Suited him, his mood tonight. He could merge or stay on the periphery, listen and watch. Yeah, listen. It suddenly occurred to him there was no loud music to punish your ears, or cause conversation to be held ten decibels above normal.

This was good, he could handle this. He began to enjoy the atmosphere, overhear some of the chat.

'No use buying old vinyls now, they're out of bed.'

'What's in, then?'

'Autographs, 'specially sports stars. I sold a small album at auction last week. Got six hundred for it.'

'Nice one,' said his pal.

Josh moved over to the other side. More antique dealers he thought, listening to their chat. All about what was in and what was 'out of bed.' He finished his drink, gently pushed his way over to the bar again. Gay boy was ready for him.

'Same again, love?'

He nodded, risked a smile but nothing too encouraging. Live and let live, but certainly not his preference. He handed over another five-pound note, then asked, 'One for yourself?'

His colourful friend beamed a Russell Grant grin. 'Love to. I'll have a half.'

Josh took back the fiver and offered a tenner. He wondered what the half would be. Gin, maybe?

'That'll be five-o-two, call it five for cash. Thanks for the tipple.' He gave Josh another five-pound note, tilted a small tumbler at him and mouthed 'Cheers'. Josh eased himself back into the room. He felt good, the best he'd felt all day. Even better when a good-looking woman smiled at him. *Bet she's been around, and back a few times, and knows what to do with the experience.*

'You're new here,' she said.

He smiled. 'Is that an accusation or an observation?'

'Whatever you want it to be.' Her face dimpled when she smiled. Mature, but distinctly attractive. She could be forty, he thought, or in her late thirties and played hard.

'My name's Annie,' she said.

'Josh,' he replied. 'Josh Swales, and I live local, when I'm home on leave.'

She nodded, sucked rather charmingly on her lower lip. 'Army, navy or air force?'

'Army, just back from Afghanistan.'

'Ugh,' she winced. 'Not good out there.'

'No, but not so bad. I've been in better places though. Like a drink?' he added, noticing her glass was almost empty.

She smiled. 'Thanks. White wine, please. Dry.'

This time, Gay Boy sniffed at him when he ordered the drinks. He'd seen who Josh was with. Battle lost. Josh pressed his way through the crowd, glasses held high above his head, to where Annie sat at a small, metal bistro-table in the window. She smiled up at him and he felt a faint pull, as if she had tied a belt around him. The effect was not unpleasant.

'One white wine ma'am.' He sat opposite her, taking in her features. Wide-apart dark-blue eyes, generous mouth and straight nose. He liked what he saw. Sue Ellen became a distant memory, history.

'So, what do you do for a living?' he asked.

'I deal in antique jewellery, mostly Victorian.'

Josh laughed. 'I presume Victorian jewellery is not out of bed?'

'No,' she smiled. 'Where d'you learn that jargon?'

'Only here, tonight. Overheard a couple of guys earlier on. They were talking about old 78 records. Apparently, they're "out of bed".'

She grinned at him. They sipped their drinks and orbited the room with their eyes.

'Was there an auction here, in Westgate?'

'Yes, this evening, at Colin's place.' Annie lifted up her bag. 'Managed to get one or two nice pieces.'

'That's good. I didn't even know they held auctions in Westgate.' He added, 'Shows how much I know of my home town. I know my Gran sometimes goes to one, in Cliftonville.'

'Ah yes, that'll be Robert Fullerton.'

'She buys odds and ends of furniture there from time to time. Went there the other day and bought a little drum table.'

'What's her name?'

'Ellie Swales.'

'Ah, I think I know her. She's quite old, isn't she?'

'Yeah, eighty-five a couple of weeks ago, Bright as a galaxy, she is.'

They had almost drained their glasses, when the barman rang the bell for last orders.

'One for the road?'

'Let me get them,' she said. 'It's my shout.' She stood up, took the two glasses and made her way to the bar. Josh admired her back view, the way her bottom gently swayed. *Wonder if she'll come back to mine tonight? Wouldn't mind a bit of mature woman. What's the old saying? 'They don't yell, they don't tell and they're grateful as hell.'*

She returned with a large white wine, a glass of Peroni and an extra bottle, just as Gay Boy called out, 'That's your lot, girls and boys. Bar's closed.' With a cheeky wave, he pulled down the shutter on his tiny kingdom, or was it queendom, Josh wondered.

They talked as they drank. Josh told her a bit about his time in Afghanistan, about Andy stepping on a roadside bomb and being blown to pieces. She listened, and he noticed how her eyes welled up when he spoke about Andy. He liked that, warmed towards her.

She told him about the antiques trade, the auctions, the fairs, and anecdotes about a few dodgy dealers.

'You got a shop?'

'Yes and no. I share a premises with five other dealers. It keeps costs down, plus I only need enough space for a table and display case.'

'Where d'you live?'

'Here,' she told him. 'In Westgate: Poundbury Close.'

'Oh right.' It was one of the newer roads, modern houses. Nice though. He wondered, *is there a Mister Annie?*

She seemed to read his thoughts. 'I live on my own since Jake, my ex-partner, and I split. He went to live up North with a seventeen-year-old.' She said it without bitterness. Josh imagined any pain she had suffered was long gone. That pleased him. He began to hope the evening would not end in this bar. The idea of spending a night with Annie both intrigued and excited him. It became an urgent need, pounding inside his head, as the noise of departing drinkers hovered on the peripheral of his consciousness. They, too, had to leave, and soon.

She was looking at him, her eyes moving from left to right across his face, as if it was a Kindle book and she was reading his mind.

'Fancy coming back to my place, for a nightcap?'

Oh glory be, she's beaten me to it.

He barely hesitated. 'Love to. I was just about to ask you the same question.

She grinned, and he read into it a hint of, what might promise to be, a very pleasant nightcap. They finished their drinks and made their way to the door. A tall, bald-headed guy swayed into Annie, causing her to stumble against Josh.

'Watch it, mate.'

'Sorry Annie. One too many tonight.'

Josh smelled more than the alcohol on him. A dank smell, like an unaired basement.

'It's ok, Alfie. You take care.' She weaved around him and Josh followed, glaring at Alfie, whoever he was.

'My car's outside,' he said. 'Just over the road.'

For a split second, she looked anxious then smiled. 'Great. Saves walking in this cold wind.'

It pleased him she did not question his ability to drive. 'Shouldn't think there's any police around here,' he said to assure her. 'They'll be busy looking for trouble in Margate. An old friend of mine got attacked there today. They beat the crap out of him, poor devil.'

'Oh, I heard about it on the radio.' She tutted. 'Mindless idiots.'

They drove in silence. He was right. The streets were deserted, and in less than five minutes he pulled up outside her house. There was not enough room to park there: he had to drive a little way further on before he found space.

'It's busy here tonight. Someone's having a party, I guess. Won't disturb us,' she assured him. 'My place is triple-glazed.'

'Bet that makes it cosy.'

'Certainly does.'

He flashed the car shut and they walked the few steps back to her house. A sudden gust ruffled her hair and she pulled her coat close to her body. *Don't worry, sweetheart, I'll soon warm that up for you.*

He followed her along a small, crazy-paved pathway, surrounded on both sides by bushes of some kind. He brushed against one and detected a herb-like smell, probably rosemary. Gran had some in her garden. A security-light blinked on as they reached the porch, allowing Annie to insert the key and unlock the door. A welcome of warm air greeted them. Annie switched on the hall light.

Josh looked around, liking what he saw. Cream walls decorated with scenes of marine water-colours, a soft, grey-tiled floor and shining white doors.

'I'm home,' she called out, which alarmed him, until an enormous Siamese cat padded through a door, from the other end of the hallway. She saw the expression on his face and grinned. 'Samuel Pepys,' she said. 'He knows, when I call, that it's time for him to go out on the prowl.'

'A well-behaved cat, then.' He thought about the dead moggy back at his place. Felt a moment's remorse, but dismissed it, as the giant Siamese brushed disdainfully past him, en route to his nocturnal activities around the quiet streets of Westgate.

Annie led Josh through to a pleasant looking lounge with two two-seater sofas, either side of a low coffee table that was full of interesting looking photos under its glass top.

'Bet that's a conversation piece.'

She smiled and nodded, slid out of her coat and casually draped it over one of two high-backed chairs enclosing a small dining table. The walls were cream-painted, like the hallway, and were decorated with more paintings of the sea. A huge square mirror hung over the marble fireplace, where there were white 'coals' inside a glass front.

'Scotch, cognac, gin or coffee?'

'Scotch sounds good,' he said.

She excused herself for a moment and went through to,

what he guessed was, the kitchen, returning minutes later balancing a tray holding two crystal glasses, half-filled with a pale amber liquid, a crystal water jug, a small bowl of ice, and a glass dish loaded with cashew nuts.

'Wasn't sure if you liked yours watered down, ice-cold, or as it comes.'

'Definitely as it comes.'

She sat next to him, and a faint waft of her perfume teased his nostrils. He took a sip and appreciated a very pleasant, single malt.

'Mmm, nice one.' He licked his lips, enjoying the taste and the intimacy. She picked up a remote control and flicked on some music. Flute music that reminded him of the calling of whales. Soothing. He felt his eyes droop and shook himself awake.

'You can always stay the night.'

Oh yes please, especially in your bed, darling.

A need seemed to grow between them, an urgent need. Glasses were put down onto the table and they embraced hungrily. They began to tear at each other's clothing. 'Let's go upstairs,' she whispered, her voice husky and soft as deep-brown velvet. He didn't need asking twice.

30

And now she was dead. Very dead: completely lifeless. Her face covered in blood, the flesh torn and battered, and horrifyingly disfigured, as if someone had laid into it with a lump-hammer.

Josh slid sideways out of the bed, naked except for some of her blood clinging to his chest and on his hands. *How? When?* He could feel panic and acid-bile rising from his stomach. Swallowed it back, but it rose again. He retched and vomited onto the bedroom floor, her expensively-carpeted bedroom floor. He fell to his knees, tears filling his eyes and sick coming out of his mouth and his nostrils. She, of course, didn't move, but Josh thought he saw movement on the peripheral of his vision. Nothing identifiable: a translucent, momentary flash. He'd seen it before, in his room after Sue died: on the river bank, after the old man pegged it. Even at Foxy's, on his doorstep as he made to leave. Just a quick, flickering movement. Gran would have told him it was a fairy or a sprite, something untouchable, something just out of your reach.

Now it was gone and he was left with Annie's body. He finished being sick, got up from his knees, wiped his mouth on the duvet cover, and turned his head away quickly. He didn't want to look at her. *Now what was he to do?*

Annie's lifeless eyes stared at the ceiling, ignoring his dilemma. She was as beyond helping him as he was her. Josh scratched his head and panted heavily. Through a mirror on the opposite wall, he saw a smear of blood on his face. His reflection stared back, dishevelled, bloody, and scared. It was a time for praying, if you had a god. Josh didn't. But he still prayed... or wished. A plea for time to go backwards, at least to before midnight, or whatever time it had been, when they sat down to drink the scotch. He was aware of the quiet ticking of a clock that gently invaded the silence around the lamp-lit room. It showed five o'clock.

Annie's spread-eagled body was not conscious of time. Nor would it ever be again. He touched her. She was still warm but only just. Not cosy, duvet warm: more cooling, as if the vitality had gone from her. Which, of course, it had.

He stumbled through to the bathroom. Turned on the shower he had used, at her invite, only five hours ago. Remembered how, standing naked, she had wrapped his dripping body in a huge black towel. Next to his, her glorious nakedness: a body that looked as if it took exercise on a daily basis. Healthy, glowing skin, no hint of fat or aging.

Now he washed away her blood from his body, turned the temperature up high,until it stung him like fire. When he could not bear the heat any more, he stepped out, used the same black towel as before, barely noticing it was still damp.

Returning to the bedroom, he was sickened by the sight that accused him. Why, why, why? Josh sat on the edge of the bed, careful not to touch her bloodied and lifeless limbs. He turned away. As if that would make the horror disappear. Only it wouldn't, it didn't. Again, he looked at her damaged body. Lifeless, the life ripped from her, along with clumps of skin and hair, even a torn ear. And fist-shaped bruises and scratches covering her naked torso. What had he done? What hadn't he done? Could he have inflicted any more pain on her? He doubted it. This was worse than looking at a bullet-riddled body in Helmand. Worse, no, not worse, but as bad as seeing the remains of someone blown up by an IED. Like Andy...

Josh shook his head, his face showing pain and disbelief. *Josh, Josh, what have you done mate?* It was like Andy speaking to him, that slightly rough voice with its East London accent. He imagined Andy's soft brown eyes looking at him, with sadness and accusation. He almost said, 'Sorry Andy' as he stumbled from the room. Or was it 'Sorry Annie?' Yes, that's what he said.

'I'm so sorry Annie... I wish...' What did he wish? What could he wish? For the clock to turn back? *That's not going to happen, Josh. You gotta get out of here, and quickly.* His mind switched to military mode. *Get dressed. Cover her up. No don't. Leave her be. Don't touch anything you don't need to.* He left the bedside lamp on, and took a final look around the room. He went outside to the hall landing, left the door ajar, not wanting to leave fingerprints. Light was coming in from the streetlight, enough for him to make his way downstairs. Quietly, he went down each step, not touching the handrail. There was no creaking. The place was almost a newbuild. He went through to the lounge, surprised to find no glasses or tray. Had she taken them through to the kitchen? Washed them up before they went upstairs? He couldn't remember, only remembered the sex. Amazing, urgent, satisfying their mutual need. Then nothing. Not until half an hour ago, when he awoke to the loathsome thing lying next to him. Blood, violence, and Annie's staring eyes.

He sighed a deep sigh. For the first time in years he wanted to cry. Nestle into Gran's arms like he used to, when something was wrong. Feel her warmth and protection as she cuddled his little-boy body. *Not any more, Josh, you're not eight any more. Twenty-nine now, and in deep trouble... Get out of here, now. Go.*

With caution, he opened the front door. A large cream and brown shape brushed past his leg, almost giving him a heart attack. Siamese moggy. He resisted the urge to kick it. Hadn't done him any harm, and Annie wouldn't like him to do that. But Annie would not like or dislike anything ever again. Poor Annie.

It was still dark outside, save for the street lighting, with a howling wind and bone-chilling, pre-dawn temperature. There were very few cars parked on the road now. Party must be over, he guessed. He looked all around him, but the street was devoid of people. Josh prayed it would stay that way. Seconds later, he unlocked the car, climbed in and started the engine, moving slowly forward, before belting himself in, and switching on the headlights.

The streets were deserted as he drove home: dark and deserted, apart from the odd ghostly flight of a seagull. He thought he saw an urban fox, slinking behind a wheelie bin, as he passed a flickering street lamp.

He drove by the café bar. Closed and shuttered, the shutters covered in humorous graffiti. No early morning commuters hurrying to the station. He glanced at the dashboard clock, not yet five-thirty. The first train to London, he remembered, came later, at six-fifteen.

It took him five minutes to get home, and another two to garage the car and get inside the house. During those seven minutes, he had seen nobody: no cars, the odd seagull, and a Siamese moggy, back from its night prowl. He had a moment of gratitude: his parents had driven themselves to Gatwick and parked their car there, so's he could keep Granddad's car out of sight.

What next? He wandered through to the kitchen, filled the kettle and switched it on. He craved strong, hot coffee. Lots of. There were no clean mugs left, so he fished one out from the cluttered sink, rinsed it under the tap, and scoured the stains away from its rim. His mouth tasted rancid. Unbrushed teeth. They hadn't been cleaned since yesterday morning. He'd have the coffee first, think about the last twenty-four hours. What had happened, where he'd been, what he had done. He dismissed the morning and afternoon with Baby Jane and Gran: they didn't count. He tried to remember how the evening had gone. First Suzie and Sue

Ellen in the deli. Then home, listening to the news about Parri Arnold; racing to the hospital, causing a late meeting with Sue Ellen. He wished now it had been her who had died, not the lovely Annie. Thinking of the café bar, the gay barman and basement-smelling dealer, Alfie, he began to panic: wondered who else had seen him with Annie. Probably lots, if they were questioned.

Who had seen his car parked in Annie's road? Or seen him driving away at something past five? Was anyone awake in his road when he garaged the car? He didn't think so. He spooned brown sugar into the cup and two teaspoons of Mum's coffee, grimacing, knowing it wouldn't be as good as Gran's. *Wonder how she is, Gran? Still got the amnesia? Bloody hope so.*

Josh could feel the room closing in on him. Too many events, too many deaths: way too many. He badly wished he was back at barracks. Maybe up in Catterick, or Germany, or Cyprus. Cyprus would be good. Warmer than the other two, certainly. Warmer than here in Westgate, weather-wise anyway. He found a bread roll that he'd bought at the Italian deli, in the fridge with the milk. Good. He'd toast it. The thought of food made his stomach curdle, especially when he pictured what he'd just left behind. Including his vomit on Annie's carpet. Idiot!

It had been a long time since he'd eaten. Those cashews, when he and Annie sat on her sofa, drinking single-malt whiskey from her expensive crystal glasses. He swallowed the lump in his throat with scalding coffee and blinked back tears. 'So sorry, Annie,' he said again.

The hot roll tasted good, generously spread with butter, not Mum's crappy veggie stuff... and thick peel marmalade, the one pleasure he shared with Dad. Mum preferred lime marmalade; too sweet for Josh's taste, and bitter as well.

He crunched the toast, swilled the coffee and wondered what to do next. Switching on the small kitchen TV, he tuned in to the news. The government had narrowly won the vote in some argument/debate. Bully for them. Drone on... Then the newscaster's voice assumed a dramatic tone. 'The body of seventy-eight-year-old John Hollander, discovered in his Highbury flat three days ago, suffered a broken neck, possibly from a violent fall. Neighbours alerted the police after Mr Hollander had not been seen or heard of for several days. The police say his death is unexplained, and are continuing with their investigation.

Josh looked up in shock. Was there anything to tie him being there? The cup he drank from? The bread and milk he'd purchased for the old man? Chrissakes... now what? Who saw him? Plenty. The no-hoper, the St Lucia woman, the black guy with his mobile and his Porsche, and Mike whatshisname, Beresford? What about old Harry and his barmaid, Maisie, Mary? One or the other. Didn't matter, they'd all seen him. Who hadn't seen him? Only Mike knew he'd been to Foxy's. And Gran. Gran, he could handle. Mike was ex-military, and ex MI5. Mike knew what PTSD could do to you. Mike wouldn't shop him, would he?

The TV announcer said his goodbye and handed over, 'to a newscaster where you are'. The ex-nationally-famous face wished his audience good morning and prepared to impart Thanet's local news. Manston Airport was expanding, creating at least 150 new jobs. More shops were closing in Margate's High Street, despite extensive redevelopment taking place. The newscaster paused. 'Police have discovered partial remains of a body from the reeds in the River Wantsum, close to where it flows into the sea. They believe the victim is a young woman. Investigations are continuing, and enquiries are being made for possible missing persons in the local area.

Josh flicked off the television. For him, the news was not good, anything but. Panic, like bile, was coming up from his stomach. What was he to do? It could only be a matter of time before they knocked on his door. Had he given them this address? Or had he fobbed them off with Gran's address? Told them he was staying with her for the rest of his leave?

He breathed in and out slowly, through his teeth. *Stay cool Josh. Think, man, think.* He stood up, paced the room, and finished his coffee. He felt restless, caged in, needed to be outside. It was barely daylight now but dull. Heavy clouds had replaced the clear blue sky of yesterday. Maybe rain was on the way. Little did he care. He needed to get away, that was for sure. But where? Where could he go now? Not London. What about up north? Where Gran came from? Would there be any relatives up there he knew? She'd mentioned a brother, but he'd be her age. Ancient. Any cousins or second cousins? None that he knew. How about... what? Train up to London, catch a National Express coach from Victoria to practically anywhere in the UK. Even Europe. Maybe he could get an open ticket, whatever they call them, and just keep travelling around England, Scotland, and Wales. Stay a few days here and there, nowhere long enough to be noticed. At least it would give him time to think things through.

His mobile vibrated on the table and made him jump, jarred his already damaged nerves. He didn't recognise the number, but knew the voice.

'Josh? It's Mike. How are you, mate?'

'Er, yeah... good. Well, ok.'

'Have you seen the news?'

'What news?'

'The old man you visited, Foxy, real name John Hollander. He's been found dead.'

'Dead? How?'

'Broken neck, apparently. In his hallway. You didn't, did you?'

'What? Push him? You gotta be joking.'

'That's what I thought.' Then, 'Do you need any help?'

Josh sighed, breathed in and out again. *Do I need any help? Too bloody right I do.*

'Mike,' he hesitated. 'I need to get away for a few days. I didn't kill him,' he continued. 'Foxy. He was well alive when I left him.'

He could almost hear Mike thinking down the phone.

'Josh... I've got a cottage. In Wales, near the Black Hills and Brecon Beacons. D'you fancy stopping there for a while?'

Josh didn't know what to say. 'Erm, yeah... that would be good. Great in fact. Probably what I need at the moment.' He sighed again. 'I feel like I'm shot to pieces. Don't know what I'm doing.'

'Ok mate, it's yours. I'm off to the States for a series of talks. I'll be gone for a week, then I'm heading up there to Hay. That long enough for you?'

'Brilliant,' said Josh. 'You sure?'

Mike laughed. 'Yes, I'm sure. As it happens, you'll be doing me a favour, keeping the place warm, stopping the pipes freezing up.'

'How do I get in, get the keys?'

Mike explained. 'My next-door neighbours have a spare set. Penny and Glen Hopkins. Lovely couple. He's an ex-jazz musician, used to play the trumpet. They breed Irish wolfhounds. They won't intrude, but if you want anything, you only have to ask them. And they'll clue you up as to where the shops are.'

He went on to give Josh the address, warned him he'd need a car. 'Public transport's a no-no there. There's OS maps on the bookshelf in the front room, if you fancy walking the Black Hills and the Beacons. Bloody cold there this time of year though, so take your thermals,' he laughed. 'Plenty of jackets and the like in the downstairs hall closet. Boots too, if you need them.'

THE KILLING OF ELLIE SWALES

Josh didn't know what to say. Just kept mumbling words of thanks. He repeated the address back to Mike, made sure he had the right house number and postcode.

An hour later he was on his way, first dropping off some milk and bread to his grandmother. She said not to bother with anything else, she'd get the carer or Nadia, the library lady, to pick up anything else she needed.

'Where're you going, Josh?' she asked, when he arrived at her bungalow.

'Erm, up to London, to see a mate of mine. Ok if I take Granddad's car?'

'Yes pet, that'll be fine. Drive carefully, won't you?'

'Course I will, Gran.' He kissed her cheek, gave her a brief, tight smile, and was gone.

Ellie watched him drive off. She wondered where he was really going. She too, had heard the news about the old man. Unlikely, she thought, that Josh would be heading for London. Probably as well she didn't know too much, in case the police visited her.

31

It would be a long journey, 235 miles or thereabouts. 235 miles away from all this aggro. He'd printed off the journey from Google, not having GPS, and thought the time estimate was a bit too hopeful, four and a half hours, door to door. The journey from Gran's to the M25 was not too bad, then he idled for an hour or more on London's biggest car park, as the M25 was often called. He inched forward, nose to tail, until the turn off to the M40, when he could regain lost time en route to Wales and the West.

Turning off onto the local roads is when he would regret not having a satnav. Maybe he could drive into Hereford: that wasn't far from Hay, and buy one. His mind wandered. How was Gran? He still had her £400 in his jacket pocket. He'd post it tomorrow, once he'd settled in. Special delivery, maybe try to get away with no return address. Or he could print 'sorry' on the back of the package... maybe not.

The traffic began to build up again and the weather worsened. Icy rain hit the windscreen, causing Josh to slow down to 60mph. He stayed in the centre lane and switched the wipers to fast. Christ! He could hardly see beyond the car bonnet, just about picked out the tail lights of a car in front. Then, as fast as the hailstorm had struck, it fizzled out. He relaxed back into his seat. Ten minutes later it began to snow, light flurries first of all, like springtime blossom, then it increased its intensity. That's all he needed, a snow blizzard this early in the year *and* driving in unknown territory. A few miles on, he saw a sign for services. Coffee would be good: maybe a bacon sarnie as well. He glanced at the dashboard clock. One-fifteen. Ok, maybe fish and chips, or a burger with all the trimmings.

He pulled in to the service station, pulled up as near as possible to the entrance and legged it out of the snowfall. As soon as he hit the sliding doors he smelled stale chip oil. Not to worry, he could smother the lot in ketchup, even if they served it in those stupid little sachets. He was pleasantly surprised to discover the place doubled as a post office. Fine: he purchased a padded envelope, addressed it to Mrs Ellie Swales and marked the back with one word... sorry. Away from the counter and the postmistress's prying eyes, he filled it with Gran's £400. That done, he returned to the counter and asked for it to be expressed: he was relieved to learn it would arrive the next day. Job done. Now to eat...

The final part of the journey, through Herefordshire, was a series of bends, right and left turns among muddied lanes, with fields and hills providing a picturesque backdrop. There were farmhouses dotted about, some close to the road, with yawning barns and large-wheeled tractors, others along small, single-track lanes, barely visible among groves of pines. Every now and then, Josh glimpsed the Black Mountains rising above their foothills, grey and forbidding in places: a scattering of snow in others, gleaming through the deepening-afternoon mist. At least the snow had stopped.

He pulled into a lay-by to study the directions. Only a couple of miles to go. He passed a dragon sign saying Croesso y Cymru, translated beneath with Welcome to Wales. Another left turn, drive on, left again, and immediately right. Christ, he thought, the houses are pretty close to the roads here. Does no-one have a front garden? Left again at the junction, then first right. He remembered Mike's final instructions. 'Park your car where you turn into the Dingle, walk up first-left then immediately right. The cottage is on the left, about halfway up the slope.'

Thanks Mike. You didn't tell me the slope was steep as Porlock Hill. Despite his military fitness, carrying his loaded backpack meant he was out of breath when he reached the front door. He turned around to look at the view. There they were, the Black Mountains. Mike said one was called Hay Bluff, and one the Twmpa or Lord Hereford's Knob. He scanned slightly to the right and identified the Brecon Beacons. He let out his breath and relaxed, relaxed and felt safe.

'You must be Josh.'

He jumped, turned swiftly around to see an owlish face, framed with wispy, greying hair and possessing a twinkling smile.

'Hi. You must be Penny, Penny Hopkins? He extended his hand and shook hers: heard a noise of deep barking.

'Your wolfhounds?'

'Yes. Only two at the moment, Maeve and her son, Billy. We've sold the rest of her litter.'

The door next to Mike's opened and a tall, grey-haired man emerged. 'And I'm Glendower, my friends call me Glen.' He held out a hand that could cover a rugby ball, and grasped Josh's in a firm handshake. Two huge dogs nosed their way through the door and nudged him, nearly knocking him over.

'Hiya fellas,' he said, patted them and ran his fingers through their thick rough hair. 'Friendly, aren't they,' he remarked to their owners.

'Like kittens,' said the man, who called himself Glen.

'My babies,' grinned Penny. 'Would you like a cuppa? The kettle's on.'

Josh hesitated, suddenly conscious he had already been sociable towards these two strangers. Maybe he could relax for a short time, let down his defences, this far away from Kent.

'Sounds good. Why not? Shall I just bung my backpack in Mike's place first?'

'Good thinking,' said Glen. 'Got the keys there, Missus?'

She fished them from her cardigan pocket. 'You make the tea and I'll take Josh in next door, show him where the switches are.' She looked up, sniffed the air, reminding Josh of one of her dogs. 'Rain I should think, or more snow, any minute now. We'd best go in.'

The blue-painted front door opened straight into a small, comfortable sitting room, furnished with brown leather sofas and a single, matching armchair. Penny switched on an overhead light and Josh saw, each side of the fireplace, low bookshelves. One had a small TV on it as well as some books. The paintings on the other walls were modern and colourful landscapes. He wondered if they were local scenes.

'Nice and warm in here,' he said.

'Yes, I put the central heating on earlier. Didn't think you'd be wanting to walk into a cold house.' He smiled his gratitude.

She led him through a small hall, switching on lights as she went. 'Bathroom's on the left here, and stairs to the right for the bedrooms. Straight ahead here, is the kitchen.'

Josh's eyes widened. 'Wow, some kitchen.' It was long and decently wide, with built-in, custom-made cupboards either side, a stove, sink and tall fridge-freezer. Beyond it, through French doors, was an equal length of covered decking area, and further down a small, lawned garden with a dry-stone wall marking the boundary. He could just about make out fields beyond, with grazing sheep and a farmhouse on the other side, its downstairs lights all on, piercing the gloom of this wintry day. A sprinkle of frozen snow speckled much of the grassy areas.

'I didn't expect all this,' he said, and dropped his backpack onto the polished wooden floor of the kitchen. 'Mike led me to believe this was just a small place. This is amazing.'

Penny grinned. 'Yes, he's made a good job of it...By the way there's a cottage pie in the fridge, just needs heating up in the micro. I've put you some milk, butter and eggs in there as well. Bread's over there by the stove.'

Weirdly, Josh felt like crying. These people were as kind as Gran, yet complete strangers to him. He felt envious of Mike having these two as neighbours.

'Thanks, Penny. How much do I owe you?'

'Nothing. Don't be silly.' She laughed. 'You can buy us a bottle of plonk once you know where the shops are. Come on, let's go have that tea before Glen starts growling just like the dogs.'

Their adjoining cottage mirrored Mike's, and was furnished with comfortable sofas, with plaid rugs thrown over them. A cheerful fire burned in the grate and, on the shelves either side, Josh could see trophies, rosettes and framed certificates, interspersed with framed sketches and photos of Irish wolfhounds.

The two dogs, after greeting him with nudges and licks, flopped on a rug in front of the fire.

'Take a pew.' Glen carried a tray from the kitchen, complete with three steaming mugs, sugar, and a plate of sliced cake. 'You gotta try Pen's barabrith,' he added. 'It's to die for.'

Josh gratefully took both tea and cake. 'Mm, not bad. In fact, it's lovely.'

The conversation was general, neutral. They asked him how was his journey, told him a bit about breeding the wolfhounds and the ready market for them.

'I won't let them go just anywhere,' said Penny. 'I vet perspective owners before they're allowed one of our pups. Don't I, Maeve?' The bitch looked up, wagged her tail at the mention of her name, then lay her head down again next to the last of her offspring. Penny also told him she'd drawn a rough map of the small town, showing him where the shops were and a few of the hostelries. Glen told him the easiest route to Hay Bluff and which road to take for the Beacons. He also told Josh something about his life as a Jazz musician.

'Why did you stop?'

'Deafness and dodgy lungs.'

'That was tough. D'you miss it? The gigs?'

'I did for a while, but not now we do the dog breeding and showing. Plus, I have my lovely wife here to keep me from boredom.'

Josh grinned. 'Lucky man, then.'

The conversation dwindled. Josh yawned and stood up. 'Thanks for the tea and cake. Best get next door and unpack. Don't think I'll be up late tonight.' He shook hands with them both and kissed Penny on the cheek. He surprised himself by offering to take the dogs with him on one of his treks. 'Maybe in a couple of days' time?'

Glen said, 'If you want company I might join you.'

Josh nodded. 'Why not? Anyway... see you later.' He patted the dogs and took his leave.

Back in Mike's cottage kitchen, he opened drawers and cupboards, familiarising himself with their contents. He found a wine rack filled with bottles of red and, next to it, a case of beer. *Thanks Mike.* He searched out a corkscrew and bottle opener, deciding to put a few beers in the fridge, and was pleasantly surprised to find some in there already. Plus, Penny's cottage pie. He took it out ready to warm it in the microwave. Thought it might be good with some of Mike's red wine, promising himself he'd replace anything he drank once he got himself to the shops. He uncapped a beer and wandered through to the front room, switched on the TV and was astonished to hear nothing but a strange language. Then he realised the news lady was speaking in Welsh. Of course, 'here' was just short of the border. He hoped all the programs weren't in Welsh, and was relieved when local Hereford news was read, followed by an announcement of the evening's programs, all spoken in English. Just as well: he doubted he could learn much Welsh, inside a week.

An hour later, after enjoying Penny's cottage pie and half a bottle of Mike's red, an Italian Chianti, he went through to the lounge and fingered a few of Mike's books. He was surprised to find that Mike was author to three of them: two biographies and one novel. He took the novel down from the shelf, settled down in the armchair and began to read. After a few pages, and a final swig of red wine, he fell asleep, legs stretched out. It was nearer two than one a.m. before he dragged himself upstairs, to crawl into a king-sized bed and under a snug duvet. Josh slept peacefully, dreamless and no nightmares, until eight the next morning.

He awoke to a weird light seeping in through the cream linen curtains. Getting out of bed, he padded over to the window to investigate. A sheet of white greeted him with an ice-clad roof of the farmhouse beyond and whitened pines on the hill behind the farm. Penny had told him the hill was called Bryn Cethyn. Bryn meant hill, she'd explained, and Mynydd was Welsh for mountain, she'd added.

He searched upstairs for the bathroom and panicked some, until he remembered it was downstairs. He edged his way down the spiralled staircase and into the bathroom opposite. He peed forever, smelling beer and wine in the urine. He looked around him. *Nice bathroom, Mike.* Soft, concealed lights made it look larger than it was. The mirror, over the washbasin, was made up of squares, giving a slightly distorted view of his face and the bath/shower behind him.

Padding through to the kitchen he searched out coffee and a cafetiere and switched on the kettle. Its blue 'on' light pierced the gloom of the room. The overhead skylight looked heavy with a thick frost, as did the back garden beyond the covered decking area. Outside it was distinctly, a very grey day. Josh stared... The kettle was bubbling, as it came to the boil, and shook him out of his preoccupation. He spooned a generous amount of coffee into the cafetiere, added boiling water and savoured the aroma. He walked over to the back-wall worktop, opened the cupboard above it for a mug, and noticed a small radio on the work surface. He switched it on and tuned it in to a news program. The central heating kicked in at the same time, its soft humming a comforting background sound to the newscaster's voice. He only half-listened to the news; mostly about Wales and the Welsh parliament, the rising crime rate in South Wales towns, and an increase in crimes of violence from last year, followed by the weather forecast. Well, he could see what that would be. Only had to peer out of the French doors. Rain, and more rain to come, by the looks of that thick, ominous sky: maybe even some snow.

'Now the news from across the UK,' said the voice. Icy hail is causing chaos over much of the country, the road across the Pennines is closed; and some trains are cancelled. Yadi-yadi-ya. Same old, same old.

'The badly beaten body of a forty-year old woman has been discovered in her house in Westgate, North Kent, about two miles from Margate. Annie Carstairs sold antique jewellery from an antiques emporium in nearby Cliftonville and was thought to have valuable stock in her home. However, a police search of the premises indicates that nothing was taken or rooms disturbed, apart from the room where her body was discovered. Burglary has been ruled out as the possible motive. Police believe she was murdered two days ago and have questioned neighbours, who appear not to have heard or seen anything suspicious. A police spokesman said it was a particularly brutal attack and, from the evidence gathered, an arrest is imminent. They want to question anyone who frequented Westgate Café Bar on Wednesday evening, as they believe Ms Carstairs was in there that night.

Josh stood still, paralysed with shock and fear. The hair at the base of his neck bristled. Annie had been found... he desperately hoped Mike's next-door neighbours weren't listening to the news: drew some relief when he heard the two dogs barking and saw Penny and Glen through the front-room window. They were warmly wrapped in heavy jackets, scarves, woollen hats and gloves. Each of them held an excited wolfhound as they slipped down the slope to the main road, on their way out to walk them. Josh breathed easy. Maybe they hadn't heard the news. And even if they had, he reasoned, they wouldn't necessarily connect him with the murder. Why would they? They didn't know where he lived. He hadn't mentioned Westgate, had he?

Maybe they assumed he lived in London, with or near Mike. *Bloody hope so. Don't panic Josh. Drink your coffee. Go back to bed for a while, nothing to get up for. Shops won't open till nine, Penny says. That's if you can ski on the ice. Course you can, they've just gone out, haven't they?*

He walked back through to the kitchen, topped up his mug from the cafetiere, and sat at the table, hands clasped around the warm mug. Time to think. What to do now?

32

Back in Acacia Avenue, Ellie Swales was also listening to the news. Unlike where her grandson was, there was no ice outside. The freezing weather that was gripping most of the country seemed to have left Thanet alone. All she could see through her opened curtains was a smooth, blue sky that was gradually lightening, as the sun made its way up from the horizon.

She cuddled a mug of tea and listened as the carer prepared her breakfast porridge.

'You stay tucked up, Mrs S,' the woman had said. 'I'll bring you breakfast in bed and get you up and dressed after.'

She prattled on about it being brass-monkey weather out there: how she'd nearly come off her bike, skidding on a patch of ice. Ellie only half-listened to Tracy as she tried to catch the news. She found it irritating, scarcely hearing what the woman was saying out there in the kitchen, banging about with the pots and pans. Ellie caught the piece about an antique dealer being brutally murdered, but not where. Tracy came through with her porridge that was steaming and smelling of the honey she had drizzled on top.

'Did you hear the news, Mrs S?

'It's on now.'

They both fell silent as the newscaster read out more details of where the victim lived.

'Blimey Mrs S, that's only about a mile from here. Second murder, if you count those bones they found in the Wantsum this week.'

Ellie nodded, lost for words. All she could think of was

223

Josh. Was he involved? Why had he suddenly taken off yesterday morning? Where was he now? Questions, questions, going slowly round her mind, tormenting her. The porridge congealed, untouched in its rosebud-patterned dish, until Ellie remembered it, and began to spoon it into her mouth.

'I'll give the front room and the kitchen a quick tidy, then I'll come back and get you up and dressed,' said Tracy.

Ellie listened to her mumbling to herself about murder, mayhem and the Lord knows what's happening in the world. She smiled, despite the seriousness of the situation. Tracy, in many respects, was quite old-fashioned. Maybe she had been a product of older parents?

Her thoughts returned to Josh. She hoped he was safe, her only grandchild. Yes, she felt more secure with him out of the immediate vicinity. Didn't think for one moment he was in London, but had no idea where else he might go. Poor Josh, he had so few friends really. Is that what a life in the army did for you? Kept you from making friends? She had no fear of him anymore, despite knowing he had been the one to ransack her place, the one who caused her to have a nasty fall. The bruises still showed but she had no pain from them anymore. Plenty of day to day pain, though. That wouldn't go away until she did. Far away. Up there with Ben...

'Time to get you dressed, Mrs S. Finished your porridge?'

'Yes dear.'

'Right then. What colours would you like to wear today?' Tracy enjoyed choosing outfits for Ellie, liked matching the clothes with her bling. 'How about that nice blue sweater and your dark-blue trousers? They go lovely with that multi-coloured scarf your friends gave you.'

Ellie tried to think what scarf, and who had given it to her. Oh yes, Robert, and Nadia, the library lady. Lovely, exotic Nadia and her handsome husband. The scarf was as exotic as those two and yes, it did go prettily with her blue sweater. She could wear matching bling, a set of blue-glass beads with matching bracelet. Nadia had called them Lapis lazuli, but Ellie wasn't so sure.

Less than an hour later, Tracy was gone and Ellie was left to the quiet of the front room. She could see a clear blue sky, with wheeling gulls, and swaying trees lining the avenue. The Royal Mail van drew up outside her property. Her favourite postman climbed out and waved to her, holding a padded envelope and indicating it was for her. She mouthed through the window, 'Door's open,' and waited for him to come in.

She could smell the cold on him and gave a little shiver within her lovely warm room.

'Hello, hello George. What have you got for me today?'

'Special delivery, Mrs Swales. I need your signature.' He tapped something into a handheld machine and handed it to her. 'Can you sign in that box, please?'

She laughed. 'Well I'll try. My writing's not up to much anymore. You'll just have to take my word for it that it's my signature.' She struggled to make the wiggles and lines that should resemble Ellie Swales. 'Not great, but it'll have to do, young George.'

He laughed, 'I like the young.' He handed her the padded package.

'Oh, I don't think I can manage to undo that with my arthritic fingers. Could you oblige me?'

'Course I can. Here, give it over, we'll soon get that opened. There's a word on the back of the envelope, says sorry.'

'Sorry?'

'That's what it says.'

'Where's it from?'

'Hereford sorting office, far as I can make out.'

They both made shocked noises as the postman undid the

225

package and a thick bundle of notes fell out. *So that's where you are Josh.*

'Bloomin' heck,' said George. 'You got generous friends, Mrs. Swale.'

'Mm. Yes... well... erm.' For once, Ellie was lost for words. At least, she didn't quite know what to say to the postman. She knew where and who the money had come from, but it wasn't something she wanted to discuss with this man.

33

The snowfall was a mischievous trick of a premature winter. A one-day wonder, giving rise to mockery in the newspaper headlines. 'TWENTY-FOUR HOUR SNOW AND BRITAIN FREEZES TO A HALT'

Josh stayed hidden in the cottage, hoping Penny and Glen would not play the good-neighbours card and come knocking. A search through the food cupboards and fridge told him there was enough basics to survive on: tins of beans and tomatoes, one of salmon, one sardines, some linguini pasta and a compact, microwaveable container of rice. He had milk, bread, butter and eggs, plenty for several days if necessary, and a rack full of wine, plus the beer.

Later, he heard them return from their walk. A glimpse through the front-bedroom shutters showed him two muddied dogs, their shaggy, grey hair hanging with baubles of the stuff. The couple had glowing faces and puffed out their misty breath from the exertion of conquering the slope.

Josh stepped back, even though he was sure they couldn't see him through the partly-closed, wooden slats. He had no inclination to socialise today. The radio announcement he'd heard disturbed him greatly. He imagined every other word the newscaster uttered was a hint, a suggestion, that it was him they were looking for. *Bet the Thanet news station is making more of it than the national. How much do the police really know? Who have they interviewed among the antiques set? What about the old-queen barman? What about Gran? They been round to hers? Asked her where I might be?*

The questions, running rings round his mind, were giving him a headache. *Get a lot of those lately, don't you Josh? Reckon you might have a brain tumour?* He grabbed an armful of clothes, searched in Mike's wardrobe for a warm sweater, found several, plus some thick plaid shirts. He chose one of each and went downstairs to shower. Looking towards the front door, he could see a note had been pushed through the letter box. Must be from them next door, he guessed. Curiosity beat the need for a shower. He unfolded the piece of paper and read, 'Cheese, bacon and more bread on doorstep. Enjoy. Icy roads treacherous, best stay in. P&G xx'

He swiftly opened the front door, grabbed a Co-Op plastic bag from the frost-covered step, and just as quickly closed it again and moved in to the warmth of the house. The few seconds exposure prompted him into the shower, first leaving the shopping and his clothes on the kitchen table.

Ten minutes later, refreshed and dressed, he began to make himself a breakfast: fried eggs and bacon, with two fried slices. He added half a tin of beans and the same of tomatoes, slid everything onto a large dinner plate and ate hungrily, mopping the egg remains with another slice of bread. He washed it all down with a mug of steaming tea and felt better than he had thirty-six hours earlier.

An hour later, he surveyed a pristine cottage. Bed made, bathroom cleaned, washing up done and all the kitchen surfaces wiped down. He'd even folded his unpacked clothes on a chair near the bedroom window.

The television reception was a joke. He gave up. On one of the shelves above the TV, apart from Mike's books, there was an assortment of DVD's, including several box sets of *Spooks*. Fine, he could watch one of them. Easy enough to ignore the TV, though he really needed to keep up to date with the news. He remembered Mike had said there was an office upstairs in the attic, complete with broadband internet on the computer. Maybe he could keep up with the news on that.

He took a last look around the ground floor: everything tidy. He climbed the spiral stairs to the first floor. The front bedroom looked out over the Black Hills, now partially covered in a thin layer of snow, and the distant Brecon Beacons. A further staircase took him up to the office. A complete surprise. It ran the entire width of the cottage and was half as deep. The angled sky window overlooked the farm and Bryn Cethyn, and the adjoining cottage gardens at the back of the house, where there was an assortment of sheds and greenhouses, gleaming with melting frost, and sitting areas or vegetable plots.

A large, glass-topped desk at the far end took up the width of the room. It was furnished with a PC and printer and several trays of paperwork. Shelves beneath carried reams of copy paper, envelopes of all sizes, a box of business cards and metal pots with pens and pencils, paper clips and so on.

Josh sat on the office swivel chair and fired up the computer. Ten minutes later he was watching the BBC News channel and flicking through some of his host's in-trays. He remained in the office for much of the day, hardly noticed the earth warming up outside: was only conscious of a change in the weather when he heard the tutter of rain on the sloping, skylight windows.

There had been no more announcement from the Isle of Thanet Police about the murder of Annie. *What did they say her surname was? Carstairs, that's right.* And no more about severed limbs on the Wantsum river. He glanced at his watch, surprised to see it was gone three. He looked out of the window again. The snow was disappearing off the field and he could see sheep out there, grazing once more and oblivious to the rain. Even Bryn Cethyn, beyond, had shed much of the frosted snow from its pines. Perhaps he'd go out tomorrow. No point today, it'd be dark soon, gloomy enough now. Maybe he could take next door's dogs for a run up in the hills. They'd be big for the car, but he'd shove them in, somehow. He quite liked the idea of running with them.

Time now to go downstairs, read one of Mike's books or watch a DVD. Maybe have a cheese sandwich. Be nice to find some dandelions in the back garden, they made a good substitute for salad rocket. It was still raining when he unlocked the French doors and stepped out onto the covered decking. Bamboo blinds hung down each side of the reinforced plastic roof, blowing backwards and forwards in the driving wind, but still affording a modicum of shelter. Joshed noticed metal shelving adjoining the kitchen wall, where Mike kept an assortment of garden tools, solar lighting and other items: the detritus gathered over time, he supposed.

He ventured onto the garden path that divided two small patches of lawn, bound by shoulder-high privet. There was no snow or frost left on the grass and he spotted a couple of dandelion plants. Good, his accompaniment to late lunch, or early dinner. Whatever. There was no sign of Penny or Glen. Probably tucked up on their rug-strewn sofas with a wolfhound each for a 'canine' duvet. Good on 'em.

He quickly dived back undercover. No sense, he thought, in getting too wet and the Welsh rain certainly knew how to come down in saturating torrents. His feet skidded on the decking where it was exposed to the weather, but he regained his balance without falling or dropping his wild salad. Ten minutes later, he was seated at the kitchen table, munching on a thickly-sliced cheese sandwich, spread with crunched up leaves. He liked them like that... it brought out the tangy, peppery taste, and tarted up the humble cheese sarnie.

One of Mike's books was propped up in front of him, about his time as a bomb disposal officer, an ATO, in Iraq.

Josh was instantly transported back to the drama of war. The ear-splitting noise of bombs, the smell of burning flesh, the body-draining heat of day and the freezing-the-balls-off nights.

The room grew dark as he read. Looking out, he saw it was darker still out there, facing almost due north. Josh could see nothing beyond the stone wall that marked the garden boundary. No fields of sheep or pine clad hill. Just a couple of glinting lights from the distant farmhouse. He felt restless, hemmed in despite the generous size of his surroundings. Maybe a walk might be good: around the town that Penny had described as one of the smallest in the UK. He shrugged on one of Mike's warm jackets and walking boots, thankful they wore the same size shoes, and picked up Penny's hand-drawn map and directions of the town.

Turn right out of the cottage, down the slope, left down next part and right when you reach the lane. (Cars parked on rt). Turn left onto Oxford road, then 1st rt. Keep going to T junction, then left to town centre or rt to Co-op (abt 200 yds on left).

He chose the final left for the town centre, saw the town clock and roads that went right and left, either side of it. Maybe he could wander through them all. There were few people about, now that it was dark, and he shared the hushed, deserted streets with little more than the bell-chime sounds of strings of lights that weaved their way across several of the tiny streets. Maybe they were left-overs from a recent autumn book festival, Penny had mentioned? Or early Christmas lights?

Every other shop seemed to be selling books, interspersed with a few food shops, arty clothes and knick-knack shops, and pubs and cafés. He saw a butcher's shop, with nothing in its window except artificial grass for model sheep and cows to graze on. All the real stuff neatly tucked away, in fridges at the back of the shop. Same with the greengrocer's, only the grass in its window displayed a wicker-basket of plastic fruit. Further on, a Spar shop was open, with light spilling from its doorway and a hanging sign outside that said, 'Open 8 till late'.

Only the pubs had indications of life. He could hear laughter, some of it spilling out onto the pavement accompanied by a swaying body. Someone bumped into him outside the Wheat Sheaf. 'Sorry, man.'

Josh muttered, 'That's ok' and walked on past another place called Kilverts. Opposite was a British Legion club. Plenty of noise coming from there. He continued to the top of the road, back onto the Oxford road, and turned right, eventually coming to a huge car park with craft shops on its roadside and the castle opposite. Not a protective stronghold anymore, but a repository for small outlets selling yet more books and one trading in ethnic clothes.

He continued slightly downhill to the next junction where he saw a cinema that sold books, not film seats, *now there's a surprise,* and a pub on the corner. He entered the pub. Someone called out, 'Hiya, Josh.' It was Glen, Mike's next-door neighbour. He stood at the bar with two silent hounds at his feet. Maeve looked up when her master spoke, gave a wag of her tail and settled again. Billy sat up and nodded his head at Josh, almost like a greeting. Josh patted the dog's head and the huge hound settled again by his mother.

'What'll you have, mate?'

'Er,' Josh examined the beer pumps. 'Pint of local brew sounds good. Cheers.'

Glen ordered Josh's pint, and another for himself, from the young man who came over to serve them. An equally-young waitress served plates of steaming food at various tables. Josh took a quick look round the nooks-and-cranny room. A young persons' pub, he thought.

'So, you decided to brave the elements then?'

'Yeah,' he said. 'Thought a walk might be good.' He

thanked Glen when his pint was put down in front of him. 'Not a very large place, is it? The town I mean.'

'No,' laughed Glen. 'Blink and you're through it. Gets a fair few visitors over the year though. Thousands not hundreds come to the Town of Books. Mostly locals, at this time of year though,' he added.

The door opened again as two or three older, middle-aged men came in. They greeted Glen with handshakes, laughing, and slightly musical voices that betrayed their Welsh origins. He introduced them as John the Veg, Dai the Meat and Tommy the Bread, making Josh think of his old teacher, Pargiter Arnold, reciting Dylan Thomas to the class. They had the ruddy faces of country men and the cold but firm handshakes of the present weather.

'Josh is up from London,' he explained. 'Friend of Mike's.'

'Tidy, man!' said John the Veg. 'Top man, your Mike.'

Josh nodded, aware that Mike Beresford must be something of a celebrity around here. Despite his wanting to hide away, Josh enjoyed an hour with Glen's buddies. Liked the warmth of their temporary friendship, embracing him. One of them, Tom the Bread, looked at his watch. 'Bleddy 'ell, 'alf past seven. I'll be late for tea. Megan'll do 'er nut.'

They all took a step back from the bar, downed their pints and made to leave.

'Yep,' said Dai the Meat. 'Time for tea.' And the three of them made their goodbyes and left.

'One for the road?' Glen asked Josh.

Yeah, why not? I'll get them in, must be my shout.' Then offered, 'Want a chaser with it?'

'Good idea. Scotch for me, please. Won't be a minute. Need the boys' room. Old man's complaint,' he grinned. 'Can't hold my bladder like I used to.'

He told the dogs to stay and was back by the time Josh had got the drinks in.

'So, young Josh, what do you do for a living? Or did you

tell us last night? Can't remember if you did,' he grinned. 'Another old man's complaint, short-term memory loss.'

'Must be catching then. I often can't remember things either. Anyway... I'm in the army, just back from Afghanistan... a few weeks leave.'

'Not a very nice place that. Went there once myself. Odd kind of place to do a gig, but we did it. Wouldn't go back there though, 'specially now.' He changed the subject. 'What's London like these days?'

Josh was about to say he didn't really know when he remembered Glen assumed he was living near Mike, his 'cousin'.

'Same as usual: busy, noisy, crowded.'

'Mmm,' the older man paused, took a swallow of his beer and knocked back his scotch. Right,' he said. 'One for the road, then I'm off. You coming back now?'

'Erm, no. Think I'll head down to the Co-op. Pick up a few things. I'll take the dogs out tomorrow if you like. Up Hay Bluff.'

'Oh, they'd love that. I may even come with you,' he added. 'If you fancy company.'

'Yeah, why not? But leave the drink, I'd best get these provisions in.'

'Ah... the Co-op'll be closed now. Spar's just round the corner. Go out through that door over there,' he pointed to a second exit. 'Turn right and Spar's a few doors along on the right.'

'Cheers man.' Josh downed the rest of his drink, belched and left, following Glen's directions. Funny little town, he thought. Lots of ins and outs and up and down roads within a few acres of land. He passed a shop selling outdoor clothing, an estate agent, an accountant, then Spar with a book shop the other side of it, and one or two opposite. *Not a town for the illiterate, that's for sure.*

The food shop was narrow but quite long. He bought cold

meat, and two pork chops, some potatoes, a packet of frozen mixed veg, a couple of four packs of lager and, as an afterthought, he added chocolates and a bottle of wine for Penny. He'd give them to her tomorrow.

When he emerged from the Spar, he remembered to turn left, past the pub and he knew he was on the Oxford road with less than a quarter of a mile before reaching Mike's cottage. He balanced the two shopping bags, one in each hand, and suffered another soaking from yet more rain before he panted up the last slope. He felt in his pocket for the keys, panicked for a moment till he found them in the back pocket of his jeans. The cottage welcomed him with warmth and shelter away from the wet stuff. He was hungry now and had an uncomfortably-full bladder. Bathroom first, then maybe a jacket potato with some ham and the rest of the baked beans from this morning. He could pep them up with the chilli shake he'd spotted in Mike's cupboard this morning. He'd cook a proper meal tomorrow night: nodded to himself, and half smiled as he emptied his bladder. A day in the hills would be good. He'd enjoy walking the dogs, was unsure about needing the company of their master though.

34

Ellie was watching the six o'clock news and looking forward to East Enders later. She'd had her dinner cooked and served up by Tracy. Later, she'd suffered the discomfort of being undressed and getting into her nightie and dressing gown, and the greater discomfort of having her eye drops administered. She then endured swallowing two co-codamol with a spoonful of yogurt. It was the only way she could get them down without choking on the horrible things. Now she was cocooned, in a fleece wrap, and sitting by the window with the curtains drawn. She hoped there'd be no more bad news on the local TV station; no more bodies or bits of bodies discovered.

What was that? Someone knocking at the door? At this time of night? Ellie wasn't expecting anybody; the front door was locked and her set of keys were hanging up on their hook by the front door. The other set were in the coded locker outside. She struggled to get hold of her sticks, threw off the fleece and walked painfully and slowly over to the sitting-room door. The outside light revealed two dark shapes standing in the porch way.

'Who is it?' she called, trusting they could hear her through the double-glazed door.

'It's the police, Mrs Swales.'

'What do you want?'

'Just a quick chat. Won't keep you long.'

'Give me a minute,' she said and made her way slowly across the small hallway to the front door. The one who had spoken poked his police identification through the letter box.

'Just so's you know we're who we say we are.'

Ellie examined it carefully, recognising the one who had previously introduced himself as 'Just Dave', the day of her so-called 'burglary'. She lifted the keys off their hook and, holding both sticks in one hand, struggled to fit the key into the keyhole. Door open, she stepped back and said, 'Come in.' She felt the cold air blowing up from the sea, smelt it on their uniforms and faces.

They crowded the small hallway and waited patiently as she made her way, slowly and painfully, back to her chair.

'If you want tea you'll have to make it yourselves. My carer's gone home.'

'Thanks, Mrs. Swales. We're fine, just had a bite to eat in our station canteen.'

Ellie switched off the TV: hoped they would be gone before East Enders came on.

'Heard from your grandson lately?' asked 'Just Dave'.

'He's gone up to London to see some of his mates,' she told them.

'D'you know any of their names or whereabouts in London? It's a big place.'

She thought for a moment. 'I'm sure I heard him mention a place, Saint something or other.'

'St Pauls Road, maybe?'

'I'm sorry pet. I can't remember. That name doesn't ring a bell though. He had this friend called Andy, but Andy died in Afghanistan, can't recall his mentioning any others by name.'

'Andy?'

'Yes, he came from North London somewhere. He was an orphan, brought up in a children's home.'

The policeman and policewoman looked at each other.

'Did Andy have an old friend do you know? A man called John Hollander, known as Foxy?'

'Oh, I've no idea,' said Ellie. She rarely if ever told lies but she was telling one now. Foxy was dead. Hadn't she heard it on the news? 'Anyway, what do you want my grandson for?' she dared to ask, not really wanting to know the answer.

'Just for a chat. We'll catch up with him sometime.'

Now who was lying, Ellie thought. They both stood up and the woman called Katie took a small card out of her breast pocket, which gave a prolonged clicking sound as she opened the flap. Velcro, Ellie guessed. No buttons nowadays if they could be avoided.

'If Josh returns, or when he comes back,' the policewoman corrected herself. 'Perhaps you could get him to give us a ring on this number.' She smiled at the old lady but Ellie suspected it was a false smile.

After they had gone, she sat for a time in the silent room, contemplating. *Where are you Josh? What have you done?*

Josh tucked into his jacket potato with the beans spilling out from it and slices of ham edging it. He had a can of beer open, and imagined Gran saying, 'Put it in a glass, lad, you'll cut your mouth on that tin.'

Gran liked things done properly, was a stickler for good table manners. She even made him use a napkin when he ate at her place. He smiled, imagining using a napkin in Afghanistan. No chance. His thoughts grew dark. Afghanistan. Andy. IED's, snipers, ragheads. *Forget it Josh, you're home now. Eat the food, drink your beer.*

He woke to a flickering TV, with people prancing around a stage set, laughing and joking. They were making no sound as he'd turned it down earlier. His mouth was furry with sleep and alcohol. How many cans had he had? On top of the pints in the Blue Boar? He looked down on the floor by the sofa, counted six... no wonder he felt cotton-wool fuzzy. He switched off the TV, checked his watch. Almost midnight. He could hear heavy rain battering the cottage window and front door, heard the distant sound of rumbling thunder, and saw a lightning flash through the half-open slatted blinds.

Time for bed, Joshua, he said to himself, ignoring the mess around him, and made for the stairs. Clear it up tomorrow, he promised the empty room.

Josh did not sleep peacefully. The nightmares returned... clawing limbs and gargoyle heads, spewing blood and guts and worms. Large grey dogs tore at pieces of flesh and bone. His. They made off with them, blood dripping from their snarling mouths. Josh awoke screaming, tearing the bedclothes from him, fighting off the terrors of his dream. He lay there soaked in perspiration, gradually realising it was just a dream. He breathed slowly through his mouth. A grey light showed through a gap in the curtains. Dawn breaking.

He was still dressed in Mike's heavy sweater and thick shirt. He was wearing his own trousers and socks with the rancid smell of sweat and stale beer assailing his nostrils. Time to shower. There was a towelling robe behind the bedroom door. One more thing to borrow. He stripped naked and shivered himself into the robe, rubbed a hand across his stubbled chin. Yeah, shit, shower, shave and shampoo. Gotta be the order of the day.

He grimaced at the mess he'd left downstairs, and was spurred by shame to bin the cans from the front room, place crockery and cutlery into the sink, then fill the kettle for coffee. An hour later saw him showered, shaved and dressed and breakfasted. He saw Glen coming through the back gate, complete with two leashed dogs. Josh waved to him through the French doors, went over to unlock it and let the three of them in.

'Morning Glen,' he said, and 'morning guys,' to the dogs.

In the end, Josh went to the hills alone, except for the dogs. Glen's lungs were giving him trouble in the severe cold.

'Sorry old son,' he said. 'But I think walking the Bluff for me now is a journey too far.'

'Not a problem. I'll take the dogs, be glad to.'

'Thanks mate, see you when you get back.' He waved them goodbye from the cottage door as the dogs, keen to be out, pulled Josh a little too quickly for comfort down the slope. He yanked firmly on their leads. 'Oi, slow down you two.' Two prancing dogs in one hand, he flashed open the car and ordered them into the back. Even when sitting, their heads almost hit the roof. He could smell their dried-food breakfast as they panted in anticipation. He wrinkled his nose, grateful for no hangover as he reluctantly smelled something akin to rotten eggs or fish. Probably was.

Carefully following Glen's instructions, Josh gradually left the town behind and drove upwards, past clumps of trees and a gurgling stream that splashed over glistening rocks. Pockets of snow here and there, merged in with water-soaked grass and more rock. The car shuddered and rattled over a cattle grid and the climb grew steeper. The trees were left behind and through the windscreen, he could see nothing but undulating hills and valleys.

Smoke rose over the hills from distant farmhouses, but he saw no sign of any other human beings. Josh felt like he was the only one left on the planet, him and two panting wolfhounds. He quite liked the sensation. There were no sheep on the hills. Glen told him the farmers brought them down to the lower slopes beginning of winter. Then he saw it, the summit of Hay Bluff, a long, almost straight-looking ridge, a giant rearing up from the verdant valleys below, a kaleidoscope of thin snow, rust-coloured rocks, many shades of green, and pools of water shining like jewels in the thin, watery sun.

Josh stopped the car and let the dogs out. He took off their leads and watched as they ran wild with great loping strides, then stopping to sniff at rabbit holes and other interesting things that twitched their canine nostrils. He listened to the sound of silence, only the wind to perforate it. All around him was solitude and the magnificent beauty of nature. He remembered Gran once describing beauty as a warmth within your soul, and without.

As he climbed, leaving the car in a natural lay-by halfway up the mountain, he thought about Gran and inexplicably wanted to be a child again. He saw a sheep's carcass, the bones picked clean by crows and its fleece in tatters, like a torn-up rug, with bits of it impaled on sharp pieces of rock. The cruel balance of nature, one creature being fodder for another.

Gran had once spoken about cruelty: when he came home from school with a bloodied nose and his shirt collar ripped.

'Cruel people are like mud inside, Josh. There's no honey in them, only pigs' swill. You're not like that, pet. You're my honeycomb, bonnie lad.' And she had changed his shirt, washed his face, and cuddled him to her. They had fish and chips for tea that night, from the fish shop on the parade. Gran asked the fishmonger for extra bits of batter. She told Josh they reminded her of her childhood up north, when all they could afford were the batter scraps, never whole pieces of cod wrapped inside their crisp, golden coats.

Josh had never known poverty. Sometimes, when growing up, he wished he'd had more love. From his parents, not Gran and Granddad. They gave him plenty, especially Gran. His grandfather was a quiet man, who spoke only when he had something of value to say.

The summit came in and out of view as he climbed, with the dogs way in front of him. As the wind dropped, Josh looked around him, at a vista of mountains, hills and valleys, that glowed in the brightness of the morning. Lakes, here and there, shone like mirrors far below the hills. There were peaks and troughs everywhere... He knew an inner peace, like he had never felt before. He was at one in his surroundings, these magnificent hills. There was no pain, no torment of the mind, just a feeling of perfect harmony. *Why can't it always be like this? The peace, the safety of these hills. Why do I have to go back?*

Josh sat on a rock, bit into a chocolate bar and watched the dogs as they drew nearer to him after their foraging. Maeve came first and laid her head on his knee. Does she know what I'm thinking? What I'm going through? She nudged him with her muzzle, gently licked his hand. He stroked her, looked at her gazing up at him. Something, some mutual feeling – of what? – passed between them. Billy broke the spell as he loped towards them, unable to stop before he bumped clumsily into Josh and disturbed the moment. Josh forgave him, patted his head and stroked Billy's long grey back. He thought how much they resembled the creatures they were named after: Josh had admired wolves ever since, as a boy, he had read Jack London's White Fang. Ironic really, he thought, these two have been bred to hunt wolves, but Irish wolfhounds? When did they last have wolves in Ireland?

He stood up, cold now and slightly damp from sitting on the lichen-covered rock. 'Time to go, fellas.'

The descent was no less hazardous than the upward climb. Josh trod carefully, aware of the hidden dangers under and between the pockets of snow that might disguise rabbit holes or jagged rock pieces. A cracked ankle now would not be good.

Just before he reached the car, he put the dogs back on leads. There seemed to be some kind of activity in the small lay-by, involving an ambulance and a police car. What's going on, he thought. Anxious now, the police were the last people he wanted to encounter. Weird, he thought, seeing them here in the middle of nowhere. He reached the car, carefully controlling the dogs who were as curious as himself. Two paramedics were stretchering someone into the back of the ambulance, an old guy by the looks of him. A woman hovered nearby, tearful, probably his wife. She looked anxious, unsure. Josh felt a twinge of sympathy for her as he made to move to his car and disappear from the scene. One of the two policemen waylaid him.

'Morning sir, enjoy your walk?'

Josh nodded. 'Yeah, it was great... what's going on?'

'Not from around here, are you?'

What's that meant to mean? 'No, I'm not. Just staying in the area for a few days.'

'And where's here sir?'

Josh resented his tone. 'Just outside the town, in the Dingle.'

'Ah, the Dingle.'

Slimy individual. 'What's happened to the old man?'

'Taken bad he was. Luckily the wife had her mobile with her and was able to call us and the ambulance. You didn't see them arrive?' he added.

'No, there was no-one here when I got here.'

'Right...' *Right what?* 'What about when you were up there?' The policeman indicated the Bluff. 'You didn't see them then?'

'No, too busy climbing, and controlling these two,' he added.

'Yours, are they?' he thought the cop sounded a double for Rob Brydon.

'No, my cousin's neighbours.' *Here we go again, my cousin...*

'And who might your cousin be?'

Josh felt like saying 'and what's it bloody got to do with you?' but restrained himself.

'Mike Beresford. I'm staying in his cottage at the Dingle.'

'You mean Mike the writer? Ex-bomb disposal?'

'Yeah, that's the one.'

'Your cousin, you say?'

Yeah, that's him... that's what I'm saying.'

'Yes.'

'Mmm... bit of a hero I hear.'

'Yeah. Diffusing fifty bombs and more, I guess that makes him a hero.'

The ambulance crew prepared to leave, taking the old man and his anxious wife. Josh stood there watching, his face a mask behind the mind that twisted and turned, trying its best to help him escape this nosey git. Finally, it was the other policeman freed Josh.

'C'mon Tommy, you'll have to drive their car back.'

'Where to?'

'Clyro. I've got 'is address 'ere.'

'Oh, all right.' He tipped his peaked cap at Josh. 'See you around... sir.'

Not if I see you first, you slimy git. 'Yeah, maybe.'

Josh let the dogs into the back of the car, climbed into the front and fired the ignition. He let the car tick over and sat there, mulling over the incident. He opened his window to let out some of the doggy smell, a mixture of sheep and rabbit droppings, and whatever the two dogs had been fed for breakfast. It smelled rancid, anyway. *Wonder if that idiot took my car number? Stupid of me to say I was Mike's cousin. They'll trace the car to Gran's address, or will they? Granddad's been dead a couple of years now: maybe Dad's paid the tax and insurance on it?* He chewed his lip, arguing back on forth to himself and coming to no conclusions. Best get back to the cottage, he decided.

'Ok, you two, settle down. We're going home now.'

The sun had gone in and the sky had taken on a yellowy, grey tinge. Ominous. Within minutes, the snow fell: soft, silent flakes until the wind blew up. It turned into a blizzard, and sent the flakes swirling in many directions. Josh hoped his memory would guide him back, because the road was all-but obliterated of its landmarks. On top of all this aggro, his grandfather's ten-year-old car clearly did not like the hilly descent with its bends and troughs, its potholes and its cattle grid: it slipped and slid its way back towards the town. Josh's dislike of this homeward journey equalled that of the car. Snow gathered on the windscreen and blew in twists and whorls on the road in front of him. Even the dogs seemed to sense the hazards of such conditions. They sat stiff and upright on the back seat, the only heat coming from their breath on Josh's neck.

At last he began to pass the odd house, one here and there beyond the narrow lane he was on. Not whole rows, like avenues or drives, but he knew he was nearing the town. He caught glimpses of the castle, towering above the rooftops of shops and other buildings, the church and the town clock. He passed the Blue Boar and would have loved to stop for a beer and a whisky chaser, but there was still a half mile to go before he could deposit these two back safely with their owners and get himself out of his damp clothes. Plus, he needed food: he hadn't eaten since breakfast, apart from that nibble of chocolate back on the Bluff.

It was only three o'clock but pretty dark beyond the car windows. The snow swirled under the greyest of skies. It could have been evening instead of afternoon, a pretty unpleasant one at that.

Billy began to whine. Did he sense he was almost home? His whining started Maeve off, only her sounds were deeper, more mature than her son's. A canine symphony, Josh thought, and almost smiled. Apart from his verbal set-to with the gobby copper this morning, his day had been almost pain free: a good feeling.

Now he was parked up by the shelter of a ten-foot-high stone wall, tucked in by several other vehicles that, judging by the fallen leaves on their roofs and bonnets, had not moved all day. He climbed out, opened the back door, and yelled at the dogs as they leapt off the back seat.

'Hold on you two,' he shouted, and yanked on their leads. 'Steady fellas, you've gotta pull me up the slope yet.'

And pull they did, while he slipped and slid behind them on the icy, untrodden snow up the steep gradient. He stopped outside Penny and Glen's front door, pressed the brass and porcelain bell and didn't have to wait long before Glen opened the door. Josh felt a rush of warm air radiate from their front room, and let the dogs struggle their way in.

'My God, you look nithered,' said Penny when Josh followed the dogs inside. 'Get yourself by the fire and I'll make you some tea. You need thawing out, poor thing. Can't believe this weather, so early into winter.'

He was grateful to be led to one of the sofas and held out his hands to the fire.

'Didn't realise it was coming down so thick,' Glen remarked. 'Not until I went through to the kitchen to make a brew. Can hardly see Bryn Cethyn or the farm... we were just beginning to get worried about you,' he added.

Josh kind of grinned. 'Yeah, I was worried about me too.'

35

Josh decided, that night, to sleep in the front bedroom; quite fancying the idea of seeing the sun come up behind the snow-clad mountains that surrounded Hay Bluff. It proved to be a decision that brought him vital time.

The sun was already hovering when he awoke, and it was to an amazing blue sky, with a pink and orange glow of the rising orb that greeted him. The interior wooden window shutters were at half-mast, with the slats open, allowing him to witness this breath-taking view. When he'd had his fill, he glanced down onto the ground below, to the partially snow-covered slope that led down to the lane where all the cars were parked. There were tiny birds' feet tracks here and there, but as he swivelled his eyes to the right he knew the snow would not be virgin for long. Struggling up the slope were two navy-uniformed policemen. He guessed their destination and also surmised they weren't calling for a social chat. His stomach lurched like he was riding on a fairground big dipper and he quickly drew away from the window, grabbing his clothes and struggling into them as he ran downstairs towards the back kitchen. He prayed the two did not know about the back entrance through the alleyway, that they would knock at the front door.

What to do? Dive over the farm fence and see if he could leg it into town that way? Go to Penny and Glen's back entrance, or keep going round the backs of the cottages until he reached his car? Suppose there were more, waiting by his car? Suppose they had traced his car registration?

Josh was really panicking now. He told himself to stop,

just stop. Think logically. First things first, he told himself. *Wrap up warmly, put on two layers of clothes, in case you have to sleep rough. Grab your wallet, you'll need cash. Grab Mike's gun... the one you saw in Mike's drawer. Why the gun? Might be necessary.* But he preferred not to question why.

For once the gods were on his side. As he prepared himself for a swift escape he saw Glen coming cautiously up the garden path. Josh quickly let him in through the French doors.

'Dunno what kind of trouble you're in, my old son. Don't wanna know,' he continued before Josh could interrupt. 'The police contacted me and Penny last night. Asked all sorts of questions about you. I told 'em I didn't know anything.'

Josh nodded dumbly. He had no answer for Mike's neighbour.

'Look,' he said. 'My car's garaged halfway down the slope. Carry on down this back alley and you'll see the garage. Here's the keys.' He paused. 'You'd better leave me yours, just in case I need transport. I won't tell them you've left them with me,' he added. Josh was still dumb and numb. He handed him his keys.

'Better wind a scarf round your face, stick a hat on too... there's petrol in the car, enough to get you to at least the other side of Hereford.'

Josh shrugged into his jacket, found a scarf and beanie hat in the hall cupboard, plus some gloves.

'Thanks man,' he said. 'And thanks for not asking me questions. I WILL tell you one day... promise.'

Glen gave him a hug. 'On your way, son... and good luck.' It was then the police knocked at the front door. He saw Josh out the back way. 'Don't worry,' he whispered. 'I'll stall them.'

Josh stepped over the snow-covered path and into the small back alley behind Glen's and Penny's cottage. He saw a movement in the top window. Penny waving at him, an anxious look on her face. He waved back and continued past the other cottages until he saw the concrete garage, tucked in on a bend of the slope. The key turned first time and the up-and-over door swung open without a sound. *Thanks Glen, for keeping it oiled.* Inside was a small black four-by-four: perfect for snowy conditions, thought Josh. He got in, fired up the ignition and glided it gently out of the garage. Should he shut the up and over door? Best not. Time was of the essence. He drove it slowly and carefully down to the lane, his stomach lurching again when he saw the police car that was parked adjacent to his own, effectively blocking it in. There were two more police in the patrol car. He kept his eyes looking straight ahead, very little of his face visible or identifiable, and drove a car that was not being sought.

At the T junction, he took a right turn, away from the town and its police station, away from the officers that were knocking on Mike's door, and away from the two who sat in their patrol car. Mike's neighbours had told him he could get to Hereford this way. Then where to? Ross on Wye? The motorway towards the north? He picked out ring marks on the windscreen. Did that mean...? He stopped in a lay-by and opened the glove compartment. He almost punched the air. Yes! Result... He saw the satnav, pulled it out of its wrapper and plugged it into the socket. Once it had lit up he tapped in directions to Chepstow; he could join the M4 from there.

The sky stayed clear for almost an hour. He was now on the way from Gloucester to Cirencester. The sight of a patrol car in a lay-by had prompted him to change his mind about Chepstow. He could travel east, via Cirencester, and pick up the motorway somewhere near there. The sky had darkened, turned ominously grey. But it brought rain, not snow. A blessing at least. He could afford time to think, drive almost on auto-pilot.

What should he tell Gran about Granddad's car? Come to think of it, was it wise to go to her? Maybe the police had already been round there, asking her if she'd seen him and where he might be.

He felt sick inside. Life was such a complete mess. Josh really didn't know which way to turn, what to do next. The whining hooter of an HGV lorry shocked him out of his thoughts. It sped past him on the outside lane, the illegal lane for lorries, and he saw the driver give him a two-fingered salute. *Yeah, sorry mate. 40mph in the centre lane is not a clever idea.* That's all he needed, the motorway cops to pull him and the lorry driver over on a traffic offence. He negotiated his way over to the slow lane and pulled off at the next service station. Maybe breakfast would be a good thing. He'd missed it on his swift escape from the cottage.

The automatic doors slid open and Josh walked first into WHSmith's to buy a paper. He was still swathed in the scarf and beanie hat. Just as well. There was a full-sized photo of him on the front page, under the headline 'HAVE YOU SEEN THIS MAN?' He shut his eyes, sucked in his breath. Now what? Breakfast was obviously not a good idea. He went back to the counter with three bars of chocolate. They would have to suffice. And a bottle of water. They would have to be breakfast and lunch all in one. Pity. He could have murdered a full English. Bad choice of word, said out loud or not.

Once again, he silently thanked Glen for the loan (well the gift really) of his car. What a top man. And Penny. Such a lovely lady. He hoped one day he could repay them for their kindness. One day…

36

Josh walked back to the car, hunched against the wind and rain. Was the car at a weird angle or was it his imagination? Not imagination, but a puncture. *I don't bloody believe it. How much bad luck can happen to one person in half a day? Don't even know where the spare is kept.*

He decided to sit out the rain before attempting to change the wheel. No point in getting soaking wet, might as well wait an hour... The spare tyre, of course, was fixed to the back of the car. It would be, a four by four. And the tools for changing it, the jack and so on, were under the carpeting in the back of the vehicle.

He sat hunched in the driver's seat, ate one of the three chocolate bars and read the paper. The front page, despite the large photo of him, did not really give much away as to why the police wanted to catch up with him. It seemed to be all 'it is alleged' and 'suggested' or 'unexplained incidents'. One thing for sure, Josh knew, it had to involve Foxy, and Sue, and Annie.

He unwrapped the second bar, broke off a couple of squares and sucked on the sweetness to make them last. He'd been told by a sergeant that it made your stomach fuller for longer. Tried to remember the guy's name, or face, or even his voice. Too long ago now. Some memories fade, the unimportant ones, others stay forever, like Andy. Andy would stay forever.

Josh wished he was back in the barracks now. That all this time since he'd come home on leave, had been nothing but a bad dream, one that daybreak would take away. No such luck. Now the rain was coming down heavier, obliterating everything except the nearest parked cars, and he could only see those through the rain torrenting down the windscreen. The daytime gloom was merging into night as the service station lights came on, in and around the car park, showing a kaleidoscope of shapes and mixed-up colours.

He searched in the glove compartment. Perhaps Glen was with the RAC, or the AA. They'd come and change the wheel, wouldn't they? Once more, luck was on Josh's side. Glen was with the RAC, and 'fully comp'. Cover for himself or any other driver. Well done that man…

An hour later, wheel changed, Josh was politely saluted and wished a 'safe journey sir': plus, the rain had stopped. With any luck, and in three hours or so, he should be with Gran, safe and warm in her twenty-two degrees bungalow.

Luck, however, is not always dealt out when you need it most. He had made the journey to Westgate from the M4 service station in the three hours he'd estimated, despite the darkness and more rainfall. Except that two others had also made it to Acacia Crescent, their yellow and blue patrol car covering the entrance to Gran's drive. Josh drove past and made a U-turn further round the crescent. As he drove past his grandmother's bungalow, he could see Gran's curtains were drawn, allowing him no view of the interior. He had no idea how many police were with her, or how long they had been there. At least, if they came out now, they wouldn't recognise the vehicle he was in. Unless. Unless Glen had been quizzed and given any details away. Somehow, Josh didn't think Mike's next-door neighbour would do that. Not willingly.

What next? Take a drive round to his house, his parents' house. See whether there were more police staked out in front of it. He paused at the junction, looked in his rear mirror and caught a glimpse of two navy uniforms, with high-viz jackets on top, coming out of Gran's bungalow. He turned left and parked a few yards on. The patrol car turned right, towards the main road that led into Margate. Josh decided he would still go home, see if the place was being watched. It was. A police car parked across the road from his house and another further up. They weren't taking any chances of missing him, when and if he returned. Damn. *You could go back to Gran's now, but would they return there later on? Maybe do regular patrols for the rest of the night? Looks like you'll be sleeping rough tonight, Joshie boy.*

Using that term made him sad for a moment. That's what Andy used to call him... he could hear his friend's voice now. He'd had one of those voices where there was always a hint of laughter lurking somewhere. Andy was never at a loss to crack some kind of joke, no matter how serious the situation, how dangerous the moment. *I miss you, mate.*

He really wished Andy was with him now. He'd know what to do, where to go. Even though a city boy, born and bred, Andy seemed to sniff out the secret country spots, places where trees grew that you could bend around you and make a hidden bivouac. No matter where they were, Josh's friend always found drinkable water, had learned how to snare rabbits and other small, edible animals. Ok, so Josh wouldn't be going that far tonight in his survival program. Lighting a fire, for a start, was a no-no, a sure way of being discovered.

The four x four would have to be his bed. But where could he park, without prying eyes and the police seeing him? Josh wondered if Parry Arnold was out of hospital. Maybe he would give him a bed for the night? Probably still in hospital after such a brutal attack, poor devil. *How did it all come to this? Where did I go wrong, let it go pear shaped, tits up? Was it Andy being blown up? What about the little Afghan girl? What I did to her came before Andy. How d'you justify what you did to her? So many circles in my mind, like the insides of a watch, all interlinked, all ticking away like a time bomb. Only mine has already gone off, detonated, exploded to jangled bits. I don't know how to pick up the pieces... or even if they can be picked up.*

Josh drove on auto-pilot for several miles after he left his parents' road. It came as a shock to realise he had driven as far as Pegwell Bay, to the entrance of the coastal nature reserve. If he remembered rightly, there was a small car park, one that had areas not visible from the road. He could be well-hidden there, and undisturbed for the night. He pulled off the road, and drove carefully over the gravel towards some stunted trees and bushes. Winding the window down, he could hear the distant sea and glimpse the odd winking light from a trawler far out there. He could hear the splash of waves, and saw ghostly shapes wheel and dive through the darkness. There was no moon or any visible stars in the overcast sky, just total blackness beyond his dipped headlights. He stopped the car, switched off both ignition and headlights, gradually adjusting his vision to pierce the darkness.

The wind began to howl and threaten to become gale force. Josh shivered, tired and cold enough to rewind his window. He felt in his pocket for the last chocolate bar. Breakfast, lunch and dinner: three bars. Nothing like variety.

Josh slept. He had let back and lowered his seat, folded his arms and pulled his jacket closer around him. He dreamed, of all things, about waving palms on a sunlit beach: how they freckled his face in and out of the sunlight as they fanned him high above. He opened his eyes. No sunlight, but an eerie moon that flickered through the small trees beyond the car park's periphery. A fox barking stirred him further awake. He looked at his watch: two o'clock... and shivered. He curled himself into a ball and tried to get back to sleep again. No chance, his rude awakening had brought on the hunger pangs. Three bars of chocolate were not sufficient for a day's intake. All that food he'd had to leave behind in Mike's cottage. And the beer. What a waste. How he would appreciate it now. Well, he couldn't get anything until tomorrow morning, not unless he went back onto one of the motorways to an all-night service station. *Go back to sleep, Josh.*

37

Aubrey Penhaligon, once a Franciscan monk, had discarded his robes and walked away a free man from the monastery. But he kept his God: he saw no reason to reject his Creator, the Creator of all things. However, he adapted and wore much more colourful clothes than the drab, grey habit he'd previously worn. He liked purple suits made from soft velvet, pink cotton shirts and rainbow silk cravats.

He exchanged his script-writing pens for sable brushes and painted richly-coloured portraits of the famous. He once painted the entire cast of the Royal Opera House's Madam Butterfly: just Butterfly, the cognoscenti would say. There was not a daub of flesh colour anywhere in these portraits. Rather, he had captured the inner colours of each sitter's spirit or soul, as he told the viewers when the paintings were shown.

Aubrey used striking hues, rich magenta, gold, butter and lemon yellows, viridian and cerulean blues. A deftly placed spot of titanium white, and the subject's eyes would come alive and follow a viewer everywhere. Aubrey could show those same eyes as fiery, powerful, arrogant, or just gentle and trusting, depending upon which character they portrayed. The finished painting revealed that character completely, and all were satisfied with the result.

He also painted landscapes, towns and villages, mountains and streams, and he loved trees especially. He tried to bring them alive as he sketched their fragile leaves, make the two-dimensional into three, so the leaves would almost quiver as they might in a breeze.

Aubrey met Lally, his wife, in the cathedral of trees at Milton Keynes. She was standing by a holm oak, so still that he thought, for a foolish moment, she was a worshipping statue, part of the atmosphere within this church of nature. Unknown to him, she was recovering from a disastrous marriage and an equally devastating divorce. Aubrey stood silent, regarding her and sensing her sadness. He quietly sketched her, somehow managing to convey a peaceful solitude, a healing stillness that went beyond her torment and pain.

When she became aware of his presence, she temporarily shed the hurt and became curious enough to ask him, 'Can I see it?'

'Of course,' he said and beckoned her over.

'You've given me tranquillity in that,' she said of his drawing.

'Yes...' he answered. It was a prolonged yes. That was how he spoke when he was in a thoughtful, pensive mood.

'How did you manage that?'

He smiled at her, a sweet smile that reminded Lally of her long-ago father. 'I seem to possess the ability to calm storms.'

She regarded him, eventually asking, 'Have you always been an artist?' and adding, 'I used to paint once.' She drifted off and he reached for her, to bring her back.

'No. I was a Franciscan monk who lived in: in the monastery. I tended the vegetable garden by day and wrote scripts, by hand, at night.'

Lally nodded: she could imagine him in just such an environment. Peaceful and silent, yet creative and forward-thinking. Another pause. 'Why are you here?'

'I've been commissioned to paint the city of Milton Keynes. Given a free hand, really,' he added, 'to paint the aspects of it that interest or intrigue me. They're going to produce a book of my paintings and comments.'

'And will you include me in it?' She smiled at him and he thought her smile illuminated her face in a very attractive way.

Six months later they married. Aubrey took Lally back to his seventeenth-century cottage near Ludlow in Shropshire. He continued his painting and she never painted again. Her last effort hung above the fireplace in the cottage front room. It was a portrait of a Canada goose standing in front of a lavishly-framed ormolu mirror, the bird's feathers so life-like they almost ruffled in a make-believe breeze.

Instead, Lally became Aubrey's agent and manager, organising events and exhibitions for him the length and breadth of the UK. On that cold autumn morning, they were driving back from one such successful exhibition held at Dover castle. Finding an early morning bakers, they had purchased freshly-baked rolls and had their thermos flask filled with hot coffee. Inside a tiny fridge that plugged into their Range Rover they had milk, butter and ham. They stopped in the car park at Pegwell Bay.

Aubrey climbed down from the vehicle and looked out onto waving grasses that bordered the seashore.

'I think I'll paint this after breakfast,' he told Lally.

A muffled figure climbed out of a nearby vehicle, walked behind it and Aubrey heard the sound of a man urinating, could even smell it in this cold, crisp air. He turned away, respecting the man's need for privacy until his stream stopped. When the man reappeared Aubrey wished him 'Good morning'.

Josh mumbled a reply. His head suddenly shot up as he smelled the coffee Lally was pouring. She looked over to him, smiled and said, 'Morning,' and added, 'Would you like a cup?'

He wondered how they got their facial scars: had a fleeting thought of Foxy... and Harry, the publican. Maybe these two had been involved in a car accident, or a fire?

Whatever. Something about them told Josh they could be trusted. He replied to her offer, careful not to stare at either of their faces. 'Yeah... cheers. I'd love one.'

She handed a steaming cup down to Aubrey, who passed it over to Josh. The ex-monk in him saw one troubled and furtive human animal. It intrigued him. When the man pulled his scarf off his face to drink, Aubrey saw the stubble, noted how the man's hands shook. He guessed he was running away from something, could feel his pain.

'Would you like a ham roll?' he said. 'The rolls are still warm, baked this morning.'

Lally was already buttering them and filling them with thick slices of ham.

Josh accepted one with caution and hunger, but with little grace. He devoured it while Lally buttered and filled a second one for him. He took that too, this time eating slowly with evident gratitude, and thanks.

Aubrey chewed on his own roll, slowly, contemplatively. In between bites, he sipped his coffee. He dared to ask, in a conversational way, 'Are you from around these parts?' Privately, he wondered why the man was sleeping rough, even though he had an almost-new vehicle and was decently dressed.

'Kind of,' answered Josh. 'Erm. Nearly anyway.' He hoped he gave nothing away with that answer, trusted also that these two had not seen a newspaper. Having spotted and identified the canvasses, in the back of their car, he said, 'You an artist?'

Aubrey nodded. 'Er... yes. We've just exhibited at Dover Castle these past few days. Home now to Shropshire. Reason we stopped here,' he added, 'I thought I might do a few sketches of the nature reserve and seashore.'

'More coffee?' said Lally.

Josh nodded, managed a smile, and held out his plastic cup. 'Thanks. I'm home on leave,' he suddenly blurted. 'My

Gran lives up the road. Thought I'd pay her a visit.' Then regretted saying it. Maybe they *had* read the papers, heard the news. Maybe Gran had been mentioned. After all, the police had wasted no time going round there to her bungalow.

Aubrey's face remained passive. He waited for the man to add to his statement, yet understood if that was all he wished to tell them. His calm silence encouraged Josh.

'I'm home for a couple of weeks from Afghanistan.'

The artist nodded. A breeze whipped up, ruffling Aubrey's sparse hair and a shy, wintry sun glistened on an icy puddle at his feet. 'Will you be home for Christmas?'

Josh gulped his coffee, stamped at the cold beneath his feet. 'Don't know yet... yeah... probably.'

Aubrey knew better than to probe further. He sensed a panic in the young man, a deep fear.

'I'm Aubrey by the way, Aubrey Penhaligon. And my wife is Lally.' He indicated her with his cup.

'Josh, Josh Swales.' Josh licked his lips for stray crumbs and tasted the salt from the ham. He could easily eat another of those. Lally seemed to read his thoughts.

'We've more rolls and ham. Could you eat another?'

Josh struggled to appear nonchalant. 'Be silly not to.' A trace of humour. Yeah, he did like these two, friendly without being too intrusive. Loved their coffee and rolls, that was for sure.

Another car rolled into the car park. Josh panicked. Time to go. He said a swift goodbye to Aubrey and Lally, thanked them for the food and drink, and was gone.

38

Now he was walking. He had left Glen's car in the middle of a busy supermarket car park, hoping it would not be noticed, traced, or identified too quickly. He strolled the concrete promenade, until he descended, on rusting steps, to the beach. The sand was still wet from the outgoing tide, with little rock pools where green seaweed clung to ancient pieces of chalk, once part of the cliffs until erosion tore at them and clawed them into the sand.

A thin, watery sun struggled to show its face through bad-tempered clouds. It did nothing to warm the earth's temperature. Josh shivered as he walked, partly through cold and some through worry and lack of proper sleep. He wished he was back in Afghanistan, to a time before Andy stepped on the roadside improvised explosive device (RIED); before the blackouts had started, and the devastation that seemed always to follow. *Before the little Afghan girl.*

Sooner than he expected, he was in Margate. He climbed back onto the pavement, shook the wet sand from his boots. When he licked his lips, he could taste salt. The Blue Elephant's windows shone in the early morning sun. Not that early when he heard the town clock strike eleven. He wondered if Sue Ellen was already at work. Decided to give the Blue Elephant, and her, a miss. There were few people about, some shopping, two or three making their way down to the beach with dogs on leads: drivers and cyclists on the road. And buses. All so normal. Not like him and what he had done. Maybe. No, for sure. There had been no one else involved, not unless he had been drugged senseless, and that definitely bordered on the ridiculous.

He left behind the main shopping centre and the seafront, to wander into back streets and lanes. Ugly, impoverished little backstreets of Margate, unlike the richer 'Lanes' of Brighton. He noticed boarded-up shops, people leaning against scruffy houses with paint peeling from doors and windows. People who spoke in foreign languages, languages that he partly recognised but did not speak. He guessed eastern-European. Further along the mean little street, a pub door opened, spewing out shaven-headed, red-faced men with bloodshot eyes. Men who had topped up last night's drinking with this morning's 'hair of the dog'. Mean faces, belligerent, bellicose, itching for a punch-up.

Josh could not help walking towards them, it was the only way to go. He badly wanted to turn around and escape this ugly street, flee down some alley to escape them. Someone called out, 'Hey, soldier boy.'

How come they recognised him with the scarf covering much of his face? He knew he could be in big trouble, knew there would be more than one voice. Were these the Margate Boys he had encountered only days ago? The ones that probably had beaten his old schoolteacher half to death? Life was being distinctly unfair to Josh Swales.

They blinked as they emerged into the wintry sunlight, unshaven, bald-headed, tattooed and belching. Despite his dread of meeting them, his lips curled. What an ugly bunch of wasted humanity. How he wished Andy was by his side now. Between them, they would pulverise this lot. But Andy wasn't with him, nor any of his platoon. Josh was on his own in a very unwelcome situation and, to him, an unknown district of this seaside town.

A girl emerged with them. Josh's stomach dropped down to his boots; the girl was Sue Ellen.

'Bit out of your way, aren't you Josh?', she sneered. She was holding onto one of the guys' arms. He was running to fat but still had plenty of muscle, plus he had back up of at least half a dozen mates. 'He's the one who came into the Blue Elephant with your Sue,' she said to the guy.

'What, my little cousin?'

'Yeah, *and* he denied it when I asked him.'

'That's not a very nice thing to do, what's your name? Josh?' He closed the gap between himself and Josh. 'What have you done with my cousin, mate? We haven't seen her for days. Not like her to go walkabout.'

'Nothing, I haven't done anything with her. She was ok last time I saw her.'

'Oh yeah, and when was that?'

Josh hesitated. When had it been? Seemed like a lifetime ago. 'Dunno, mate. Three, four weeks?' He edged his way backwards, not conscious of what was behind him. The what became a who, one of Sue's cousin's mates. He kicked Josh behind the knees, making him lose his balance and fall to the ground. He hit his elbow on the edge of the kerb and sucked in breath as pain shot through him. There was much more to come; long minutes of sustained beating and snarling from a vicious pack of animals in human form. Minutes that felt like hours, so sustained were the kicks and blows rained upon him. He was kicked in the ribs, in his spine and his kidneys, and on both kneecaps. One of them stamped on his hand, repeatedly, with steel capped boots, until his fingers cracked and surely broke. Sue's cousin kicked him in the face, splitting his lips, and causing a gaping wound above his left eye. He felt the blood spurt, tasted it. There was more to come. They had smelled his blood and wanted more. They grunted in their effort. *Yeah, ten out of ten for effort, lads.*

Just remember it's me under all these blows. But they knew that. There was pleasure in their exertion: you could tell from how many times they said 'yes' or 'bull's eye' when they hit a preferred target. They seemed to know where his kidneys were, and his rib cage. Oh, for sure, these thugs understood about street fighting and where to hurt their enemy most. Today, Josh was their enemy. Their number one foe.

Mercifully, he lost consciousness, unaware of how long the beating continued: did not hear Sue Ellen say, 'Enough fellas. You don't wanna be had up for murder.' Josh didn't see her sudden revulsion at the bloody pulp his face and body had become. Or realise that people were gathering and making noises of shock and disgust. It was their appearance on the scene that saved him from further punishment. The gang disappeared. A man said to others in the crowd, 'Someone give me a hand to get him up.' Josh barely felt himself being lifted and carried to a nearby bench outside the pub. Neither was he particularly aware of the pub landlord coming out with a bowl of warm water to mop up, at least some of, the blood.

He spat out a tooth, grazing his lip as he did it.

'You ought to go to hospital, mate. D'you want me to call an ambulance?'

Josh shook his head and wished that he hadn't. The throbbing agony was unbearable.

'I'll be ok,' he croaked. 'Could you call me a tackthi? I wanna go home.'

The man who had picked him up said, 'It's ok, I'll run you home, mate. Where d'you live?'

'Wethtgate.'

'Right. I'll just fetch my car, it's round the corner.'

So there were still decent folk about.

Josh sprawled on the bench, wishing the pain would go away, or even some of it. In a short time, the guy drew up next to him, got out of the car but left the engine running. He helped Josh to his feet and persuaded him into the passenger seat. He went to belt him in until Josh cried out in agony. Decided against it and walked quickly round to the driving seat.

'Not long now, mate.' He wished he had a clean rag on him, or a clean handkerchief, noting the blood still seeping from the poor sod's head wounds. Josh was barely conscious, and lolled against the window, leaving bloodied smears on it.

'Can you tell me the address, mate? Where do you live?'

'Yeah,' he coughed, and bloodied-spittle dribbled down his chin. 'I think I'm...' he didn't get the words out. Instead he vomited over his own lap and onto the car mats at his feet. His driver scowled, all decency disappearing at the smell and the mess that would have to be cleaned up. *Thanks mate,* he muttered to himself.

Josh managed to say sorry but not to blush or feel shame; he was too injured for social niceties. They had almost reached Westgate.

'Where to now?'

'Acathia Avenue, number dwenty fi...' Subconsciously he had given Gran's address. Better. She'd take care of him.

'That's Birchington isn't it?'

'Yeah, thorry.'

His rescuer pulled up outside the bungalow. Josh all but fell out of the car, leaving behind his blood, and the remains of his breakfast rolls that the artist's wife had made for him. He was unable to shut the car door, but his benefactor leaned over and shut it, then opened the windows to let out the smell of vomit. Josh crawled across the pavement, and pulled himself upright on the trunk of the holm oak at the beginning of Gran's drive. He staggered and crawled, in turn, along the lawn's edge, until he reached the front wall of the bungalow.

Ellie peered at him from her riser-chair in the window, a look of horror growing as he came into her focus. She hoped her morning carer had left the front door unlocked. It would take her a few minutes to reach it and if she had to unlock it with her arthritic hands... they were acting up today, more painful than usual.

She heard him stagger in through the front door, and his hoarse whisper as he called, 'Gran.'

She was halfway across the lounge on two sticks as he stumbled into the room.

'My God, pet. Who did this to you?'

Josh shook his head, fell into an armchair. 'I don't know, Gran... who they were or anything. But they beat me to a pulp.'

He began to cry, 'I hurt, Gran.'

She leaned over him, gently stroked his head. 'All right, bonnie boy. You're safe now. Gran will make it better.' She thought he was anything but her 'bonnie boy'.

'Climb up on my bed, son.' She managed to persuade him to crawl towards it, giving him little support, apart from her words. 'That's it, pet, well done. Bit more.' She watched as her grandson dragged himself painfully over the carpet, leaving droplets of blood that she chose to ignore. A carpet could always be cleaned. It had taken all her effort to persuade him along the hall, wanting to scream out in her own pain as he leaned on her for support. He could barely walk and several times fell onto his knees, still crying like a baby and saying, 'I hurt Gran,' every step.

At last she was able to push open the door and persuade him through into her bedroom.

'Go on son,' she urged. 'Get onto the bed and I can bathe your wounds. Make you better, like I did when you were little.'

He whimpered as he inched his way to the side of her bed.

His cuts gaped open, ugly, bleeding, needing badly to be stitched to stem the flow. Josh was a long way from a doctor. Close only to the loving grandmother he had almost murdered. Now she was helping him, trying her frail best to save his worthless life. Why? What for? What use was he to anybody, least of all himself?

He managed to grip the bedclothes and haul his agonised body onto the bed, with her pulling and tugging at his ripped clothes in a feeble effort to get him on top of the duvet. He sank back, head on her pillow that smelt faintly of lavender, her smell. She took out a hankie from her cardigan pocket and gently dabbed away some of the blood, hushing his moans. 'I'll get you something for the pain in a minute, pet. And clean all your wounds.'

She put the hankie back in her pocket, ignoring his blood on it. 'Right, bonnie lad,' she said. 'I'll go and get you something to make you feel better.'

He was in too much pain to ask what. Hardly wondered and dismissed even that fleeting thought, reluctantly returning to his throbbing, tortured body.

Ellie Swales hobbled, on two sticks, to her kitchen. Apart from immediate first aid, she knew exactly what her grandson needed, freedom from the pain that was so racking his poor, injured body: freedom from his tortured and twisted mind. She had just the antidote for both. Something she should have dispensed to him a long time ago, especially after she had learned about Foxy and Sue and the old fisherman who had sat so innocently on the banks of the Wantsum. Even the cat had not deserved Josh's vicious kicking to death. It was one of the things he was confessing to her in his pain, telling his Gran what a terrible thing he had done, just because the cat had scratched him. She wondered what Trish and Paul would have to say on their return, knew it would all be too late then. There was no going back. Too many people, plus the cat, had suffered.

And who was this Annie he kept mentioning? Mark you, she thought, did her grandson deserve to suffer the raging PTSD that was ruining his own life? Had he deserved the nightly punishment of his horrifying dreams?

'Bloody wars,' she muttered, then castigated herself, mentally, for swearing.

It was brighter in the kitchen, with a thin, wintry sun peeping through the window. In the distance the sea appeared calm, untouched by the usual high winds of winter. Ellie nodded, accepted a feeling of peace and rightness. She moved over to the work surface, opened her little medicine chest where, apart from plasters and bandages, she kept her pills, prescribed for her own, permanent agony and pain. She took out a whole strip of high-strength co-codamol. In the cupboard beneath the work surface she carefully lifted out her pestle and mortar. It was heavy, but she needed it in order to crush the tablets. She switched on the kettle. Best make Josh a nice cup of tea, strong and sweet, just how he liked it.

In a few moments, she had crushed all the pills to a fine powder, added them to the mug with two heaped spoons of sugar, then waited patiently for the kettle to boil. Josh was moaning softly in the bedroom.

'Won't be long, pet,' she called out.

She poured boiling water over the concoction, her hands shaking with nerves and old age, and stirred it until it resembled nothing more than black tea. She added just the right amount of milk. Watched it swirling round and round, like he used to when he was a little boy. Remembered how he would ask her, 'Why does it go round and round, Gran?' And she would say, 'Because it's magic, Josh, a whirlpool for the fairy folk.' And he believed her.

For her journey back to the bedroom, she would have to manage on one stick and carry the mug in her other hand. Best not to fill it too full then. It was a struggle, but she managed the few yards walk to her grandson's side without spilling a drop of the precious liquid that would free him from his pain. In her cardigan pocket, she carried plasters to temporarily dress the gaping wounds. Briefly, she wondered who had done this to him. Some of those Margate gangs were murderous swine: she'd read about them enough in the local journal, and often marvelled how they were never caught and put away. Maybe Josh had been set upon by them? Seeing him when he fell in her front door, she thought he looked like he'd been flung into a cage of ferocious dogs, dogs that were accompanied by men wielding machetes or some such vicious weapons. He was that badly injured, she marvelled that he had managed to reach her bungalow... the car driver had all but dumped him outside. *Wonder if he was one of the gang. No, he looked very kind, too kind to do anything like that.* She wondered where her dead husband's car was. No matter, her grandson was here now, and safe in her bed. Just like when he was a little boy and she would read to him before he dropped off to sleep, with his little tousled head flopped on her pillow.

She reached the bedroom and winced again when she looked at his injuries. There was blood everywhere, on the carpet, the bedclothes, and on the pillow where he rested on his half-torn off ear.

She hobbled over to him, put the mug on the bedside table and sat beside him on the bed.

'Poor, poor boy,' she said. She gently patted his hand, winced when she saw how swollen it was. Probably his fingers were broken. *Wicked, wicked men!* 'Gran will make you better, just like she always has.' She helped him into a sitting position, lifted the mug and brought it to his lips. 'Here, drink this, pet.' She nodded in encouragement.

Too sweet, always too sweet. He liked one sugar but he knew Gran always put one and a bit in his tea. For the life of him, he did not know why. Perhaps she felt it was her way of showing her love for him. Old people did that, Mum had once said. How she knew it was beyond him.

The rim of the mug hurt his bruised and split lip. He could feel the state of his mouth with his tongue. If he had been in hospital, like his friend Parri, they would have given him a drinking straw, a heat-resistant straw that did not melt in hot drinks. Gran wouldn't have any straws. Why would she?

Bitter too, it tasted bitter. She was stroking his head, carefully avoiding a gaping wound above his left eye.

'Go on, son. Drink it, it'll do you good. Help take away the pain.'

He wanted to ask, 'Like medicine?' but felt too broken to say anything. He would just obey her, she knew best. Didn't she always? Hadn't she always?

Ellie gently held the mug to his lips, carefully wrapping her hand around his broken fingers that were puffed-up like fat pork sausages, only they were purple in colour. He drank half the liquid then rested. He looked up into her little blackcurrant eyes that glistened in the light coming in from her bedroom window. His face puckered.

'It wath me, Gran. I did it.'

'Did what, bonnie boy?'

'I took your money. I thought you were dead and... I panicked... made it look like you'd been burgled.'

'Hush now, pet. We'll sort it after.' After what she did not know.

'I thent it to you,' he struggled to say between swollen lips and a cut tongue where he had bitten it during the beating.

'Shush, shush,' she whispered, stroking his head with one hand and gently pushing the mug to his mouth again. She nodded and smiled at him, encouraging him to drink more. He obeyed, as he always had. When he finished the last drop, he kind of knew why she had made him do it. There was something in the tea, something more than 'one and a bit' spoonfuls of sugar. The something that tasted bitter.

He knew what he should do now, push the mug away; stick his fingers down his throat and make himself sick. Drink a pint of salt water and bring up more vomit and, with it, the poisonous barbiturates she must have crushed into his tea. But he had no strength left. Or the will.

'I'm thorry, Gran,' was all he could say before he lost consciousness. Soon he would take his last breath and she would be there holding him, cradling the grandson she loved so much. She gently placed the pillow on his face... and pressed.

It wasn't Ellie Swales who was dying, it was her doing the killing, 'the killing of Ellie Swales'. A few minutes later, she looked at her dead grandson, peaceful now, despite his wounds. She patted his lifeless hand and nodded. It was good what she had done. Now she needed to sit down, listen again to the news, in case there were more developments. Though they *had* said the police had made good progress and were expecting to make an arrest in a matter of hours. It would be too late then, she reasoned; their prime suspect dead, out of their reach. No matter, there would be no more murders. She gently covered him, pulling the pretty floral duvet up to his bruised and battered face, tucking his broken hands inside. She noticed a bulge in his jeans pocket. Pulled out a wad of money. Unbelievable. A miracle those animals hadn't robbed him of it. She counted it while he slept the deepening sleep. £300. She nodded to herself. What did her Ma used to say? 'God always pays his debts.' But of course, it wasn't her money, Josh had already repaid that. It was no use to him though, she reasoned. Perhaps she'd give it to charity. Help for Heroes was a good one, she'd heard.

Ellie smiled tenderly at her grandson. 'I forgive you Josh.' She kissed his forehead, pushing back a lock of blood-soaked hair, gently stroking him as he lay finally asleep. Maybe later, they would arrest her. But not yet. Plenty of time left for resting... The tiredness swept over her, just like gentle waves on the beach. Ellie yawned, limped her way slowly, painfully, from the bedroom through the little hallway and into the lounge, to her riser chair by the window. She was out of breath. Sat down quietly until she could breathe easily again. Time for a little nap now. Later she would make herself a strong drink... then call them, the police. She hoped it would be those nice officers, 'just Dave and Katie' as they'd called themselves. Her eyes fluttered and her chin drooped towards her chest. Sleep now, Ellie, your work is done...

THE END

THE KILLING OF ELLIE SWALES

THE KILLING OF ELLIE SWALES

·

ABOUT THE AUTHOR

Olga Merrick has owned pubs and restaurants, including a film-land pub near Elstree Studios, north of London. Here she met and served real-life 'cops and robbers', as well as famous actors and film-stars, who inspired her to write crime novels and psychological thrillers.

Olga's last restaurant was in Hay-on-Wye, the famous 'town of books' in Wales, where she met famous writers, and more actors and stars of stage and television, at many of the town's annual Literary Festivals.

She has also dabbled in the antiques trade, worked briefly as a school teacher, a market research interviewer, and as personal assistant to an explosives expert. Today she lives in Shropshire with her partner and their small poodle.

The Killing of Ellie Swales is Olga's third novel. She is currently writing her fourth, for publication in 2018.

ACKNOWLEDGEMENTS

My thanks, as always, to my editor and partner, Geoff Thatcher, for his encouragement, sound advice and ever welcome glass of wine at the end of each writing day.

MORE FROM OUR AUTHORS†

chadgreen books

UNTOUCHED DEPARTURES
a psychological thriller by Olga Merrick

A RAKE OF LEAVES
Olga Merrick's second psychological thriller

TALES OF ROMANCE
The Phantom Reborn and more
by Rosemarie David

FROM THE MOUNTAINS TO THE SEA
More tales of romance
by Rosemarie David

SHROPSHIRE SHORTS: Books One, Two, Three and more
A series of anthologies filled with stories and a few poems by
creative writers and mature students from Shropshire, UK

Coming next Spring (2018)
SPARROWHAWK
another psychological thriller from Olga Merrick

† For further information about these titles, please email

    chadgreenbooks@yahoo.com